Eve of Ascension

The Fall of The Ascendancy, Volume 1

Daniel McMillan

Published by Vector11Studio, 2019.

EVE OF ASCENSION

First edition. April 19, 2019.

Copyright © 2019 Daniel McMillan.

ISBN: 978-1725935440

Written by Daniel McMillan

For all of the people in my life who inspire me. You know who you are.

(Keep it up.)

My deepest gratitude, as always, to my incredible wife, Tahera. You make all things possible.

Acknowledgements:

Cover Art by Ramzan Artsikaev
https://thebookcoverdesigner.com/designers/ram-art/

Special thanks to Kelsey Pohl, Sheryl Sasseville, Gil Pitre, and Norman Morrel for their contributions to this book. Your input was invaluable, and I cannot thank you enough.

Thanks also to Deborah Derksen Avery, Mark Maxon, Bonnie Alston, Barb Coughlin, Jake Kulgawchuk, Pat Hudon, Lisa Abbassi, Jaime Lombaert, Nicole Koroluk, Lisa Gorowski, Kathryn Old, Kerry Clermont, Mychelle Pycha, Rick Harrington and John Dale for their assistance and support.

None of this would have happened had it not been for the continuing encouragement and support of my parents, Bryan and Audrey McMillan.

I am grateful to all of you.

Introduction

THE GREAT CATACLYSM occurred several generations ago when an asteroid collided with the Earth.

Before that devastating event, technology had blossomed, and society evolved. Eventually, their baser instincts guided them into a global war, pitting the common people against an upstart World Government.

But on the day of the asteroid, in a single clamorous breath, all of humankind was equalized. Billions of people died, the atmosphere was scorched, and life on Earth would never be the same.

The grim conditions and scarcity of food, water, and resources in the dismal times that followed made many of the those who survived the initial strike wish they had perished that day - and a great deal of them had that wish granted slowly and painfully.

After some time, though, the relatively few who remained saw the world replenishing itself. Food gradually became more available, and rain fell and collected on the ground again.

Living was still not easy, but it was manageable. The human population started to increase again. The generations born into this unusual environment had no basis for comparison and were content to live in constant survival mode, until the coming of a saviour in the form of ambitious new leadership.

The fledgeling government, which developed into the Ascendancy, had raised great round walls in a dozen locations across the globe. Each of them was closed off from the savage world beyond and offered shelter and resources for anyone who settled there. All they asked in compensation was for the settlers do what they could to ensure the safe zones continued to develop and evolve. The more anyone contributed, the higher comforts they received. This sounded like an attractive opportunity to people who endangered their lives to have food and water every day.

The Ascendancy developed the 12 cities of the modern world, and none of the Ascended asked how the sanctuaries had originated. No one knew where the high, round walls that harbored them came from. The sole factor that interested them was that they felt much safer inside the new havens than they had outside them. As far as they were concerned, the Ascendancy had rescued them.

The neophyte governing body also provided a renaissance of high technology and the protection of newly developed robotic Guardians. The fresh inhabitants, indebted for the luxuries of civilization, endeavoured to improve and develop their newfound home alongside robotic counterparts and nanotech.

But, not all survivors wished to partake of the Ascendancy's accommodation. Those who remained outside the cities became identified as Sylvans - people of the woodlands. They established villages and lived off the surrounding land, meeting the daily harshness of the new world head-on.

The Ascended grew complacent about their safety. The only fear they held was the one that the Ascendancy ensured it cautioned them of at every possible opportunity: that the Sylvans could come over the walls at any moment and take all they had built.

The Sylvan threat loomed over the Ascended, and eventually, the cities were enclosed by plasma domes that arched over a magnetic field high above the living spaces within.

Finally, the people of the Ascendancy felt safe, wholly separated from everything beyond the crackling plasma that shielded them from the world.

The woman who developed the dome technology became ascended to the highest status and was granted access to the best the Ascendancy offered. The occupants of the cities applauded her loudly and worked harder than ever to live up to the precedent she set.

But, unknown to the citizens, the Ascendancy was making the lives of the Sylvans more challenging than they already were. They raided villages and captured prisoners to serve in facilities outside of the cities, where the wilderness-hardened slaves attended to the needs of the Ascended. Sylvans, who had been wrenched from their homes and families, provided water purification, waste management, power generation, and everything else the Ascended needed to live in comfort.

The cities matured, and technology flourished as those within worked to ascend. The Ascendancy grew fat from the advancements the citizens presented them.

The Sylvans, contrarily, learned to be mobile and sometimes would move entire villages to evade detection by the Ascendancy.

An underground movement started within the Sylvans that called itself the Luminants. They subverted the Ascendancy whenever they could, and relayed messages to the people who resided under it, anticipating they would awaken and remove any authority the government had.

But the interferences of the Luminants did little to facilitate reform. The deceitful leadership's technology and influence, combined with the robotic Guardians that strengthened the police force, made it difficult for the Luminants to achieve any traction in their endeavors.

Despite the rebels' best efforts, an increasingly unquestioning populace continued to do everything they were told so they might advance into higher status and luxury.

Prologue

THE RUINED CITY SHAWAN Forander found himself in had been in that state for generations, deserted after the Great Cataclysm had blighted it along with the rest of the Earth.

Nature was doing a thorough job of reclaiming the spaces between the decrepit buildings and heaved pavement. Vines and plants slowly tugged at the railings and ancient structures that leaned precariously out of the ground while trees and grass split and pitched the walkways between them.

Shawan came to this abandoned place that lay between the villages of Sylva and the cities of the Ascended to upset a balance of power that had consistently been Ascendancy-heavy.

Pre-Cataclysm cities were no longer safe places and had been passed over as too unstable for homes. The Sylvans started over rather than working to revive them, preferring to establish more suitable towns from scratch in convenient spaces of the wilderness.

Within the former metropolis, animals inhabited impromptu caves that were formed by the rubble, now that the habitats of humanity decayed. The birds that roosted in the remaining balconies had no fear of being shooed away by angry broom wielders or having things flung at them by children.

There had been no children here for a long while, nor women, nor men.

Right now, the only remaining human in the jungle-city showed no interest in the animals or plants here, except those that got in his way as he ran for his life.

Only minutes ago, Shawan met his contact in the neglected city, and the transaction between them had gone smoothly. The merchandise he obtained was smaller than he guessed it would be, but it was intact and in proper order, and the courier had deemed his payment adequate. They reached out to one another to shake hands, and the man he was dealing with stiffened briefly, and his eyes widened, still catching Shawan's squarely. Then the fellow's gaze fell, along with the rest of his body, as he died.

Shawan watched his contact's limp form descend ungracefully to come to a heap at his feet, and he saw the black-edged hole in the man's back where an ion stream from an Ascendancy-issued rifle had burned out his existence. Looking up quickly he discovered the fatal beam's origin: a Guardian - a robotic Ascendancy officer in the form of a shiny, athletic woman - was recovering its balance after the first shot, working to retrain its rifle on him.

"Halt," the officer called out in a firm, alto voice as Shawan dodged and bobbed. He scrambled to the nearest cover while shots impacted around him.

The female form of the officer was designed to make people feel at ease around it, but all he could see when he looked at it was a killing machine produced by an unscrupulous regime, created to keep people in line without humans having to do anything distasteful. It was a 'non-threatening' construct that would end his life with no reluctance or remorse.

So he ran.

He made it away from the initial assault because the officer robot - or O-bot as they were called - had fired from a precarious position and briefly lost its footing, but that would not happen again. His survival had been a gift of Providence, and from now on he would have to earn the right to go on breathing. The bots were not super intelligent, and could be outwitted, but they were strong, fast and implacable.

Shawan could not fail. He needed to keep moving, had to finish this for the good of everybody - Sylvan and Ascended alike. The package must get to Shadaar; he would know what to do with it.

He proceeded through the rubble and forced aside any notions of failing, becoming focused on the objective. The things he learned in a lifetime of training came surging into his mind. He had to prioritize. He must make it to a Gate at the bottom of a small pit outside the city which would transport him to his village of Nylen, providing his escape.

Shadaar had designed the pit as an escape hatch after Shawan had a close call, and was almost followed back to the village. It was merely a hole in the ground with smoothly sloping sides, to allow critters to climb out, with a Transport Portal Gate at the bottom. The Gate transported anyone who crossed through it to a place on the peripheries of Nylen and then would seal itself off to preclude any pursuers from following. All that mattered now was getting there; preferably in one piece.

As he ran, he called for his backpack to come to his chest, and the millions of nanobots it was composed of shifted their positions, moving around him under one arm as they kept all the objects inside in their proper places. He reached into a compartment on the pack and removed a device. He triggered the small instrument and dropped it onto the roadway as he continued to run.

Hopefully, this would buy him a brief rest before he carried on. He had to make it out of the city and reach the pit. It would be hard to manage a balance between pushing forward at breakneck speed and preserving enough strength to get all the way there.

He sidestepped into a narrow alcove alongside one of the last streets of the city. The buildings were modest here, and farther apart, so he needed to take advantage of shelter when the opportunity presented itself. He peered back around a corner to get a peek at his mechanical pursuers.

Damn. Four O-bots were tracking him; more than he had prepared for. They slowed as they neared and on the faces of each, electronic eyes scanned for any hints of movement.

As the Guardian on point came a little closer, Shawan thought the officer looked at him. It stopped searching in his direction, and took a tentative step as it locked on a high-probability location.

The device Shawan left on the street exploded. It was a primitive, home-made bomb, and only took out the officer who had observed him. Flying debris flailed the others, but they single-mindedly continued past the still-twitching limbs of their debilitated counterpart. Shawan wished he could use Electromagnetic Pulse grenades to knock out their circuitry, but he recognized that the same EMP that would fry the officers' electronics would also ruin the article he was endangering his life to protect.

The moment of confusion gave Shawan an opportunity to advance, not toward the edge of the city, but laterally, as he attempted to get to a better offensive position and gain the upper hand on his pursuers. The backpack returned to its customary place between his shoulder blades when he told it to, making it easier for Shawan to run. He sprinted to the end of the block he was on, then curved left to curl around the relentless officers, hopefully coming up behind them. The ancient, derelict construction stood precariously with its top portion sheared off and piled in a heap beside it. Debris caused him to stumble as he charged into a darkened entrance. A staircase inside the door beckoned to him, and he made his way upward.

He scaled the stairs as far as he could until they broke off at what was now the top floor. There had been a hallway there, but the mangled remains were now open to the sky above. Moving to the edge of the building and looking down, he discovered that the remaining officers had split up.

There was one beneath his position and one further up the street where he had been hiding a minute ago. The third one was nowhere to be seen as he scoured the road from his location.

He was only three stories up and still not far enough away to risk dropping an EMP grenade - the blast radius may include his current position. Shawan brought it along as a last resort; a contingency plan if push came to shove.

He conducted a quick inventory of the weapons he had with him: two impact grenades, a timer-detonation bomb, his rappelling piton pistol, and an EMP generator. These were all useful things to have - Shadaar equipped him well - but none of them was the right tool for the job. He wished he had a gun, but he had decided not to bring one as a show of good faith to his courier.

Then it occurred to him: the proper tool for the job was lying on the ground beside the disabled O-bot down the street. He shouldn't have come up here; he should have gone around the officers and taken that abandoned ion rifle. It was too late for that now. He would modify his plan as he made his way back down to the ground.

There was a clamor behind him - metal against metal - and Shawan turned to catch the shadow of the officer he had lost track of moving up the wall of the stairwell. He would have to improvise.

Shawan took out his piton pistol and sprinted across the ruined top floor as the officer moved far enough up the stairs to see him. "Halt," it said while bringing its rifle around toward him, trying to get the weapon aimed at

Shawan. It bound up the remaining stairs as Shawan dove over the lip of the building.

Shawan spun his body as he cleared the edge to face his adversary. He fired his grappler piton into the side of the building, and the carbon filament line pulled him in toward the collapsed wall as the officer on the open 3rd floor fired a shot. Shawan's abrupt change in orientation caused the ion beam to miss narrowly, and he turned his attention to what he would do when he arrived at the rapidly approaching wall.

Once the filament had slowed him sufficiently, he cut the cable loose from the pistol, and arced downward such that he would not hit the wall. He would still be travelling at a significant rate when he arrived at the ground.

He realigned his body for the jolt, and upon connection with the earth he pulled himself into a tucked position and rolled before coming to a stop. Shawan looked to the building. The officer wasn't at its upper edge yet, but would certainly be there in a short interval.

He scrambled to his feet and dashed back to where this had all started, this time staying off the street, electing instead to go around, behind the buildings where foliage would afford some additional security.

A pair of shots missed him as he went between two trees, and a branch caught his jacket, tearing a hole in it and scratching what would be a new scar someday into his arm.

As he exited the treed area to find more substantial cover behind a building, another shot hit the corner of the structure next to him from a different angle. The O-bot closest to him on the ground had a bead on him as well.

Shawan ran behind the building and turned to face the street. There was a broken staircase protruding from the debris there, offering temporary cover, and beyond that, he could make out fragments of freshly destroyed android, and the ion rifle lay on the edge of the road, beckoning.

He ran toward it, summoning his pack to the front once again and removed an impact grenade from inside. He set it and continued closing the gap between him and the rifle. An officer appeared on the far side of the street, stopping across from where the gun lay. Shawan aimed and threw the explosive.

He was not trying to hit the Guardian, but a point halfway between the officer and the rifle. His calculation was a long shot, for sure, but if it paid off, he would accomplish two goals with one grenade.

The officer was raising its weapon as the device reached its mark on the street, and the blast sent it flying back, away from Shawan. It also sent the ion rifle careening toward him.

Shawan ducked and covered himself while the gun and a hail of debris flew past him. He twisted and followed it as it flew into the branches of a shrub behind him, dropping to the ground only a few meters away. Shawan scrambled to it on all fours, snatched it and rolled onto his back, pointing the weapon toward the street.

The officer was recovering, but it had lost the arm that formerly held its weapon, and as the metal menace rose, Shawan put an ion beam into its torso. Sparks flew out of it and bolts of electricity arced between its joints, its bright eyes blackened, and the Guardian fell forward in a heap. Two down, two to go.

The officer from the roof was coming, presumably the same way he had, and the other, that had been further down the street, was likely right behind the one he had shot.

He quickly surveyed his surroundings and saw, at the bottom of the broken staircase at the end of the building, an ancient door hanging ajar on its hinges.

He did not falter. His legs tightened, pushing him toward the only way out of the present predicament. He knew that every moment he remained alive was an affront to probability and, realistically, his life was likely to come to a conclusion very soon.

He struggled to open the old door, and shots from the rear of the building glanced off it as it finally gave way. A greasy, burning smell of fried metal filled his nostrils, and he covered his face with his arms against the sparks that emanated from the door as he ran inside.

The inside was in poorer condition than the one he had been in before. There were chunks of concrete and building materials haphazardly strewn throughout the otherwise vacant space before him.

He sought the path of least resistance and ran as swiftly as he could. He sidestepped a pile of rubble as he heard the door behind him being ripped from its ancient hinges, then hurdled over an old girder that had probably been part of the roof but had since come down, doing considerable damage where it fell.

In flight above the steel beam, a shot took him in the ribs, and he lost sight of where he was for a fraction of a second. He hit the fractured and crumbling ground on the other side with a crash. The aged and damaged floor gave way to his weight and momentum, and he plunged through, into the murky space below. He reached the floor of the level beneath and heard fragments from the fresh hole falling around him, and the surrounding illumination lessened.

Shawan thought it was over for him. There was light entering through the hole above him, but it wasn't sufficient to determine the extent of his new wound. It hurt like hell, but he could still move, so that's what he did.

He shoved aside the scraps that had crashed around him and rose to his feet, and when he peered ahead, he discovered that the Cosmos had smiled upon him yet again.

He was in an underground parking area and looking at a Phantom 3850, one of the hottest airbikes of its time. It was upright and appeared to be unaffected, despite all the other vehicles around it being damaged or altogether demolished. If this thing started, he would officially consider himself a favored child of God and ultimately invincible.

Shawan approached it and found the decomposed body of its previous owner laying beside it with a piece of wood jammed though him front to back. He shifted his attention back to the bike and heard the two officers above clearing debris out of their path so they could maintain their unwavering pursuit of him. The keys were sticking out of the ignition, and he flung aside the helmet that dangled on the back of the seat and slung his rifle there. Mounting the vehicle, he grasped the key and closed his eyes as he twisted it. The engine was amenable and fired up with a roar. Shawan lost his balance as the airbike rose from the floor to its operating height, but he instantly had muscle memory take over, giving him appropriate reactions to the weight shifting under him. He spun the bike around, leaning it to the side, and searched with the headlamp for an exit.

There were a couple sharp thumps in the area with him, and as he rotated, the headlight showed two shining figures rising to a standing position before him. He could also see, beyond them, an old sign hanging by one corner that had the word "EXIT" imprinted on it in red letters, taunting him to try for it. Shawan punched the throttle and launched forward.

The officers raised their weapons, but had to dive out of the way hastily, one to each side as Shawan recklessly bolted between them.

The grateful new owner of a used airbike looked over his right shoulder as he rode away from the Guardians in time to see them rising. He turned his awareness to where he was going and floated through the opening under the sign at the end of the room, then around an abrupt bend that bore him upwards as he circled into the increasing light.

He exited the parking structure at the edge of the road and habitually checked both directions before making a left turn onto the street. Looking over, he saw the O-bots through a window.

They were back on the main level and still on him. They ran alongside the airbike through the interior of the building for a brief time, then vaulted out, shattering a brittle window as they returned to the heaving sidewalk. Shawan tried to reach for the rifle, but his burning ribcage would not tolerate it. The ordeal wasn't over yet.

Shawan opened the throttle as much as he could while still navigating the debris-packed streets and the hazards they created. He knew the officers were practically as fast as the bike on an open stretch, and his slowed progress meant that they would be on him once again, and relatively soon at that.

A shot glanced off some broken pavement ahead of him and to his left, accompanied by two more on his right. When he looked behind, he saw the officers putting the straps of their guns around their necks and over their shoulders and dropping to all fours, speeding up in a heartbeat to a pace that rivalled the airbike.

Shit! He didn't know they could do that!

He took a sharp right turn, struggling to remain mindful of where the pit was relative to his position. He made a quick left, followed by another, and worked out that he had to go five or six blocks before making a right again to travel straight out of the city and then to his liberation.

Shawan let go of the throttle to use his good arm to get the rifle from the seat back, and slung it alongside himself. An officer exited the street ahead of him to his left, still on all fours; it must have cut through when he made those two successive turns. Shawan fired at it, then swung down an alleyway and was not impressed to learn that it dead-ended.

He stopped. There was an unsuitable exit behind him, a dead-end in front of him, and buildings stretching down either side of the alley with doors at intervals. If he turned around, he would head straight toward the bot behind him. If he tried to go to the end of the cramped passage, he would be boxed in, and that was no better.

He was contemplating trying to shoot his way out when the Guardian, now reunited by its companion, came into the alley and reared up, slowing as they returned to two-legged runs and reaching for their shouldered weapons.

Shawan ran the bike between the haphazard rubble and slid it sideways as he approached an open door in the building on his left. He gunned it again, bouncing the bike off the steel railings on either side as he headed up the steep stairs that led to the door.

Inside, there was a long corridor ahead of him that concluded in a staircase leading upward. Energy bolts flashed, but they were nowhere near hitting him as he ascended the rest the stairs. He steered down a few more twisting passages, searching for exit signs.

When he finally saw one, he veered toward it and headed down the stairs he found there, careening the airbike off the walls the whole way down. The officers were not behind him anymore, but he went on without slowing. They would never quit, so neither could he.

He arrived at the bottom of the stairs and pulled the bike up beside the double doors there so he could kick them open. Shawan pushed the bike back, angling it so it faced out of the building, and set off again, down the stairs that led back out to the street.

The O-bots came out of the exit, firing bolts of blue energy at him. Shawan got down as low as he could to the bike and lurched as he accelerated wildly. A beam hit the front of the bike, and his rifle fell and clattered away in smaller fragments with each successive bounce.

He looked past the cowling, and even though there was smoke issuing from a hole in its side, the panel in front of the turbine was all that had been affected. If this had been a newer model with a nanobot body it would restore itself, but as it was, he would have to proceed with the dark blemish and the smoke it created.

Lifting his head to look over his shoulder, Shawan saw the robots dropping again to all fours with their weapons slung over their shoulders.

He opened the bike up to its maximum speed as he was leaving the city - the wreckage was not as hampering as it had been amongst the buildings. He checked behind again and saw that he was extending the distance between himself and the mechanical officers. Good.

Shawan knew that once he got far enough outside the city, heading off the roads and toward the pit, he would have to leave the bike behind when the scrub there became too dense for it.

With the gap growing between Shawan and his stalkers, he put his head down and lowered the arm closest to his injury so that it rested on his lap. He could manage the throttle with his other hand, and he urged the airbike beyond all limits as he left the city behind.

He cruised up the highway as far as he could as the sun settled on the horizon, oblivious to his predicament. By the time he arrived at the exit that would take him to the pit, he was in significant pain. His ribcage was shrieking at him, and he touched the wound there experimentally, causing a new jolt of agony to make him grimace as he pulled his hand away.

He rode a short distance off the highway before the trail was too grown-in for him to continue on the bike. Stopping, he dismounted while cradling the injury on his side. He was thankful for the old airbike. There was no way in hell he'd have escaped without it.

Despite his pain and the urgency to proceed, he had established a habit of considering his daughter while he was doing jobs out of the village, and he did so even now. He touched the eject button on the console of the bike and waited for a second. A disk emerged, and he took it, sliding it into a compartment in his jacket that was stitched in for just this purpose. If he lived through this, she would be pleased.

He staggered to the edge of the brush and cleared undergrowth out of the way with his still-functional arm, while the other one was pulled in tight against his side to protect his ribs from any further harm.

The going was slow, and he still had a long distance to travel, especially considering that there were two homicidal androids hot on his tail. He pushed farther into the woods, and the sun turned the horizon a bright red-orange as it pressed into it. He advanced along the trail, fixated on reaching the pit.

Shawan advanced as quickly as his injuries would tolerate. The sun continued to set, and he became increasingly aware that 'as fast as he could' was becoming slower as the pain he endured and blood he lost affected him.

He drew closer, and was able to identify the spot where the forest opened into the clearing where his salvation lay. He was going to make it.

As Shawan stepped into the clearing, a newfound sense of positivity entering him. A couple dozen meters more and he would be there. Everything would be alright.

There was a familiar crackling behind him. The blast that came with the sound caught him in the thigh opposite the ribs where he had already taken one. Shawan fell forward, and a second blast passed overhead. He braced himself as he dropped, then promptly collapsed from being on his hands and knees to a fully prone position. His hopes were shattered in a moment. The O-bots were nearing.

You're frikkin' kidding me, he thought. *After all this, these idiot bots are gonna take me now?* He snickered as he reached into the backpack, still in front of him, for the EMP grenade. It would send out a pulse of electromagnetism, frying all the surrounding electronics, including the device he struggled to defend. And then he would perish here, laying in the grass, with two burned out androids as the only witnesses to his passing.

He removed the fist-sized grenade and armed it, but then had a glimmer of inspiration. Once he was through the portal-gate that rested at the bottom of the pit, it would close, as Shadaar programmed it to do, to stop anyone that might try to follow him through. If he went into the Gate, but left the EMP behind, there would be no further trouble out of these particular Guardians. And the prize would remain unscathed.

They lingered over him, and one of them gave him a kick, which brought him back to his hands and knees. He coughed and howled in anguish, then hung his head while he clutched at his throbbing side. Tears leaked from his eyes as he tightened them, and he issued a lamenting groan.

The robot farthest from him had its rifle pointed at him, but the other shouldered its weapon with one hand as it grasped for him with the other.

Shawan gave a kick of his own, donkey style, which sent the unarmed officer back and into the other, knocking them both off balance. A shot streaked upward and into the dusk as the bots fell over together.

The wounded Sylvan used what little remained of his strength to lurch forward. He rolled down the incline of the pit and hurled the grenade into the last of the daylight.

He tumbled through the Gate a split second before the EMP issued its circuitry-disabling wave, leaving the officers above as useless heaps of expensive metals and electronics, heaped together in the tall grass as though they had been lovers who died in each other's embrace.

Shawan came out the other side of the portal, transported to the paired Gate outside his village of Nylen, and landed unceremoniously. There were two of his devoted friends and his daughter there waiting for him, and as they rushed to meet him, he said, "I got it. Contact Shadaar," before his inner world closed up on him and blackened.

Chapter 1

THE SKYLINE WAS BEAUTIFUL, backlit by the softly crackling plasma-dome over it. It was night, and there were few shadows in the streets below, uniformly illuminated as they were by the gentle light that emanated from Enswell's protective covering. The sky beyond the dome was always obscured and occluded from view, as though the Ascended were a shiny gift wrapped in frosted glass. A bright spot traced its way daily across the dome as the sun travelled overhead, and every evening the arcing blue-white luminescence of the shield over the west end changed to a delicate pink for a while as it set.

Those less ascended lived on the perimeter of the city and were used to the light and sound of the dome, but the people who rose into the more centrally located areas didn't have to deal with it as much. It was good to rise.

There was little doubt that Candace Clarke's ascendance to the downtown core had been fueled by her husband's creation of the Gates - the portals that allowed instantaneous travel between distant points. They were complicated, and William had tried to explain them to her on many occasions. She was partly befuddled by them but mostly indifferent.

All that mattered to her was that his work had granted them the greatest luxuries of ascension - a central home high in the core, and all the latest amenities, entertainment, and comforts.

Most of all, it gave the Clarke family prominence, and on this night Candace was entertaining Ascendancy dignitaries and celebrities in her home in honour of her son, Baxter. He had been awarded for his academic achievement and contributions, and was the first ever Ascended to achieve Level 25 at the age of 26.

Candace was keen to show off her family's accomplishments and had invested a lot of time and employed many people to ensure that tonight went off without a hitch.

Some details of the setup for tonight had not been carried out to her satisfaction and made Candace upset, but she had to overlook them for now. She would circulate with the top-shelf crowd coming to her home and direct their attention away from those elements, but she made a mental note to deduct some Ascendance Points from what she had pledged to the coordinator. A-Points were for individuals who merited them.

She forced the thoughts aside to bask in her big day. Baxter's Award of Excellence came with upgrades to his cerebral implants, and he had also gained enough points to move up a level. Perhaps she could pick up a few points herself if she pointed out to the appropriate people what she had contributed to Baxter's progress.

Candace looked impeccable, as she had planned to. Her style maven would undoubtedly receive some additional A-Points for this.

Two hours ago, Candace stood in her undergarments in front of what was a blank wall otherwise, but now was producing a mirror image where she could see herself in the various outfits, makeup, and hairstyles her stylist had recommended for her. Although she was nearly naked in the room, the projection of her on the intelligent wall was of her wearing a vibrant red dress with a floral overprint that swayed gently in an unseen breeze, shifting around to match any movement she made. She shifted to study at herself from different angles, and the flowers on her dress moved along with her, and she concluded that she didn't like it.

"Kyla, next dress", she commanded the wall, and her virtual assistant appeared next to her image and took the dress away. Candace's semi-nude form flashed for an instant, her assistant switched the attire she was holding, and then the aide flung the new garment toward her reflection, and it became covered with a royal blue dress.

This one was more form-fitting than the last gown she had tried, and featured a white bird about the size of one of her hands that fluttered around the heart of the dress between her hips and shoulders, but stayed off her breasts so as not to call unwanted attention to them. The fabric clung to her until halfway down her hips, where it flared slightly and continued to the floor in a gentle cascade that hid any trace of her movements inside the garment, making it appear that she was floating when she moved.

"I love this one, don't you?" she queried Kyla. Kyla responded that it was the very latest design and assured Candace that no one else attending this evening would have anything like it. There was no need to try on another; this was the gown she would wear.

"Superb," Candace resolved. "Now, on to hair and makeup."

Kyla gestured toward a door on Candace's left, which opened to expose the blue dress in all its splendour. She was eager to get on to the more delicate points of her look for the evening, but the dress enthralled her.

"Sorry, Kyla. Let me get dressed first. Then we'll look at the fine-tuning."

"Very well, Madame."

The front of the dress opened itself from top to bottom, along with two more openings from the center line to the ends of the sleeves. Candace stepped back into the garment, aligning her arms with the gaps, and the dress stitched itself back together around her. As it finished, she returned to her place in front of the wall, where Kyla waited.

"Okay," Candace cooed, "Let's get on with it."

Candace gleefully continued, trying out different hair and makeup styles on her smart wall reflection until she was satisfied that she would be the most glamorous woman at the celebration. Along with nano makeup that adjusted to best suit whatever expression she made, she elected to ferrous-infuse her hair and suspend it in a magnetic field. Once fully assembled, no one could equal her.

She asked Kyla to check on the ballroom, which had been formed by having the walls in the flat move back to the perimeter, creating one ample open space, with only the bedrooms remaining unaffected by the rearrangement. Kyla gestured to a spot on the wall beside her, and a window appeared there with real-time video and audio of the central area. Some guests had already arrived and were being served refreshments and food by the household drones. There were no VIP's yet, so Candace waited a while before she went out. She was about to inquire where William was, then checked herself, knowing her spouse would be in his workshop and presumably still not fit to receive guests.

"Kyla, please send a reminder to Mr Clarke that he needs to get ready now."

"I will notify William immediately." The avatar on the wall nodded. "Done. Is there anything else I can do for you?"

"Thank you, Kyla. That will be all for now."

Kyla faded from the surface along with the other images that had been there, leaving a peaceful beach scene in its place.

Candace turned and stepped out of the dressing area and into the bedroom. It was quiet and dimly lit, and she called for better lighting on herself and another full-length mirror to appear on the wall in front of her. She rechecked herself, and her makeup shifted slightly as she simpered at the image, contented with herself and confident in her ascendance.

Her mother had advised her well. Before Candace married William Clarke, a man well on his way to high ascension, her mother, Emily Rhodes, taught her the power of rising.

Emily and her husband, Gerald, lived in a moderate flat in the Fourth Circle of Brighton, a vicinage as close to the fringe of the city as the core, and Emily had done everything in her capacity to get that far, herself having been raised in the Sixth Circle.

Ascension was everything to Mother, and Candace remembered hearing her declare that the purpose of life was to ascend as high as you could so that those who came in your wake might make it further than you did. Candace's father had worked his way up to a supervisory position at a facility just outside the city, making the trip to his workplace every day by monorail, before Gates made them obsolete and the tunnels were sealed off. Emily had pressed her man to rise as much as was possible, and Candace remembered that some of the most intense arguments she ever heard between her parents had to do with how they should deal with things to maximize their ascent.

Emily worked as well but put in a lot of time seeking potential suitors for Candace. She knew better than to try marrying her daughter into households that had accumulated ascension beyond the Third Circle; there was no way the computers would authorize such a union. She looked instead for exceptional young men in the middle class - Fifth, Fourth, and Third Circles - whose potential was greater than their current status.

She came across a youthful, Fourth Circle man in Enswell who had some fascinating ideas that could lead to a possible leap forward in travel. The young man held incredible, and as yet untapped, potential.

Candace was a biologist working on the issue of human ageing and attempting to advance some older theories on Engineered Negligible Senescence, a process by which age-affiliated damage to human tissues was repaired periodically, postponing age-related conditions for as long as the therapies continued. She made some modifications to the process, but nothing that significantly changed how it was practiced. Her most noteworthy contribution to the field of research was the synthesis of the existing material into a more manageable structure, making it easier for others to study. That provided progress in the overall research, and marginal ascension for Candace, but nothing compared to the potentially life-altering theories the young man in Enswell put forth.

Emily used all of her available resources to have someone acquainted with the computer systems that set up matches for marriage hack the associated algorithms (Candace was pretty sure Mother also slept with him, as inconceivable as that sounded) and lo-and-behold: Candace Rhodes was to be married to William Clarke the following year.

Candace met William frequently before they wed, but she never really hit it off with him. He had a sense of humour based on obscure scientific references, and Candace laughed when it seemed appropriate to do so. He also devoted a lot of time to his studies and research, but Candace saw that as a virtue. It meant that once they were married, she probably wouldn't have to see a lot of him.

William seemed more interested in his work than in women, but he knew he would be wed someday and the computer Artificial Intelligence had presented Candace as a suitable match, so he accepted that there must be something to it.

They were married none too soon. If it had been a couple of months later, Candace would never have landed him. William created the Gates, brought instant travel to the Ascendancy, and his status shot through the roof. There was no way the computers would have recommended her pairing with him after that; lascivious hacker or not.

So it was that Candace Clarke was launched from the Fourth Circle of Brighton to the First Circle of Enswell. Then William went on expeditions to initialize his new portal technology between the city centers, and once they were working and direct transport between the cities became conventional, Candace found herself moving into a stylish flat in the Core.

Her parents were able to move to the Second Circle, and Father died soon after that. Mother lived for another few years, and passed away at the age of 148, having carried out her life's mission, even if she had to make extreme sacrifices along the way. Candace was honoured and indebted.

Now, she was on the cusp of ushering in a new era for the next generation, with Baxter moving ahead in his ascension more brightly than anyone before him. It was good for her, and also made her more forgiving of William's quirks, as she admitted that much of what Baxter knew about thinking creatively came from observing his father.

Baxter wanted to be Captain of the Avalon - the first Earth ship to promise to spread humanity beyond their fragile home planet. Not only would he be ascended beyond all ascension, but he would also be a celebrity and a hero. Candace could not be more pleased.

She broke from her nostalgic reverie and took her Resveratrol as she did every day. It was available to anyone who attained Level 70 or higher and stimulated the body's immune response to counteract aging. Between her youthful looks and fantastic apparel, all would envy her as they should.

She studied herself one last time and, delighted with her appearance, made her way out of the bedroom and down the corridor she had configured into the Ballroom Layout of the flat that allowed her to make an impressive entrance into the party to end all parties. The party with which she would declare to all the distinguished people - the people who mattered - her arrival at the top of the food chain.

Candace flowed into the open ballroom with her suspended blonde hair changing to match the lighting and shadows she found herself in. She was cordial, but not too much, moving through the lower guests ("Oh Candace, I love the way you've configured the place!") and addressing the cliques that collected the most significant people. Lower people were to be envious, not to engage her in any consequential way. Besides, points collected from them in attempts to get on her good side were still points, and she would take them any way she could get them.

"Good evening, Mr Burke," she said as she edged her way among the surrounding people, who promptly gave way to her. Her makeup changed itself to become more radiant and shifted to highlight her eyes. "How are you on this wonderful evening?"

"Ah, Candace Clarke, I find myself in an excellent state, thank you. My wife and I extend our most sincere congratulations on the upward movement of your son. Level 25, I hear."

"Yes, that is correct. He may ascend further even than we have been able to."

"Actually, Level 25 qualifies him for an implant. Has he chosen an enhancement?"

"Not yet. He will weigh his options before he decides. He wants it to be significant."

"I understand. He should get a processing implant. I think they overrate memory expansions. But, who am I to wheedle a young genius such as he is. He will make an informed and prudent decision, I am sure." The surrounding people displayed their corroboration, and Burke scanned the room briefly. "Actually, where is the man of honour this evening? I should like to extend my congratulations in person while he will still actually speak to a no-goodnik such as myself."

Candace laughed precisely along with the others around them, and her makeup changed to best frame her haughty response. She feigned slapping his chest coyly. "Michael Burke, you embarrass me! I will always ensure that Baxter pays the appropriate respect to someone in your position." The group laughed politely once again. "Baxter is on the balcony with his friends. I'll see to it that he comes around to receive you. Michael, please say hello to your fine wife and family for me, and now, if you'll excuse me, I have pressing matters to address. Enjoy our hospitality, all, and Ascend."

The circling people beamed at her, some bidding her to Ascend also, and she left the group as elegantly as she had come into it, pleased that the first person she had engaged was Michael Burke. He was a representative of the Chancellor himself, and someday he could ascend into that leading position, between his contributions and the influence of his influential family. The Clarkes would do well to have an ally in such an exalted place. She would make sure that Baxter paid him proper consideration before the night went on much longer.

Where was that boy? She hadn't done all of this for him to have it go to waste. He could spend time with his friends later.

She progressed through the crowd, smiling and greeting as she moved ("Candace, did you move the windows? They look great!"), and then she spied her husband, William, standing beside a buffet counter. He was chewing and tapping his foot to the soft instrumental music that seemed to come from everywhere, but also from nowhere specific. He was not looking around the room, but rather his gaze was cast downward at the surface of the appetizer table.

"William, will you please pay some attention to our guests?" William jerked his head up, and Candace could practically smell him trying to formulate a response. "I understand that this is taking you away from your projects, but tonight isn't about you, you know. It's about me. So get out there and show our friends some hospitality." William quickly swiped his reading material from the surface of the table and faced her again as she went on. "I didn't do all this work so you could stuff yourself with appetizers and try to disguise the fact that you redirected your research from your terminal to the other surfaces in the house. Don't think I haven't noticed."

He waited for her to finish her tirade, as he invariably did.

Candace had learned to love him over the years, and she appreciated that his achievement had ascended them beyond her wildest dreams. It drove her a little crazy, though, that he did not value proper etiquette as he should, especially now that he was a person of considerable import. "I am sorry, Candace. I will do my utmost to entertain our company."

She relaxed instantly. "Alright, William. Thank you. Do you know where Baxter is? I told Michael Burke that he is on the balcony, but I do not believe that to be the case."

"It is indeed the case. He is out there now with Kent and Lila."

Candace smiled at her spouse and also left no doubt that she was issuing an order. "Would you be a darling and go fetch him? He should be in here."

SYLVA HELD LITTLE INTEREST for Timoth Forander. He could admit that the forest that hemmed in the village was beautiful and that the people of Nylen were generally relaxed and content, but he was the type to speculate about things beyond his present scope.

The earthen streets between the portable homes seemed dirty to him, and he found the mirth of the children who played there corrupted by the barrenness he perceived. The rest of the world, he knew, contained much more than Nylen - or all of Sylva for that matter - could ever afford him, and it ground away at the back of his mind like a mortar and pestle in an apothecary.

The Forander family gathered at the kitchen table in their modest yurt-style home, trying to enjoy the meal Mother had prepared. A wall divided the central living, kitchen and dining areas from the bedrooms and a small washroom on the other side, cutting the circular house in half. The planked floor was invariably kept clean, even though people went in and out of their home steadily throughout most days. They had all they needed, and nothing more.

They were usually a composed and lively household, but today there was an edge of unease in the room. They all knew that Father's wounds were mending, but the visible bandaging Mom had carefully wrapped over them, and Dad's evident discomfort, made them difficult to overlook.

Timoth was the youngest of the two children, but at 19 years old, he hardly regarded himself a child. His sister, Raishann, was three years older than he and, after years of training and scavenging with Father, was just starting to go on Luminant missions. Timoth himself might be invited to accompany them soon. He hadn't determined yet whether he would. He was skeptical about a number of things.

Raishann acted like she was pretty tough, and she talked a continual stream of rants and bluffs, but Timoth knew that it scared her to shift from the relative security of searching around for items they could exchange or re-pair, to the uncertainties of going on missions where real harm might arise. He glanced at his father, saw the seeping that issued through his bandages, and winced at the prospect of losing him, or Raishann, for a cause he was dubious about.

There were no fans of the Ascendancy in this house. Raishann thought the residents of the cities - or "the zoos," as she called them - were feeble-minded and spiritless, even though their parents had explained to her that those people did not know what was happening behind the scenes of their everyday existence.

They had no notion of the alternate history that the Sylvan elders told, or of the disturbing things their beloved government perpetrated against the people of the woods. But then, Timoth had no means of knowing if those reports were accurate, either.

The Ascendancy gave the people in the cities all kinds of comforts and a safe place to live. Was it so terrible that they asked for some loyalty and respect in return? He recognized that the Ascendancy had done awful things to the Sylvans, but the people of Sylva also hurt the city people. They tried to impose their beliefs on them by hacking into their systems and sending them all kinds of messages about how they should think and live. So, were the Sylvans any better?

Timoth shook it off and returned to his meal. His chopsticks had been pushing his food around in his bowl, and he didn't want to look like he was too worried, so he grabbed some noodles and a fresh piece of broccoli and put it in his mouth. He looked back at his father, who was eating quietly and very much favouring his left side, even when he chewed.

It wasn't the first occasion that this, or something like it, had cropped up in their family. Mom didn't go out on missions anymore, outside of occasionally scavenging with Father, because she had been seized by an officer bot just as she went into the pit, and she appeared on this end of the portal with the Guardian's severed arm still clinging to where it grabbed her leg. The mechanical arm had to be forced off of her, and she wouldn't wear shorts, even in the peak of summer. But, she felt she was fighting for a just purpose; that's what they believed.

Since then, Mom mostly passed her wisdom to the children of the village, and had become one of the preferred teachers in Nylen. It kept her useful, and as safe as she could be as a Sylvan and a member of the Luminants.

Now that he considered it, he was surprised that Dad would be taking Raishann out for missions. Timoth supposed that Dad must figure somebody had to do it, but might change his mind, in light of recent events.

There was never any pressure from his parents to become a Luminant, and he was grateful for that, not because fighting with the rebels scared him, but because he wasn't sure he maintained the same assumptions they did.

Timoth tried talking to his buddy, Kasih, about it a couple times before, but Kasih said that he was not concerned with politics at all. He was just content to not live under the Ascendancy, judging from the things he had been told about them.

One time, Tim had talked Kasih into sneaking to the boundary of the nearest city with him to see what it was like there, but when they arrived, they discovered that they could only make out vague shapes of the buildings inside the crackling blue electric dome that traced the skyline's contours in the air. Kasih hadn't cared much, and just wanted to go back to the village to chase girls, but Timoth had been very disheartened.

Everyone at the table was exceptionally quiet, and Timoth's mother, Aellana, broke the silence by addressing what she knew everyone was thinking. "He's gonna be fine. He's been in worse shape than this before." She regarded Shawan, who nodded his agreement. "The important thing is that he got the package and survived to tell of it. Luminant intel says this device can put a stop to the Ascendancy. This could end to the fighting. Finally."

Timoth looked at her and saw that she was smiling. A real smile. Not some painted-on-for-the-sake-of-appearances smirk, but a sincere, comforting smile.

Dad and Raishann had turned their attention to Mom, also, and Raishann looked hopeful, too, as she reached for Mom's hand and gave it a gentle squeeze. Dad was home intact and had procured the object he sought. Timoth knew that the article - whatever it was - was significant. Supposedly, it could destroy the Ascendancy, and that was no small deed.

But the more Timoth reflected on it, the more uncertain he became that the Ascendancy was as evil as the Luminants made it out to be. All things considered, the Sylvans seemed to be just as toxic to them.

BAXTER CLARKE LIVED in a world of dreams. Everything he needed or wanted was provided to him through the marvels of the latest technology, sometimes before he even knew he needed or wanted it. Food, health, entertainment, and anything else, including cleanliness, came easily from drones and computers so that he was always comfortable.

All he had to do in return was ascend. As long as he was rising so that the Ascendancy as a whole rose along with his efforts, all the newest developments and amenities would continue to come his way. Even his feelings could be regulated so he was never anything other than content and pleased. Theoretically.

Baxter did feel uneasy, however, and it wasn't just because he had stopped taking the daily medications that kept the Ascended healthy and on an even keel.

He was gifted, much like his father, and was already setting new milestones for ascension through his achievements and well on his way to living among the elite of Enswell and the other eleven cities of the Ascendancy. Everything was looking good for his projected future.

His issue wasn't with the amount of effort he had made or the things he had developed that put him in this position. He was born into a highly ascended home, and he had no problem with that, either.

His father was an incredible genius and had built something that earned them the right to live in the city core with all the latest tech coming into their home.

In his artificially enhanced surroundings, and encompassed within the plasma-dome that sheltered the Ascended from the outside world, Baxter simply craved something real. He wanted things to happen or exist that hadn't been pre-planned or artificially produced.

Nanobots could build everything and anything, but they couldn't provide an experience that was meaningful or a feeling that was organic. He was worn from the weight of all the critical decisions in life being prescribed to him by protocols and algorithms.

It was inescapable in every facet of a person's day, from arising in the morning to retiring for the night. People were protected, sheltered and guided both toward the acceptable and away from the undesirable. As a citizen of the Ascendancy, you are free to make all the insignificant decisions you want. All the important things would be taken care of for you in your presumed inability to be able to - or even want to - handle them alone.

If something did hurt him or make him feel bad, he wanted it to take place as a matter of course and not be preordained.

Ascending wasn't the reason Baxter did the things he had done. His intentions began with thoughts other than the idea of putting something together to earn points and perhaps move up a level by producing it.

The budding genius had ideas that were worked on for days and nights without realizing how much time passed while he was engrossed in them. He was driven by the intellectual pursuit of solving the issues that kept those plans from working. Like his father, he could not rest until he figured out a problem. That was what made him push through the frustrations and challenges of the creative process. That was what led to his premature ascent.

And that was also what prompted him to be troubled about his feelings over the whole matter.

He felt no need to be placed on a pedestal for what he had done. His ideas were for the benefit of all and, more as a byproduct, they also benefitted the Ascendancy. He didn't want accolades. He didn't want the latest gizmo. And he certainly didn't want the division and separation that came with ascension.

But he simultaneously understood the need for people to rise. It was necessary for the betterment of humanity, especially since the Cataclysm.

Humankind, before that near-apocalyptic event, had lived for individual, personal gains and it had nearly led them to extinction. Baxter was reasonably sure that was not what those people wanted for themselves, despite having created it.

Just as certainly as he didn't want the party that had been put together for him tonight to celebrate his achievement of a new level of ascension, even though he had created that. This gala event was in his name, but in all honesty, it had been planned by his mother and was for his mother. She loved this kind of tosh.

She planned the party specifically for tonight because a breakthrough in Holographic Projection that generated much more realistic and robust looking renderings than had ever been seen before became available today, and this afternoon the Clarke home was the first to have a system installed. There would have been a party tonight even if Baxter hadn't attained this goal, but now his mother got to write the whole affair off as being for him.

That made things even worse for Baxter. At least when his mother's inane parties were only about her showing off, he could make an appearance and then disappear without getting too much flak from her about it later. But a party in his honour - that was something he would have to endure from start to finish, smiling like a fool until it hurt.

His only real saving grace was that the two people who were closest to him, lifelong friends Lila Riley and Kent Thompson, had received invitations and would be able to mitigate the damage.

He was wearing the suit that his mother's stylist had designated for him, and even though he had been somewhat dubious at first at wearing something that someone else was choosing for him, he had to admit that he liked it. The most exceptional ascended people were filtering into their home, dressed in their most beautiful and modern clothing and Baxter reluctantly admitted to himself that what he may have selected for tonight would not have been up to par. As it was, he felt like he fit in and that heightened his comfort level.

Kent and Lila had been at the apartment for several hours now, and they spent that time outside on the balcony with Baxter, who was waiting until he was beckoned to come in by his mother, putting it off for as long as he could. They were able to talk openly, and Kent did his usual excellent job of breaking the tension, which he could do in any situation.

"If you keep this up, you may not have to sell part of your brain to the Ascendancy for supplemental processing power," Kent guffawed. "You may even be able to procure a position in a refining facility."

"Very droll, Kent," Lila intervened, rolling her eyes. She leaned over to Baxter and fussed with the collar of his suit. "Don't let Kent's jealousy of your intellect obscure your focus, my dear." She looked into his eyes briefly, then focused on arranging his clothes perfectly. "Maybe you should bring in the gather of your waistline a little," she added.

"Increase waistline gather by three percent," Baxter ordered, and his suit waist altered itself to match his command. "Better?", He inquired, looking at Lila and holding his arms away from his body to give her a clearer view. Lila examined him, leaning back slightly and then giving her approval of the alteration.

Kent had already expressed his disdain over the idea that catapulted Baxter ahead of the rest of them, because it was one of those things that, once heard of from somewhere else, seemed obvious and made people wonder why they hadn't thought of it first.

Baxter knew that once the Gates were installed throughout the Ascendancy, they no longer needed telecommunications towers outside the walls to get past the interference from the plasma shields, which stopped radio transmissions. They could now send wireless signals from one city to another because they went through the Gates and radiated out from there. Baxter had postulated that if one force could travel via the portals, then maybe they all could.

He set up computer simulations that included a Gate rotated so it was parallel to the ground, and its mate, likewise turned, under the floors of the Avalon spacecraft. Sure enough, gravity travelled between the Gates and exerted a diminished downward tug on objects on the Avalon. He then moved the Source Gate in the simulation closer to the center of the Earth and found that by placing the Source Gate at a depth of about a kilometer, the Gate under the floors of the Avalon would give a 0.9G pull. It meant that the Avalon's decks would have to be curved so that all points on the floor were perpendicular to the Gate, but nanobots and android technicians were already making changes to the architecture of the orbiting ship to accommodate the new design.

Baxter had delivered gravity to space. Combined with the accumulation he already had, the corresponding ascension points moved him further ahead than anyone his age had ever gone. The new development made him the youngest citizen to reach the milestone of earning an augmentation. He could get an implant of his choosing, which would enable him to do even more.

He was excited about the prospect of expanding his abilities through enhancements, and hadn't yet decided what to have done. Memory expansion, processing speed, visual or auditory enhancements, device interfaces, and so many other things were available that he was having difficulty picking one. He supposed he could get other upgrades later on, but for now, it was important that he choose wisely, as this would be his only augmentation for a while.

Because stopping to eat distracted him and took away from his work time, he was considering a synthesizer for glucose. The process was like photosynthesis, in which amino acids and vitamins were produced from degradation products, so a person could go for weeks without food. It would eliminate what seemed to him to be the most frustrating thing he encountered in his travails.

All of that would come soon. For now, he would put aside those decisions to focus on getting through an evening of tedious hierarchical snobbery and subjecting himself to flattery he never desired.

Baxter became aware of his immediate surroundings again. Lila was smiling at him with every fibre of her being, and Kent was merely happy to be along for the ride.

Baxter, Lila, and Kent leaned on the railing of the balcony with the temperature-controlled night air gently circulating around them. It was nice to stand in the breeze quietly and be engaged with the moment.

Baxter was delighted with what he had achieved, and he knew that his friends supported him unconditionally, even though their interests and areas of expertise were highly differentiated from his. It gave him a sense of peacefulness amid the turmoil of his mother's party.

Music softly wafted out from the open patio doors that led to the party that was starting behind them. The glow from the plasma-dome illuminated them enough to allow them to see clearly, as they were pretty much as close to it as a person could get.

The Clarke home was near the center of the city, and very near the top of the building they occupied. It was a marvel of contemporary technology and had all the latest entertainment and comfort features. The inside could entirely reconfigure itself to create any layout that suited them. Right now it was arranged according to one of the presets, which was an open concept. All the rooms not being used had everything in them ambled into spaces around their respective peripheries, and the walls that separated those places from the rest of the household moved themselves toward the outsides of the home, leaving the center of the apartment open, ballroom-style.

The home possessed several features that showed the Clarkes' level of Ascendancy, as well as all the modern standards.

With data from the entire inside of the house continuously monitored, cleaning drones made their way around the environment from time to time when the artificial intelligence that ran the systems in the home deemed it necessary. They were handy and hard-working, but sometimes people would ask them to return to their charging docks to get them out of the way when they became a nuisance.

The appliances were all self-repairing, and Mother was quick to judge anyone who ever had to have a technician come into their home for any reason.

Food was available by verbal demand, and was prepared and served quickly in the kitchen and dining area, but could also be delivered by drone to any place you were within the home.

The new windows mother had insisted on having installed could be moved with tiny nanobots moving around inside the wall to make space where the window was going and then filling in any gaps left behind after it had relocated. The opacity of the windows was also adjustable, and these brand-new ones even had a feature that allowed for different scenes to be shown within them, giving the illusion of being anywhere in the world. Or outside of the world, for that matter.

Their entertainment was state-of-the-art. There was a modern virtual reality system inside that worked without headsets. It was tied into the new holograph projector, and the renderings it promised were supposedly beyond belief. The constructs were interactive, reacting to users by tracking their location and position. But, because they were laser renderings, a person could not touch or feel them. There was no warmth to a holographic character and no roughness to a laser-generated rock.

Mother was showing her friends the usual high-end hospitality, including the best food and most sophisticated music, but after dinner, she planned to wow them all with some savoury displays from their new projection system. There was no doubt they would be impressed.

Baxter enjoyed all the frills that came with living in such an ascended family, but he did not like the crowds of strangers that his mother assembled when they had an excuse to show off their latest purchases. Mother would find him soon enough, telling him to fulfill his social duties, or more likely, she would send Father to do it.

He turned and looked at Lila, who was already smiling at him in her coy little way. "So?," she asked casually, leaving him open to respond in any way he wanted.

"I am not sure. I mean, I know what I want in the long run, but I am not so sure what comes next. I will get an implant, which is very savoury, and I will continue my schooling. I am not so worried with the accumulation of points, I suppose, as I am with doing something worthwhile with my life."

"The eternal benevolent," Kent said, leaning down to look at him past Lila. "You are most noble, my good sir," he added, smirking. Kent was just as concerned with ascension as most were, but he seemed to be doing a decent job of it.

"Go dock yourself," Baxter retorted to his sarcastic friend. "Once I become the Captain of the Avalon, maybe I will procure for you a position as a cargo clerk on the ship. And if you show me the right respect, I will consider not having you discharged from an airlock in deep space."

"Thank you, kind Sir."

"You are most welcome."

Lila interjected. "Stop it, you two drones. And Kent, I don't I appreciate your verbal assault on my future husband." She leaned over and jabbed Kent in the ribs with her elbow and turned to give Baxter a wink. "We are both very proud of you. Pay no attention to this blockhead." She gave Kent another little shove with her hips, and they all laughed.

Baxter occasionally forgot his assigned marriage to Lila. It had been announced almost a year ago, and honestly, he was not opposed to the notion. Lila was smart and fun to be around, and though not quite as ascended as he was, she had done well for herself in computer technology and artificial intelligence, and she would be a frontrunner in that field some day. It made sense that he be paired with her, although Lila seemed to be more enthusiastic about the idea than he was.

For Baxter, it was a matter of course; the logical conclusion of the Ascendancy based on the available data. Lila had not only accepted the suggestion; she had embraced it. When he pictured in his mind's eye the woman he wanted for himself, Lila was the closest he knew to someone who was a good fit. She would be more than adequate.

Lila was proud of Baxter, and it was clear to everyone who knew them that Lila was pleased that they were assigned to one another.

He was better off in that regard than Kent. He would marry a girl from Haven that he had only met face-to-face once and holo-chatted with a few times. Kent had stated to Baxter afterwards that talking to her had been awkward and a little painful. But, he was marrying into a more ascended family than his own, and the girl was lovely to look at and possessed of some physical features that Kent preferred, so he was inclined to accept the assignment. His work as an astronomer specializing in exoplanetology gave hopes for advancement, but the odds of making a remarkable discovery were low, and dependent on sheer luck as much as anything else. Kent was not as smart as Lila or as innovative as Baxter, but he was savvy, and joining a higher family would provide him with the best possible opportunities in life.

Baxter was also acutely aware that his future vocation would have him away from home quite a bit. The Gates on the Avalon would deliver him to and from work every day, but he knew that being a Captain of the first starship would mean putting in much more time than his regularly scheduled hours. It would be worth it. The Avalon would take humanity to the stars, and he would be part of that.

"I really mean it, though. I want to do something that has a purpose and moves humanity forward in some aspect. It is not nobility or anything like that. It is just, well it would be a calling I suppose. And it surely is not meant to please my mother, despite her constant reminders of how important I can be." Lila and Kent chuckled, knowing how much pressure Baxter was under from his over-encouraging mother.

"There is no need for you to explain yourself to us, Baxter," Lila said as she put her arm around him and squeezed.

"We have known you for your entire life," Kent added. "So we know fully that you are a smothered, over-achieving drone who lives under the oppressive thumb. Do not worry about it." Baxter looked at him past Lila, and it took a second before he laughed, and then the three of them chuckled together. "In all seriousness, Bax, you have nothing to be concerned about. I'm sure your contributions will be notable."

"Many thanks, my good friend. I apologize, I suppose I am being affected by the formal tone of the evening."

"Speaking of which," Lila said, turning to look behind her, "Here comes your father. I presume we are to be called inside now."

Baxter shook his head slightly. He knew Mother would send him out here. Oh, well. Time to enter the party for him that he didn't want.

Chapter 2

THE SUN GLEAMED IN the sultry air, dancing through Raishann's auburn hair as she made her way along the earthen streets of Nylen.

Father feeling a little better, and Mother had insisted on her getting out of the house for a while, as there was nothing further she could do, anyway. She had asked her father if he was sure there was nothing else she could take care of, and he reiterated Mother's urgings. Maybe they needed some alone time.

Raishann greeted her neighbours as she walked along, playing a game with herself that demanded she not kick up any dust as she stepped, as per her combat instructor's lessons. The roads were hard-packed, but any dragging or shuffling of her feet would send off a slight cloud of dust. Though she walked quickly and happily, she remained mindful of her lessons.

Nylen was one of the few villages located this close to an Ascendancy city to have stayed in one place long enough for the roads to be well travelled for a period sufficient to make them this comfortable to walk on.

There were more stable villages to the North and South of Nylen, but most of the towns in this part of Sylva had moved because of Ascendancy raids in which they took people away and caused substantial damage to everything else.

Everything in the village was portable for that very reason, from the houses and other buildings to the water pumps and even the crematorium.

The Sylvan villages far enough away from cities to be beyond the interest of the Ascendancy were still ready to roll out on short notice. It had become part of their culture.

Raishann was old enough to remember Nylen relocating when she was a child, but Timoth had only been a toddler at the time and had no recollection of having lived anywhere else. She was comfortable in the village and enjoyed the town itself, and some of the places nearby, but the wheels under everything served as a reminder that her home was only temporary and they could be forced to move on any given day.

She put the idea out of her thoughts as she continued along, kindly addressing the people she met while she proceeded to the edge of town.

She was supposed to spend time with her best friend today, but Laena's father wanted her to help with some chores. Raishann had offered a hand, but Mr Reisatra assured her that he and Laena could handle it on their own. Raishann looked at Laena and shrugged her shoulders, and Laena flipped her off as she followed her father to the shed behind their home. Raish had been looking forward to time with her closest confidant, but now she would instead go to her secret spot and spend some quality alone time there.

Her sanctuary away from home was an old bunker that her father said was from the before times, used by ancient men to protect themselves from the wars they created.

It was one of the first places Raishann scavenged with her father once she was old enough and sufficiently trained for Shawan to take her with him. Together, they had picked it clean of anything valuable to the villagers - who got the first choice of what they found - or for trade to Luminants in the cities for things they could not get anywhere in Sylva.

Shadaar himself kept a lot of the artifacts that came from them. Books, electronic devices, clothing, and other relics that were not wanted by the Sylvans made their way to him. Raishann wasn't sure if he kept them or re-traded the artifacts to others, but she sometimes wondered how he could live in a city and be able to maintain such a volume of items hidden from Ascended eyes. He had proven to be most inventive, though, and probably had some way of dealing with the issue.

Raishann continued out of the village, past the small farms on the outskirts, and into the trails of the forest beyond that would lead her to the river. She knew every path intimately and had even helped to clear some of them after the rebuilding of the village. She adjusted the sword sheath across her back and proceeded into the woods.

She was excited to get where she was going and eager to find out if the new disk from Father would work in her player. If not, she would watch some of her favourite movies again.

Among the things she and her father had found on that day after literally stumbling over the protective hatch that served as the entrance to the bunker was a device wrapped in several layers of plastic. It had been carefully stored in a thick, sturdy chest along with some other, smaller boxes that were likewise packed and protected. Raishann sat and unwrapped the device and the packages and, not recognizing them, asked her father what they were.

The apparatus was about the size of a hardcover novel and it opened like a book, revealing controls on one side and what appeared to be a viewer screen on the other. Father said it was a player for the objects next to it that also looked like books, but when they were opened, contained flat, shiny plates with holes in the centers. There had been other ways that people had stored data, Father said, but only plastic disks kept in safe places had lasted this long.

She implored him to keep the device and the disks, and he told her that they were probably highly desirable objects for a collector, and would likely fetch a good trade. When Raishann looked at him beggingly, and he could see her fascination with them, he agreed but told her to leave them behind rather than bringing them home.

They told no one about the place they found that day or the things in it. Later, her father helped her to hook up an appropriate solar panel and battery to the viewer. She watched all the shiny plates and had become very enamoured with what she saw.

Some of the disks had movies on them that she watched on the tiny screen of the viewer. Others, when played in the device, had no picture, but only contained audio files of music such as she had never heard anywhere else. She loved it, and though she had to admit that not all of it was the work of a genius, even listening to the worst of them was time better spent than an afternoon with anyone other than Laena or her family.

When the trail got close enough to the edge of the river, Raishann left the path and headed down the rocks along the shoreline and followed it for a while. The river diverged from the trail, which swung back up and around the other way, turning to the left where the river went right. She had learned this trick from her dad, and stayed on the rocks to avoid breaking a visible path from the trail to the entrance of the bunker.

Once she was around the bend in the river, she went up the hill from the embankment and came to the place where a large steel tube emerged slightly from the ground, mostly covered by grass and scrub. It was the door she had tripped over years ago when she explored the area with Father.

She got on top of the sealed hatch, careful not to disturb the natural cover too much, and turned the wheel that unlatched the door on top. Once it let go, she squatted with her feet on the edge of the tube and grabbed the wheel with both hands before standing, pulling the round hatch cover open as she rose. It flopped over opposite her, and she turned around and pulled the bottom of her sword sheath close to her, lowering herself into the breach. There was a ladder there on one side, and she went down a couple of rungs before reaching down with one hand and pulling out the solar panel that was stowed there. She climbed back out and carefully withdrew enough wire from the hole to get the panel into the small bush next to it. Once the power source was adjusted to catch as much of the sun as was reasonable, she descended again, being careful not to tug on the homemade cable while gently closing the hatch. A dim light came from below, and the muscle memory of hundreds of repetitions of descending the ladder kicked in, guiding her down confidently.

At the bottom, the wire was pegged along the ceiling of the open space and led to a lightbulb, and from there it went down to a rickety table that displayed her most prized possession.

She crossed the room to the table and removed the lid of the wooden box she had made herself to protect this valuable commodity. A hole in the side of it was well sanded to allow the wire to pass through without marring or cutting it.

There it was; player on one side and a small collection of boxes marked as "DVD's" and "Compact Disks" on the other. There were all the original ones she found with the player as well as a few more that father had scavenged for her.

Shawan often brought cool things back from scavenging runs, and if she hadn't been with him, she exercised patience as they meted the haul out to people in the village until she could be alone with him. Then she would find out if he had brought anything especially for her. She was positively giddy when he did, even though she discovered that most of the ones that were taken from scavenge sites didn't work.

Some weren't shiny anymore, and she had learned that they had to be polished to play right, and others were scratched or cracked or both, and they would not play either. But, occasionally, she got something new to watch or listen to, and nothing pleased her more. This was one of those days.

The front of the disk was all black, except for a white triangle at the top with a white line entering it on the left and a rainbow coming out on the right, like a prism refracting light. She placed it into the player and started it. There was no picture, but the music was outstanding. Part of her wished Laena had joined her to hear the new disk, but she was enjoying sitting back and listening alone. She would play it for her best friend later.

Laena was the only person she ever trusted enough to bring to the bunker, and since then, she had never once gone there without Raishann. She had been so cool about the whole thing that Raish never worried about her secret going anywhere beyond her confidant.

No wonder all the boys in Nylen were crazy about her. Laena was exceptional. She could, and sometimes did, have any guy she wanted. Laena exuded confidence and calmness, and everyone around her picked up on it. She was in the good graces of every person in Nylen, except for those girls who were envious of her. There was one group in particular that had given Raishann and Laena grief whenever they could, but they were a small, although exceedingly obnoxious, exception to an otherwise stable rule.

Raishann could have her pick of men, too, but the few relationships she had been involved in were uninspiring and short-lived. She spent more time in training than the lot of the local guys and paid more attention than most, knowing that she couldn't solely rely on physical strength to do the work for her. She became a master of technique and combat strategy, and she was confident that she could have taken any of her admirers in a fight - fair or otherwise. None of them stood out to her in any way.

The whole courtship thing was very dull, though she did want a husband and children someday. She would not marry someone she didn't love, however, merely to have those things.

Raishann had heard people saying that life was too short for this or that, but she held the belief that life could be very long if a person made foolish or rash choices about how to manage it. For now, she was content with her family and her friends, and the romance that came to her vicariously from her DVD's.

She was waiting for someone to surprise her. And waiting was getting tiresome.

CHANCELLOR MARSHALL paced across the end of the table where Doyle Morgan sat with another advisor, Michael Burke. The Chancellor seemed uneasy, which was not his go-to modality, and Doyle was interested to find out what had prompted him to this state.

Marshall had called Burke and Morgan into the vast and sparsely decorated office, offering no reason why they were to be there. It was after regular hours, which meant this was significant, but when Marshall directed Burke to close the door in what was now a vacant department, Doyle knew it was going to be serious. He gave Burke a sidelong glance and shrugged his shoulders, his chubby face expressing mild confusion. Michael repeated the gesture back to him.

Doyle thought Burke was an idiot, but he had to concede that being as well-connected as his counterpart was often made him aware of information that he, himself, was not able to access.

"I have been speaking to President Windsor," Marshall began, glancing up, "And she is not pleased." He sat down at his desk and adjusted an art piece that was meant to be impressive before he looked into the eyes of Burke and Morgan. "She feels we have been too soft on Enswell. Though the city is generally performing well, there has been an upsurge of online searches that reflect criticism of the Ascendancy and alternative conduct choices. There is always some online chatter of this nature and, of course, we monitor it very closely. But she says that our averages are far above those of the World Ascendancy cities, and she wants it culled. Suggestions?"

Doyle continued directing his attention toward the Chancellor, but noticed peripherally that Burke had turned to him - as he often did when he had no ideas of his own to share. He felt like he should keep count. This would be yet another occasion when he had to make them both look good. "I'm confident we can come up with something reasonably soon, your Worship," Doyle said, hoping to buy time to mull over the issue before jumping into anything too hastily.

If Doyle was going to ascend, he had to be right. Every time. There was no room for mistakes for someone in his unique position. Burke could mess up all he wanted because of his family ties, but he didn't have the deck stacked against him as Doyle did.

"The citizens count on us to keep them comfortable and secure," Marshall continued. "But we must also maintain order. There is a precarious balance, and it must constantly be preserved. If there is too much security, the people will notice our influence. Conversely, as is the case now, if there is too much comfort the people feel like they can do whatever they want."

"I agree, Mr Chancellor," Burke interjected. Whether or not he truly agreed was irrelevant, because he would always tell Marshall that he aligned, no matter what he really thought. Doyle sometimes wondered if Michael might be an android programmed to augment their director's ego. "They are much too complacent. They actually take their freedom for granted."

Chancellor Marshall squinted and pursed his lips a little. "That is not entirely true, Michael. The people simply can't deal with real autonomy because they don't want the responsibility that comes with it. They would rather give away that control and accountability to us, and preserve the capacity to blame us when anything goes wrong."

"So they need to be reminded of the benefits they derive from the Ascendancy, so they do not question it," Doyle stated. "I'm sure we can devise something that will have the desired effect, your Worship."

"Good. Time is of the essence, Doyle," The Chancellor declared, "The President seems quite concerned, and I would like for us to ease that. We alone are ultimately culpable for the smooth inner workings of our city. It is, after all, your job to catch these things and inform me so we can move forward appropriately. Maintain the balance, you know."

Doyle didn't appreciate the insinuation that the current circumstances were their fault. He had done everything in his power to take care of things accurately, but he had dead weight for a partner, which meant he had to do all of his own work, plus two-thirds of Burke's, so they, collectively, could keep their heads above the waterline and avoid drowning. "You don't have to remind me, your Worship, but you may want to repeat that last statement for those in the room who may not be as aware."

As soon as he said it, he knew it was a mistake. Michael Burke was a golden child of sorts and was protected actively both from within the city and by powerful forces on the outside as well as his highly ascended family.

Michael stiffened and drew in a breath to retaliate, but the Chancellor beat him to it. "Mr Morgan, you should be more concerned with your own affairs than those of Mr Burke. He belongs here, and here he shall remain. You, on the other hand, would do well to remember your roots and how fortunate you are to be in your position at all. Things could have been very different for you."

Doyle knew that all he could do was swallow this criticism and ensure that nothing like it ever came out of him again. It was alright to entertain these thoughts, and it was even okay to present them to Burke directly in the form of insults that the oaf would not understand. But he must never express anything unflattering about Michael Burke, Golden Boy of the Ascendancy, out loud if there were anyone around who was prone to kissing up to the high-ranking idiot.

"We'll fix this, your Worship," Doyle said, looking straight into the eyes of his boss. "You can count on us." What he meant was 'you can count on me', but he left that thought in his head.

"Good," Marshall added, "I did not become the Chancellor of a city by surrounding myself with incompetents. Enswell needs you. Don't disappoint me." The leader turned to face the window behind his lavish desk and paused for some time before deciding he was finished. "You are dismissed. No. Michael, you can leave, but Doyle, I need to talk to you."

Burke left, and closed the door. Doyle waited in his chair, not sure of what was coming.

Marshall regarded him seriously and, after checking that the door was shut, he began. "You have come a long way from where you were when we first met."

"Thank you, Sir."

"You have strived for ascension more than most, and your efforts shall not go unnoticed."

Doyle straightened in his chair. He had been working for an opportunity to rise to the top since he was a young man, and he anxiously anticipated the Chancellor's next words.

"If you prove instrumental in assisting with this issue, there may be a Chancellorship opening in one of the cities."

Doyle was beside himself. "Which city?" he got out without sounding too zealous.

"This one," Marshall said. "Do right by me in this time of need, and my good fortune may become your good fortune."

THE PARTY HAD GONE as smoothly as Baxter could have hoped, and Lila and Kent had lived up to their roles as intermediaries between him and the overzealous guests admirably. He had been gushed over, coddled, and questioned beyond all reason, and without his friends there to buffer him, it would have been unbearable. Lila had been more attentive to him than Kent, which Baxter expected. Kent was there for him, but also used the opportunity to talk to high-ascenders, looking for potentials for his rising. As it was, he was grateful for their assistance, having made it through without too much difficulty and now was able to relax.

The flat had been returned to its original configuration, with the vast space once again performing its usual function as a sitting room, dining and living room, and it was more like the home it was intended to be rather than the entertaining area it had been for the evening.

The unveiling of the new holoprojectors was a hit. The guests had never seen such solid-looking images in full light. Usually, when people wanted to view a holo, they would darken the room to increase the illusion of tangibility to the otherwise translucent forms.

When Mother asked for the attention of all the visitors and introduced the woman who appeared to be standing next to her before passing her arm right through the rendering, there was a moment of awe within the audience while they tried to discern what they had just seen, followed by robust applause. Mother loved it and for the rest of the evening, images of exotic animals and impossible scenarios intermingled with all in attendance. The guests delighted in their bravery in the face of computer-generated beasts and inappropriate jokes made at the expense of people who weren't really there.

Baxter was not impressed with the reactions but had to admit that the tech was pretty savoury, himself not having seen it until its unveiling at the party.

He was relieved now that the whole thing was over and his social expectations had been met. It was nice to sit with his friends and not have to stave off bootlickers or weigh the communal impact of every chosen word. He could just be himself again.

No one spoke as the three of them relaxed in the living room. Lila chose a serene landscape to surround them on the walls, and though she had been tempted to add holographic embellishments to it using the projector, she left the space as it was. Baxter would not have denied her the opportunity to play with the new toy, but he was grateful that she had chosen not to. Lila always knew what to do to make him feel better.

Kent broke the silence, laughing to himself. "Did you see Mr Lancaster's wife roar into the holo-lion's face? That was priceless. And, in case you missed it, I recorded it. We can watch it again and again until we can't come up with any more awful things to say about her. It'll be fun."

Lila giggled. "I saw it, and from the way she had her hair done, there was an instant where I had issues discerning one from the other."

"Who are we talking about?" William asked as he entered the room. "Mrs Lancaster, I presume?" He came to the back of the sofa, between where Lila and Baxter were sitting, leaning on it as he waited for a reply.

"I have video if you'd like to see it," offered Kent, but Mr Clarke just waved and shook his head.

"I saw enough of her this evening, and have no desire to relive any of it, thank you."

Lila turned to look at William, and the sofa shifted its shape to accommodate her new position. "Will you come and join us, Mr Clarke?"

"Thank you." William made his way around the end of the sofa and Kent moved over to provide a space for him between himself and Baxter. Sitting down in the open place, William continued, "I was trying to work on my project, but after all of that sensory overload, I can't find it in myself to process anything of any value."

"What are you working on, Mr Clarke?" Kent implored.

"I'm developing an augmentation for the Gates."

"Aren't they as efficient as they could possibly be?" Lila interjected. "How much faster than instantaneous do people need to travel?"

"The Gates work fine as they are, but I am trying to make them better. Right now, the Gates work in pairs. You enter through one and immediately exit through the other. That's fine, but limiting, because for a pair to be usable, you have to make the first trip to where you want to be transported to in person and physically bring the exit Gate there." Father then looked upward, going into a momentary reverie.

Baxter knew about the original Gate placements because his father had been involved as an advisor in the expeditions. He had travelled by air from one city to the next until they had built a network that provided transport from any of the 12 cities to any other. Once the principle sets were operational, they used those portals to bring more things through for the Gates that would operate within each town. Father had regaled him as a child with all his tales about being outside of the cities and seeing the sky and the forests and wild animals.

Baxter loved hearing the stories when he was younger, but he had heard them so many times now that he could tell them to himself verbatim if he so chose. He still realized, however, how significant it had been. Since then, moving from one city to another was as easy as stepping into a Gate and exiting wherever you needed to be in any of the cities.

Shopping complexes were now immense, as each one was linked to every other, and a store owner could expand his place of business to another mall in another city just by having a Gate installed to connect the two or more locations.

William leaned ahead with passion in his eyes, and Baxter smirked, knowing that his friends had set Father off, and there would be no stopping him now.

"What I want to do is to have a single Gate that can project to another point without having a receiving Gate there."

"Well, that would make your precious spaceship obsolete, wouldn't it?" Kent joked to Baxter.

"No kidding," Baxter agreed. "Maybe the Avalon will be launched before it comes to that. The Gates are a miracle, but this is beyond reckoning."

Lila nodded, and Kent said he didn't even begin to simulate an understanding of the workings of the Gates.

"They're truly not all that complicated," William went on. "The math and theory for them all worked on paper, and all that was needed was a way to bring that concept to life."

"The whole process is ingenious in its intricacies, but not that hard to grasp as a concept," added Baxter.

Baxter was amazed at what his father could produce. As brilliant as he knew his father was, the otherwise erudite man's rambling thoughts and forgetfulness sometimes surprised Baxter. Father would occasionally stand in the kitchen with an empty glass in his hand, or something similar, and appear to be unsure of what he was doing. When Baxter was younger, he had suggested that William see about getting an implant to address the issue, but his father had just told him it was part of the creative process and best left alone. Baxter did not argue. He knew how ingenious his father was and accepted the answer, although he was sometimes afraid that he was not as smart as Father because he did not share that trait.

"Well, why don't you explain it to us, Bax?" goaded Kent. "And Mr Clarke can fill in any gaps or correct any mistakes you make." Directing a squinty-eyed grin at Baxter, he waited for him to begin.

Baxter knew a lot about the portals from sitting with his father while he worked on them; more than most, he suspected. But he felt like he was cutting in on his father's enthusiastic conversing. "Father could explain it better."

"Nonsense," William interjected. "I'd get caught up in the minutiae of it all and lose the overall concept. Go ahead. You know as much about it as anybody."

Baxter supposed that was true. Although his father had not always been present when he'd have liked him to be, he had been available enough to answer questions, or to point Baxter toward a resource that could help to illuminate his curiosity. He began.

"Well, the Gates are a set and one thing at the same time." He looked tentatively at his father, who nodded his agreement. He carried on. "Quantum physics has always allowed for one object to exist in two places at once, but it usually only happens at the smallest of scales. However, the relevant theories allow for the possibility of that happening with any object, no matter how big it is." He was getting excited, and if he had been looking at William then, he'd have seen his father recognizing himself in his boy. Baxter's attention went back and forth between Lila and Kent as he continued. "What Father did was to find a way - a process - that creates conditions for that to happen to large objects. The key to the whole thing is creating a quantum field of heavy energy. You don't have to know what that is. What it does is the important thing. You suspend a plate in the field, and it becomes one thing existing in two places at the same time. Not a copy, like another thing that's over there, but another instance of that same object existing at another location within the field."

Baxter looked at Lila, who seemed to follow, but he saw some disbelief on Kent's face. "It's authentic," he directed at Kent. "So when the plate is quantum entangled with another one of itself, the field is shut down and it leaves you with two plates."

"But they're really just one plate, right," Lila queried.

"Yes, that's right, and that's what makes the whole thing work. Because those two plates are one thing, when you touch one, you affect them both. So, the plates are stabilized in the Gate frames so they avoid decaying. Then, whatever you do to one happens to the other. And Father, please correct me if I get this wrong, but when you touch one of the plates you become one with it, which in turn is one with the other plate. So you can move from one to the other because your body's total displacement in the quantum entanglement is equal to the distance between the plates plus the distance you have moved." He looked at Father, who was nodding. "It seems so natural to go through them because it moves you in space with no differential in time. You go in one side and come out the other. Done and done."

"Very good," William said, applauding lightly.

"Wow," Lila and Kent overlapped one another.

"So, what was the augmentation you came up with, then?" Lila inquired, looking at William with some degree of hero worship.

"I want to make them one-sided, I guess. I want to make one Gate that will take a person in and send their energy out, so they arrive at the point the Gate is projecting to."

"Like teleportation without a Gate at the destination?" Kent asked.

"Exactly," confirmed William. "But it turns out to be much more troublesome than I expected."

"Did you try tuning the heavy energy to a point beyond the wavelength of the plate so it extends out past itself? Wouldn't that turn it into a beam?" Baxter inquired.

"That was one of the first things I tried, and it does project outward, but it's almost as though the projection has a surface tension, and when it gets to a certain point, it pops. If you do that to a portal, you end up with a Gate to nowhere. It would take you in, but then it would disperse your energy evenly to the surroundings." He shrugged and made a thoughtful face. "It would be a peaceful way to die, I suppose."

Baxter was only slightly disappointed that he had not been helpful. He knew there was no way the first idea in his young head would hit on something that William Clarke had not already thought of. If it had been such a simple problem to solve, his father would not have been interested in it. At least his suggestion made enough sense that his father had previously tried and dismissed the idea. It wasn't entirely irrelevant.

"Can the Gates be dangerous if that were to happen spontaneously?" Lila challenged with some concern in her voice.

"No, it cannot simply 'happen'; it would need to be programmed into a Gate explicitly. Portals are much more stable than people realize, but the possibility of phenomena like that is an excellent reason why they should not be tinkered with by untrained personnel."

"Maybe you should try marketing it that way to the Ascendancy," joked Kent, causing Lila to recoil somewhat.

"Problem with that," William gravely stated, "is that they would be happy to have it."

They all sat silently, drinking the remark in. That was, indeed, the problem with that, wasn't it?

THE WALK BACK FROM the bunker was serene and calm. The new music Raishann had just heard was still playing in her head, and she sang quietly as she walked, while maintaining her ever-vigilant awareness of her surroundings. She always had to be aware of the potential dangers that lurked in the forest, even though the peace within herself overwhelmed her. She was happy, not stupid.

She heard the sounds of the wilderness around her and smelled the freshness of the woodland air. Flashes of light on the forest floor touched the undergrowth, passing between the leaves of the gently swaying taller trees. She felt the stability of each of her footfalls - the result of a lifetime of training and diligent practice. Raishann was confident and secure, and giddy with a renewed sense of the connectedness of life. She hummed the new music and saw beautiful little flowers between the roots of the old trees that she hadn't noticed before.

She carried this delight with her from the river, up to the path, and through the twists and turns of her journey home.

Then the shadows of the forest grew smaller, and there were more significant patches of brightly sunlit forest floor. In the distance, she could see the opening that led to the farms and the village beyond.

Then Raishann heard the distinctive crack of rifle fire from ahead, and she slowed herself, reaching over her right shoulder to the handle of her sword, straining to see better, and moved off the pathway to conceal herself within the leaves and branches as she made her way to the forest's edge.

As she got closer to the end of the trail, the sounds of critters and wind in the trees became replaced with yelling, weapons discharging, and chaos. The smell of the forest air interchanged with the acrid scent of smoke. She began to understand what she was seeing, and her sense of joy converted to anger and fear.

The Ascendancy was invading the village.

She knew, theoretically, that this was something that happened occasionally, but now that she could see it clearly, she didn't know how to respond. Should she charge in? Was it more strategically correct to hang back? Go for help?

She pulled her sword all the way out of its sheath and stood, weighing her options and studying what transpired before her. For all her training in combat strategy, she couldn't find it within herself to decide how she should proceed. She noticed herself being paralyzed by her own indecision.

It wasn't too far from her hiding spot to the small farm at the edge of the village. She could see some of what was going on and make out some noises, but nothing specific. What she heard was aggressive and woeful, though, and as much as she always said she would be great in a fight, hearing those sobering sounds just made her want to retreat or at least cover her ears, so she didn't have to listen to it anymore.

She could see people, most of whom were armed with various hand weapons, engaged in combat with Ascendancy soldiers and O-bots with ion blasters. Where were the Luminants? They had projectile and energy weapons and knew how to use them. They should stop this from happening. Raishann wished she had a rifle, so she might engage from where she was, or find a point from which to act as a sniper. What could she do alone and armed with only a sword?

She saw amid the smoke and dust that the Ascendancy forces were withdrawing. They were falling back, rejoining their units and travelling in groups toward the other end of the town, where the trails led to the city.

She kept her sword out as she exited the underbrush at the forest's boundary, slowly making her way into the fields.

She ducked behind a tractor in the field about halfway between the forest's edge and the village and confirmed the Ascendancy's retreat. She could now see faces more clearly, and there were people stopping their defence of the town and allowing the Ascendancy to leave. Some chased the soldiers and Guardians as they marched away only to be met with ion beams. The people looked beaten, and she felt guilty for not having contributed during this time when her neighbours needed all the help they could get.

Oh, shit! Mom and Dad! Timoth! Were they okay?

She picked up her pace hesitantly, still wary of any signs that soldiers or O-bots might still be there. The farther she progressed without seeing any, the more quickly she trotted and she broke into a full run once inside the small town.

Most people ignored her as she went past them, and the few that noticed her went right back to what they were doing, giving her no attention.

Raishann hurried home, burst through the partially open door of the house, and called for her mother and father, but no one answered.

She ran through the area at the front of the round dwelling, moving toward the smaller rooms in the rear, still calling out.

There was no response from any room and no signs of struggle or fighting. She went back to the door, looking out among the faces she saw for the ones that mattered most to her, but did not see them.

She slowly left the open doorway behind her, wandering into the soot and debris outside and imagining horrible scenarios in which her family did not live through this attack.

Raishann climbed onto a tipped-over wagon to be better able to see around her. She convinced herself that the smoke that rose from the ground was the reason for her tears, and called out again to her mother. This time, she got a reply. Raishann turned to face the direction of her mother's voice and saw Mom and Timoth helping Father up the street, slowly moving toward the house.

Raish jumped down to the ground and on the way to meet them, she passed Mrs Reisatra, Laena's mother. She looked longingly at Laena's mom, but went past the crying woman to her own family, and hugged them all, then moved to her father's side as they helped him to walk home.

When they made it back to the place where Mrs Reisatra was, Aellana indicated to Raishann with a gesture that she should go to talk with the distraught woman. Raish went to her, stooping as she covered the short distance to the Reisatra matriarch, who was sitting on her heels outside their house and sobbing into her hands. When Raishann called to her, she opened her arms, getting up to her knees and opening reaching out to receive her.

Raishann kneeled next to the woman who had been a second mother to her for as long as she could remember and put her arms around her, hugging tightly and rocking slowly. "What's wrong?" she asked through a face full of dishevelled hair.

"She's gone," Mrs Reisatra sobbed. "They murdered my husband and took Laena." The woman exploded into tears and squeezed Raishann so tight she had trouble breathing. The crushing embrace, combined with the shock of the news, made her pull back slightly before she could speak again.

"Are you sure?" Raishann inquired, knowing immediately after the question exited her mouth how dumb it was. Of course, she was sure.

Mrs Reisatra didn't answer, but instead fell back to her original position and continued to wail. Raish joined in, and the two of them remained entwined until the young woman backed away and wiped her eyes.

Raishann stood, still dripping with tears, and offered to help Mrs Reisatra to get up. Laena's mother waved Raish away, stating through her tears that she would be okay, and that Raishann had her own family to look after. Raish hugged her one more time before turning to follow her sibling and parents. She resolved to go back and check on the woman again, as soon as they settled things at home.

Her family was settling at the table in the kitchen, with Father being helped into his chair before the others sat down.

Raishann was still dazed and crying, and she spoke into the silence. "Will we have to move?"

"I don't know," replied Aellana as she rose to comfort her distressed daughter. "Maybe."

Shawan shrugged his shoulders. "We'll have to get ourselves pulled back together before we make any resolutions. A lot of people would move right now, but they may change their minds once we have everything taken care of."

"Laena's gone. They took her." Raishann hung her head and tears rolled off her cheekbones and onto the cloth place mat before her. "Will we do anything to get those people back?"

Timoth had been quiet up to this point, but now spoke his fear, one that was shared by most. "We can't take on the Ascendancy head-to-head. They'll wipe us out."

"We can't take on the Ascendancy yet," Shawan corrected. "But we do have something that can give us the advantage." Everyone regarded him, waiting for him to clarify. "We have to get the artifact to Shadaar. He'll know what to do with it, and we'll move forward from there. Maybe we can put an end to this once and for all."

Chapter 3

DOYLE MORGAN WENT INTO Marshall's office with Michael Burke, and an old, many-times-used idea that he was sure would not impress the Chancellor.

Doyle had been inclined to use a public relations campaign combined with the release of a new program offering tours of the nearly completed Avalon to distract people. It would give them something to do and discuss; keep them otherly occupied. Replace the chatter of discontentedness with excitement for a new era.

But Burke had wanted to go with another option, and Doyle let him run with it, thinking it may be an opportunity to shine some light on his partner's ineptitude.

He had waited patiently for the appointment to come, as he was sure the Chancellor would disapprove of Burke's tactic, which would then open the floor to him making his well-prepared presentation.

"Sit down, Burke, Mr Morgan," his boss said, indicating the chairs on the other side of the large desk, "Let's hear what you have for me."

Doyle sat confidently as Burke settled into the adjacent chair and drew in a sharp breath. Doyle breathed calmly and waited for his moment to come.

Burke began. "It actually seems to me that Enswell represents a hub where some of the complacency in other cities comes from, on top of it being the issue it is here. The citizens need a reminder that not only do they share a common enemy, but that they also actually need the Ascendancy to protect them from it."

"Are you saying we should provide them with an enemy and then save them from it?"

Doyle repressed a smirk and waited for the inevitable rejection. He was not averse to harming people in the pursuit of accomplishing a task, but he was certain that the plan would be seen as foolish and poorly thought out when weighed against its potential long-term effects.

"Yes. We should arrange an act of terrorism within the city and then hold the Sylvans responsible for it. There hasn't been a real assault from the heathens in a long time. Hacking into our A/V and sending messages denigrating the management is not actually life-threatening. But, it does remind the citizens that they still exist; that they are out there lurking. But if we can set off an explosion in one of the outer vicinages near the rim, there will be casualties, but it will hurt no one of any import. And then the people will beg us to protect them by any means we can provide, which is what we actually wanted in the first place."

Doyle winced in anticipation of the recoil.

"Good," Marshall agreed. "It is decisive, quick, and logistically easy to implement. The damage seems acceptable compared to the payoff, and we can make the people come to us. We can then put something in place publicly, but hesitantly, and they will love us for it. Make the arrangements." It surprised Doyle that the Chancellor would approve such a tactic. He knew they sometimes had to be ruthless, but he had been so sure that Burke's plan would be seen as impulsive and derivative he had to recover before he was able to interject. "You don't think that to be somewhat short-sighted?" he disputed the Chancellor as he was turning to face the window. "There is a possibility of a severe backlash from something like this."

Marshall returned to his initial position and leaned forward as he spoke. "It is extreme, but this is an extreme situation. Not only will this put an end to what is happening in Enswell, but word will spread from here, and we can have a positive impact on the whole system. I think the President will be happy if our efforts here result in better numbers throughout the Ascendancy." He reclined and folded his arms across his chest. "I expect that you will do your utmost to fine-tune a plan for implementation and ensure that it is carried out without issue."

"Yes, Mr Chancellor. We will see this through." Doyle heard himself say the words reflexively, but he could not believe that things were moving in this direction. Burke was coming out of this better off than when he came in. Shit.

"Keep me apprised of your progress and ensure that no one hears of this who does not have to. Keep the circle as tight as possible."

"Yes, Sir," Doyle and Burke replied in unison. They rose from their seats together and exited the room. Burke was beaming. He didn't deserve it.

Doyle would have liked to knock that stupid, smug grin off Michael's face right then and there, but he would instead allow the socialite to fail of his own accord and expose himself. Then Doyle could have a smug smile of his own.

WILLIAM WAITED UNTIL Candace was out shopping and Baxter left the flat to do some research into augmentative implants. They would be gone for long enough. He retrieved the key that hung in secret in the back of the room that served as his home workshop, then went to the opposite wall and placed his hand on it.

A section of the surface opened when the nanobots that bound it together scurried out of the way as they had been programmed to do. They were sensitive to the combination of the close presence of the radio key combined with the physical contact that provided his DNA.

There was one other individual whose genetic code was registered into the system, but that person did not have a key. Not yet, anyway.

The new gap in the wall revealed a Gate he had built when they were still early in their development, and he had kept without anyone knowing. It was small, and William crouched as he went in. When he came out on the other side, he was not in his home anymore - not even within the city.

Once he was through the portal, the wall back in the shop re-sealed itself, and no one who looked into his home office would ever know what had happened.

As he entered the small room, the only light came from the soft glow of an emergency light that was on all the time and powered by the unoccluded sun that shone overhead. The whole place had been put together very carefully, and the work that was done within it was more valuable than anything else he could ever hope to accomplish.

When William went on the expeditions to establish the first portals, he asked for some time to enjoy the wonders of the wilderness and also do side research into the natural phenomenon outside the cities.

It had been approved, but what he actually did in the forest had nothing to do with the proposed experimentation. A man as brilliant and celebrated as William Clarke was at the time would not be questioned about anything he said he wanted to learn.

Alone, he had used a portable disintegrator to excavate a hole in the earth. When it was finished, it was six meters long by four wide and about five meters deep. Then, every day following, he brought as large a piece as he could smuggle with him as he assembled a small portal - the other half that was paired with the Gate in his home office.

He returned from his jaunts with some random twig or interesting-looking rock as a "sample". There were notes on his pad that appeared to have been taken in the field, which in reality he had created at home in his off-hours and hidden in his gear so he could pull them out after his excursions as justification for the time he spent away.

None of the Ascendancy soldiers in the work crew knew the difference and they never questioned what he was doing.

Once the hole was dug, and the portal was in place, he stopped going to that spot while he was with the Gate Initialization Team. He did, however, continue to make side trips in different directions every day until they installed the new Gates and completed the contract.

From then on, he could bring the pieces he needed to finish his work at the site from his home, through the Gate. He framed the hole securely with lightweight, super-strong carbon fibre beams that would not rust or decay, and built a sealed roof before filling in the shaft's top with debris. In time, nature would completely cover his activity there.

He installed solar power and a self-cleaning ventilation system that would never have to be maintained. He built the inside walls and floor before bringing in his equipment and the modest collection of artifacts he had collected up to that time. In a couple of months, he completed building what he started calling his "Nest".

He had already developed the key and DNA scanning system that kept his portal hidden and secure, and once that was installed, he programmed the house to always move the concealed entrance in the wall as a single unit. The facade would never open and reveal its secret while the flat was in any other configuration than its default room setting. He covered all traces of the home systems having been tampered with, and double checked that he had been extraordinarily thorough.

Now he had an invisible room with no direct access. It was a place he could go to tend to the business of being Shadaar - contact and collaborator to the Luminants.

His dealings with the rebels were well concealed. There were only a few Sylvans within the Luminants who knew who he was, and no one in the Ascendancy was aware of his secret life.

He was proud of what he had built, and he smiled as he sat in the chair at his desk and turned on the central power. The glow of the emergency light was replaced by illumination from the ceiling fixtures, and a laser scanned his eye before the terminal monitor came on and the computer initialized.

Candace had nearly caught him at the party, checking the message from Aellana Forander stating that Shawan had successfully retrieved the package from a counterpart from Belleburgh, which was on the far side of Nylen and across the abandoned ancient metropolis that lay between them. The man had made a long journey to get the device to its destination.

Even though the Luminant sympathizer in Belleburgh had been able to obtain such a prize as Shawan now possessed, he could not use it. Hence, he transported it to Shawan who, in turn, got it for Shadaar, who could do all manner of unusual things with computers and electronic technologies. Their cause would be substantially advanced.

William learned of this cause serendipitously as a young man, before the creation of the Gates, and even before Candace came into his life.

When he was in university, he came across a youthful woman one day while he was on his way home from school. She was hurt and in need of care. She said she did not want to go to a hospital, so William helped her to the university dorms where he was staying. She looked like anyone else - William had not given it a second thought - and it wasn't until he got her back to his apartment and tended to her wounds that he saw the dark skin she concealed under her clothes. He discovered that the lighter skin of her hands, face and neck was a ruse hiding a Sylvan - probably a Luminant - disguised as Ascended.

It shocked him, and he stopped administering any care to her, unsure of what to do next. She pleaded with him to not report her to the police as she succumbed to her injuries, which were more substantial than William had initially assessed. Shortly, her begging grew weaker, and then she passed out on the bed he had laid her on.

He could not allow her to die in his apartment. How would he explain what had transpired? He might end up implicated in a Sylvan plot or labelled as a terrorist. He didn't know what to do, but he knew he had to get her out of there, and the best way to do that was to have her able to get back to wherever she came from on her own. So, mostly to preserve himself, he did everything he could to treat her.

He doctored her as well as he was able, and allowed her time to recover, taking a few days off from school. When she finally awoke, and William was able to talk to her, she informed him about the Luminants. She explained to him about the origins and inner workings of the Ascendancy. He listened, dumbfounded, as everything he had been taught to believe became unravelled in his ears.

She told him how, before the 12 Cities and the Great Cataclysm, the governments of the world tried to amalgamate and enforce a One World Government and a World Army upon the people of Earth. At that time, there were people inhabiting most of the globe rather than just the zone from the Tropic of Cancer to the Tropic of Capricorn, where the 12 modern cities lay. Humanity would not accept the rule of the new order, and war broke out.

The World Army was winning the war when they learned that the People's Rebellion had turned many of their own soldiers against them. Those troops left, taking weapons and, sometimes, entire military complexes with them, strengthening the rebellion.

It was hard to dominate the people when the army you used for that purpose comprised those very people; all of whom had families who would find themselves among the oppressed once the war was over.

The strength of the Rebellion grew, and the World Army was in imminent danger of being defeated.

So their leaders changed tactics in a most sinister way.

There was a significant asteroid streaking toward the Earth. Most people knew about it. It was not on a collision course with the planet but would pass by very nearly according to all calculations. The rulers of the World Army intervened, using a technology that was developed to save the Earth in the case of an imminent direct strike.

They reversed the process and placed a large satellite near the asteroid. The gravity from the massive rocket pulled on it and changed its trajectory, placing it on a collision course with Earth.

The Global Elite withdrew as many loyal people as could be accommodated, and they retreated to space stations in high Earth orbit. They sat in comfort, fully stocked with provisions and entertainment, ready to stay where they were for many years.

When the asteroid struck the Earth, it wiped out a significant percentage of all life on the fragile planet in less than two hours.

The Dark Times that followed were terrible for the survivors of the Great Cataclysm, and those sick, suffering people struggled, unaware that the very governing body which existed to look after them had forsaken them.

The Elite stayed aloft until things settled enough that they could send down self-replicating robots, who made more copies of themselves from almost any materials they could find, to build the rims of what would become the 12 cities. During the initial phases of the construction, they eradicated any humans who wandered near, and the building continued.

This went on night and day for several years until the outer walls of the cities were entirely constructed and some necessary internal infrastructures were put into place. The robots also stockpiled food until there was enough for thousands of people to live in relative comfort.

Then the Elite came back to Earth, splitting themselves among the 12 prospective cities, and began new lives for themselves. They sent out squads to search for those who would be willing to partake of the safety and comfort they offered. When groups of people started coming, either with the troops or on their own, the Elite presented themselves as the saviours of humanity.

Many people were ready to drink it in and give themselves over to the newly formed establishment.

The World Government re-branded itself as The Ascendancy and created new social structures. The more a person contributed, the more they ascended, and the better products and comforts they availed themselves of. The citizens tripped over themselves to achieve so they might enjoy as many of the perceived benefits as they could.

The new Ascendancy even used the people who chose not to join them. Although robots could do all the work, the Sylvans were despised for their nonconformity and taken as slaves to run the waste and water treatment facilities that lay outside each city. It was a power move; a reminder to the people of the woods that they were less than the people in the cities. The Ascended citizens never thought about what happened to something they threw out, or where the comforts that came into their homes originated. They had been completely cut off from reality and sold their souls for security and entertainment and pleasure.

Marriages were assigned by the government, and they paired citizens based on algorithms that projected the maximization of loyalty, to keep as much order within the fledgeling regime as could be had.

Then, fully established, the Ascendancy maintained control of their people with propaganda and fear of a threat from beyond their borders, provided by the Sylvans.

In those early days of establishment, an Ascendancy official who could not live with the way administration was running things left his city and came to Sylva, sharing with the people the details he knew. He also had ideas about how to wake the Ascended from their dreams of utopia, and the Luminants were conceived. They started as a small group of Sylvans who knew the truth and wanted not only to defend themselves from the raids on their villages but to free the enslaved people of the Ascendancy. A new rebellion was born.

The story the Sylvan woman told from his little bed as she regained her strength had shocked him from his complacency, and William was never the same afterwards. He let his new friend, Aellana, return to her life once she was healed sufficiently to get back to her family.

Once he was alone again, William searched for proof of what the young woman had shared with him. He found enough corroboration of her story to lead him to contact her again by the means she had provided, and he joined her and her cohorts to bring individuality back to the Ascended, and end the tyranny of the Ascendancy. In all his time with the rebellion since then, there had never been a better opportunity to do that than the one before him right now.

The computers came online, and William sent a reply to the message he had received from Aellana - the one he read from the surface of the buffet table. He thought it strange that Shawan hadn't posted it himself as he usually did, now that his wife was no longer as directly involved in the operations of the rebellion.

His note to her was simple. "Hope all is well there. I am unable to leave. Meet me. Bring the package."

RAISHANN HAD BEEN AWAITING this day for a long time, but now that she was going on her first mission to a city, she struggled to hide the fact that she was frightened half to death.

With her skin lightened and her hair styled as the Ascended wore it, she barely even recognized herself when she saw her reflection. Timoth had been no help at all, making snide comments about her appearance and calling her names.

Mom told him to knock it off, but only once it had ceased being entertaining for her. She had done this many times before, but it had been a long while since the last time.

They left the village as Shawan looked on, feeling stronger than yesterday, but still not well enough to go, and surely too bandaged up to accommodate the disguise of a city person. Barring some terrible accident - an anomaly in city life - no Ascended would ever be as banged up as Dad was now, and they sure as hell wouldn't have rifle wounds. It was better that Aellana went, and as Raishann's first mission into a city, they sent her as a support to her mom.

Although it still bothered her that she had hesitated when she came upon the Ascendancy raid on the village, Raishann was still confident in her combat skills and had a lot of training to prepare for this. She was at the top of most of her classes, and she didn't want to let down any of the people who believed in her.

Among her practices, she had learned how to talk like a city person, but she would have to stay focused to ensure that she wouldn't slip and say something random that gave her away as a Sylvan. Mom had instructed her to speak very little, and to pretend that she actually lived in the city while she was there.

Raishann would have to carry herself like a city person. She could not gawk at the buildings or appear to be surprised by anything she saw.

She admired her mother's courage as they walked along the path that would lead them to the city, which was becoming visible occasionally through the trees as a small hump on the horizon. There were trails cut all over the place in the forest, as the Sylvans did not want to be easy to find, and sometimes people would walk randomly through them so that each was as travelled as the next. Mom knew the best path to take to balance getting there efficiently and staying somewhat concealed. There were no Ascendancy patrols this far out, but there might be once they got closer to the point where they would enter Enswell.

Mother knew the man they were going to connect with; she was one of the few Luminants who was friends with Shadaar. Being the only person in the village familiar with the contact, and also available to make the trip immediately, she had been chosen to go in Shawan's stead. Her training and experience was more than adequate, and this was supposed to be a straightforward transaction. They would meet the contact at the agreed upon point, hand over the package, and deliver a message before leaving. The whole thing sounded simple enough.

Raishann padded along behind her mother as they walked through the jungle, paying attention to where they were going and being careful not to snag her clothes. Neither of them said anything to the other until they passed the facilities on the fringe of the city and reached the outer wall, where Aellana ushered Raishann into the overlooked maintenance shaft that would lead them into Enswell via their infrastructure inlets.

Once they were inside and walking the streets of the city rim, Raishann found that there was no need to worry about saying anything out of place.

Aircars flew between the ultra clean buildings in the stale and strange-smelling air, and those who walked all looked like they were going somewhere important. Large holographic signs hung over the streets that said "Rise!" and "Ascend!" with images of vital-looking people smiling smugly next to the uplifting messages.

A man walked past her, talking to his companion, and she noticed the tattoo on his exposed arm. She had seen tattoos before - they were reasonably familiar in Sylvan culture - but it seemed like this one noticed her looking, and it moved around on the man's arm before coming back to its original position. She suppressed a gasp and hurried to walk beside her mother, from whom she could derive some semblance of confidence.

No, she would say nothing untoward. She had never seen or even dreamed of a place like this in her life, and she found it impossible to say anything at all.

LAENA REISATRA'S DAY began unlike any she had experienced before.

She had been away from her home in Nylen before, but knowing she did not have the option to leave the dismal place she was in weighed heavily on her. She wondered what happened to the rest of her family. She wanted to be there to help with the aftermath of the raid. And she deeply missed Raishann and hoped that her best friend fared better in all of this than she had.

Lights came on without warning, harshly illuminating her plain cell and the few possessions they had issued her. There was an annoying blare of an alarm, and the door of her cell slid open unceremoniously. She squinted into the ignorant light and rubbed her eyes before rolling up into a seated position on the edge of her cot.

Laena made sure she was at least sitting before the guards arrived. Other prisoners had told her that it was a small matter that saved a lot of potential grief first thing in the morning, and honestly, she didn't need that kind of crap to begin her day.

"Everyone up," she heard a man's voice yell from down the corridor, and the prodding to wake up continued as he made his way along the banks of cells, banging on the bars of any that contained slow risers and clomping his boots excessively on the floor.

As the heavy footsteps approached her open cell door, they stopped, and she looked up, opening her eyes for the first time. A guard with a patch on his uniform that designated him as number 482 stood before her with a stupid grin spread across his face like the paint on a toddler's artwork. "Good morning, Sunshine," he oozed to her.

"We'll see," Laena shot back to him as she scratched her forehead. "Still too early to determine." She let her hand drop to her lap once again and met his gaze. "Hope so."

"You will have a great day," he whispered through the open door, the smile dropping from his face, "As a matter of fact, I will ensure that it is fantastic. I think I will take you to work in the garbage processors today. Sounds like a good way to spend a day, does it not?" He paused briefly before he grinned again and carried on, banging on the bars a couple of cells down. "Get up!", he barked at some sleepy prisoner. "Do not start your day with a beating. There. That's better." The footsteps continued down the corridor, and Laena just knew that today was going to suck.

She got up and pulled the onesie that she had been given over her sleeping clothes and headed out to the courtyard with a stream of other people in the same garb, where they would take a head count. She didn't know why they bothered with the ritual; everyone would be there. From what she heard after being brought in and processed yesterday, she was pretty sure that no one had ever made it out of this god-forsaken hellhole, or had even really tried. Something to aspire to, she guessed.

After headcount, breakfast was served in the mess hall, which she thought was aptly named, because that's what they fed the prisoners in that room. A mess. She ate her gelatinous nourishment without paying any attention to it, choosing instead to worry about what might happen to her through the course of the day. As bad as it was to be here in the first place, and as hard as it was to fight back the tears that had always been hanging on the brink of full manifestation since her arrival, the unknown variable of living under an active antagonist made her edgy and stressed. It was not a way of existing that she was familiar with. She would ensure that her fear remained hidden behind sharp quips and a rebellious attitude.

The guard who had greeted her this morning, number 482, seemed to have it in for her since he got fresh with her yesterday, shortly after she arrived with the others taken from Nylen. He had cornered her when she was coming out of the refresher, wrapped in a towel and carrying her clothes to the change room.

He backed her up against a wall and leaned in close, putting one hand on the wall beside her head to intimidate her. But Laena wasn't easy to scare and was not impressed by his overcompensating attempt at manliness. She just dropped her clothing and punched him in the exposed pit under his raised arm. Her towel fell away from her, and even though he was in pain, his eyes widened at the sight of her bare body. She kicked him in the groin as hard as she could before she took any steps to cover herself.

While the temporarily disabled guard lay curled up on the floor, gasping for breath with his hands in his crotch, she gathered her towel and clothes. She then ran to a cubicle and threw her jumpsuit on quickly so she could get the hell out of there before he recovered.

The incident was not spoken of again. The guard would have caught a lot of shit for it, she supposed, so he probably hadn't reported it at all. But afterwards, he made a point of pushing her harder than any of the other new prisoners for the rest of the day, yelling at her and shoving her with the end of his baton.

And now, knowing that he was on duty again, she found herself walking around in a state of paranoia, wondering what form his revenge would take, and when it would happen.

Maybe it would be today.

DOYLE REALIZED THAT he was not the only person who had gone from rags to riches within the Ascendancy, but he doubted if anyone else had the same differential between their starting and ending places. It was not uncommon for people to move up a level or two, or occasionally even three, but he ascended all the way from the outer rim to the Core, and it sometimes irritated him that he couldn't tell anybody about it.

In his luxury flat in the heart of Enswell, Doyle sat back in the plush chair he was in, and it adapted its shape to support his body most efficiently. The lights were dim, and a holo was playing itself out in the space before him.

It was a bootleg program depicting a beautiful girl dancing, scantily dressed, who had a low-level Artificial Intelligence and could interact with Doyle and carry out his instructions. He had several of these programs, each with a different personality and the ability to have physical characteristics altered to match his appetite on any given day. It was usually on in the background, even though he spent most of his time at his office, either in person or by telepresence, and only came to the flat to recharge himself so he could stay focused on his professional development.

He asked out loud for a beverage, and his virtual assistant appeared on the smart wall closest to him and acknowledged the request, stating that he would have it presently.

Doyle liked having access to the good life he lived and was grateful for the choices that had ascended him. It had all been worth it.

The deal he made that caused his launch from the fringe to Fifth Circle bound him to secrecy, as much for his protection as for the discretion of the Ascendancy.

He had set his sights on getting out of the rim of Stableton at an early age, but when it became plain that the amount of work necessary to do it traditionally would take several lifetimes, he sought an alternate route. At one point, he had even strongly considered selling a portion of his brain to the Ascendancy for wireless processing enhancement for the central computer. But, he knew people who had done that and, after the augmentation in exchange for Ascension Points, they were never the same. Eventually, he discovered another way.

He espoused misgivings about life in the Ascendancy, and soon caught the attention of the Luminants. Taken into the fold, a couple of years later he found himself in a position of trust and influence in their circles. He even learned that there were members of his own family among their ranks, some at quite high levels. He never met anyone in the upper echelons, such as the infamous Shadaar, but when he knew enough that he could cause some real damage, he turned on the group and went to the police.

He would not tell the constabulary anything, and said that he would only speak to Chancellor Roberts herself. Believing that Doyle may be a security risk, the police denied him that opportunity and held him at Aldergate prison in solitary confinement. He talked to no one, and was patient, knowing the bits of information he had enticed the authorities with must also have piqued the interest of some high-level people.

Doyle was momentarily pulled from his reverie when a drone appeared, silently moving across the floor with the drink he had requested, and he leaned forward to accept the vessel it offered. The little robot asked if he would like anything else and Doyle told it to go dock itself. It tottered off, fading from sight as it moved away from the light of the holo to charge its power cells.

Doyle sipped on the perfectly chilled beverage and slumped back into his chair once again.

His waiting paid off, even though he almost lost his courage a couple of times while in Aldergate's confining cell. The Chancellor showed up one morning outside his cage and ordered the guards away, leaving him alone with Stableton's leader and an armed O-bot. When he demanded to know why the Guardian was there, she said it would record the conversation they were about to have. Doyle agreed to talk with her in exchange for a fresh start. The Chancellor asked for clarification.

This fresh beginning, Doyle stated, was to begin in the Third Circle at the very least, along with a starting position in City Administration. The Chancellor said they could move him to another city and rewrite his personal history, giving the appearance that he transferred into a new position from another town. But this would only happen if what Doyle was sharing was worth it, and she impressed upon him that his testimony had better show full loyalty to the Ascendancy. He was not to withhold any information to protect citizens he knew. Doyle was okay with that and reassured the Chancellor that what he had to share would please her.

With an agreement in place, he turned in everyone he knew - strangers and family alike - in a two-and-a-half-hour-long treatise about the internal workings of the Luminants.

His honesty delighted Chancellor Roberts, who became sure that she was getting the better end of the deal. Doyle held nothing back and relentlessly spoke against those he betrayed with his deceptions of comradery. The man was loyal to the Ascendancy beyond question.

Doyle moved to Enswell shortly after that, into a Fifth Circle flat the likes of which he had never even seen before, and quickly put to rest any guilt that may have been gestating within him. He set aside what he felt had to be done to achieve his long-time goal and got down to the business of progressing upward.

He took his low-level administrative position very seriously, staying late and going far beyond his prescribed duties, memorizing data so he could answer questions on the spot, and making himself an invaluable commodity to his superiors.

He continued to rise, eventually moving to the Core, and then into the posh flat he now called home, and he did not plan to stop climbing. There was always more to do and a higher position to aspire to.

Things had been a little stagnant for him of late, and he nearly become complacent where he was now. There were few people above him, and a lot of those were celebrities or scientists who had made useful discoveries. Some people in his office were parallel to him, but he had demonstrated that he would do anything that was necessary to win the approval of Chancellor Marshall.

It was only a matter of time before something came along that would put him ahead of the crowd, especially above Michael fucking Burke. His time would come. He had his eyes on Marshall's office and would keep pushing until he took it.

His journey had commenced at the absolute bottom of the barrel, and he would not be satisfied until he found himself at the pinnacle of ascension.

He wondered what he would do after that.

Chapter 4

MOM AND RAISHANN HAD left for Enswell and Dad was resting in his bedroom. Timoth had the rest of the house to himself and, besides having to stay quiet so his convalescing father could sleep, he could do whatever he wanted to.

Mother had requested that he not leave home so that Father would have someone to watch over him in case he needed anything or something went wrong.

Timoth thought he might invite Kasih over to visit, but the idea was fleeting, as he remembered that his friend was likely busy with the aftermath of the raid, like everybody else was.

He still could not believe that the Ascendancy had just marched into the village and taken what they wanted. He supposed they could do whatever they pleased.

Fortunately for him, Mother had asked him to help her to bring Father to see the doctor before the whole thing started. The Ascendancy hadn't bothered with the little local hospital. They weren't interested in taking people who were sick or injured, Mom told him later.

Timoth had pushed his recovering father in a wheelchair even though he could stand and walk with some help. The hospital was one of the most massive and permanent buildings in the village and on the last street in Nylen. Behind it was the fullness of the forest. Timoth did not like that he had to push the chair along the rough roads while trying not to jostle Dad too much. They should have at least taken a donkey cart. There were easier ways to do things for a reason. But Mother wanted the walk and said they were in no hurry, anyway.

The doctor told them that Mom was doing an excellent job of keeping the bandages changed and clean, and gave her a tincture to use on the mending sores where Father's skin was burned. The shots were both grazes, and had either of them, especially the one on his ribs, been a more direct hit, Father might not be with them now.

From the tiny examining room, they heard the first signs of trouble, and when it became apparent what was going on, the doctor got Timoth and his mom to help him protect the other patients. Together with the nurses and other non-disabled people at the hospital, they had assisted all the patients out through a back exit, and into a small clearing a short distance into the woods behind the building. Maybe that was why it was on the last street.

But Timoth couldn't understand why, of all the people in Nylen, they went out of their way to protect the people who were sick. Didn't strong people matter more than the local invalids?

As the attack went on, Timoth and the others were given swords, and they maintained a defensive line at the entrance to the clearing. They didn't see any action, and when it was over, they brought the patients back into the hospital, and everyone dispersed to check on loved ones and see if they had sustained any damage to their homes.

The Ascendancy had taken 18 people with them, killed a dozen, and wounded many more. None of their forces had been killed, and if any of them was injured, it had not been so severe that they couldn't retreat along with their comrades when they left.

The whole thing had been over in about 20 minutes, and though they made a mess of the village and the people in it, they had been relatively unscathed. They were a superior force and took what they needed from an inferior people.

Timoth couldn't help but think it was like watching evolution take place before his eyes. The strong overcame the weak to further their survival. It was the natural order playing itself out at an accelerated rate.

And now, his sister and mother were risking themselves again in yet another desperate attempt to preserve the Sylvan way of life. Why were the Sylvans putting so much effort into staying subservient to the greater power? Why did they fight tooth and nail so they could continue to live in filth and comparative poverty?

Timoth was tired of being on the losing side of the predator/prey dynamic.

He craved a better existence than what was accessible to him. He wanted to rise.

THE DECISION TO FOLLOW through with Burke's strategy was still bothering Doyle when they started working on it. They had pulled together a small committee - only three other people - and met in private to discuss what they would do and how it was to play out.

As it was his plan, Burke had selected the other members, and the finalized group consisted of people he trusted, mostly because they were friends of his, or ass-kissers, or both.

Doyle was there because he had to be, still believing that consequences down the road would eventually shatter Burke's designs. He held onto the belief that the idea, even if it got positive short-term results, would ultimately backfire, and Doyle wanted to be exempted from any repercussions. He washed his hands of making any significant contributions to the ridiculous scheme and was trying to remain as distanced from it as he could.

The committee discussed various plans and eventually landed on setting off an explosive device in the city. They would fake a Sylvan hack into their communications, play a falsified message of Sylvan hatred to the people of Enswell, and then, shortly after, they would explode the apparatus at a location near the rim.

Doyle had to admit when it was all said and done that it sounded like a workable plan, despite his assertion that the committee amounted to the stupidity of one of its members multiplied by the number of people present.

They decided that Burke would take this suggestion back to Mr Marshall for presentation, and with that, the meeting was adjourned.

Doyle had learned before too long within this corporate structure not to leave a meeting as soon as it was over. A lot of politics happened between adjournment and the attendees going their separate ways, and it was better to be privy to that discussion than not.

The committee members shook hands with him and Burke and each other, and they all congratulated one another on their collective brilliance. Typical.

It was not until Burke left with one of his chums, and Doyle was collecting his papers, feigning preparation to go, that he overheard the remaining two members talking. They discussed something that snapped him to attention, and he had to remind himself to appear as though he was not interested so they would continue speaking openly in front of him.

"Have you heard the latest?" the man who remained asked the lady who was left there. "Burke will ascend to the Chancellor's position if Marshall retires or leaves. His sister told my mother at the hairdresser's last week. I suppose it pays to have people of influence in your family. Personally, I do not feel he is up to it, but the bottom line is that he has accumulated enough points to put him in the running. I don't know if he even has any competition."

He had better have competition, Doyle thought to himself. *I've done more for this city up to this point in my life than he will do if he lives to be three hundred years old. Privileged little shit!*

He finished packing up his things as the difficult conversation continued in the background as though he wasn't even there. Doyle knew they were aware he could hear them, and it increased his annoyance as they ignored him. He left the room without saying goodbye to either who remained, too angry and surprised to acknowledge their existence.

BAXTER WAS GRATEFUL for the outing with his father. They had not gone out together, just the two of them, in a long time. William had invited him to go out earlier, and even though he had planned on tending to his studies, he dropped that in exchange for a rare opportunity to spend time with his father.

Baxter got his shoes on while Father waited at the door. They endured the long elevator ride quietly, and it wasn't until they were walking along the street that William broke the silence. "So, you must be pleased with yourself. That was quite a high award you received."

Baxter nodded and tried to contain his pleasure, appreciative of the acknowledgement from his father. He didn't care when he received accolades from people whose opinions meant nothing to him, but when it came from William Clarke, he drank it in deeply. They went down a couple of streets, turning here and there and discussing nothing in particular.

This continued for a while until they came to an entertainment center, and his father beckoned him to follow without even asking Baxter if he wanted to go inside. Baxter thought it strange that his father would want to go into a place that was almost exclusively inhabited by younger people, but he was glad that his father was trying to be savoury. He liked it.

They went inside, into the subdued light. There were several platforms on which people immersed themselves in Virtual Combat and other games. Projected holographs of the game worlds next to each platform allowed spectators to watch the players in action. People with headsets on gesticulated wildly trying to achieve game-based goals while others admired the players' prowess or picked up on new ways to handle certain obstacles when their turn came.

They wandered around, and William seemed distracted but asked Baxter if he wanted to play a game. Baxter politely declined and queried his father as to what he thought of the games. William replied that it was too easy to become immersed in a false reality that was not of your own making. Baxter thought that was a strange answer to a relatively simple question, but he recognized that Father wasn't paying attention to him, but instead continued to scan the arcade, as though for something in particular. Perhaps he had just answered the question reflexively or misunderstood what he had been asked. Then, Baxter spotted an older woman with a young lady who was about Baxter's age. They seemed a little out of place, but the younger of them was breathtaking, and as he surveyed her, he noticed that she gave off an indefinable energy such as he had never encountered before.

He was trying to decide whether he would approach her and say hello when they walked straight up to his father and the older of the two greeted him amiably and with a distinct familiarity.

"Hello, William! I have not seen you for quite some time. How have you been keeping?" Baxter lost his ability to speak.

William looked delighted and extended a hand to her. "Hello, Alana. I am very well, thank you kindly. And is this lovely young lady with you today Rachel? My, she has grown into a striking young woman."

"Oh, my apologies," the woman said turning to the girl who accompanied her. "I do not know if you remember Mr Clarke from the Foundation. Rachel, this is William Clarke, and even though I have not met this young man, judging from his good looks and confident manner, I presume him to be Baxter?"

"Oh yes, that is correct. This is my son, Baxter. Baxter, this is Alana and Rachel Forester. Alana and I have partnered on some projects in the past, and Rachel would come to visit us at work from time to time."

Baxter reached out his hand to shake Rachel's, leaning past her mother to do so. "Hi. I am very pleased to meet you."

Rachel reached out and took his hand. Her skin was firm and soft and she caught Baxter's eyes nervously. "Hello. I am likewise pleased." She dropped her eyes and smiled, and Baxter had not stopped smiling since he first saw her. His face flushed, and his cheeks were getting sore.

"I am tremendously sorry we could not attend the party," Alana continued. "We had a previous engagement, but we do have a gift for Baxter." She turned and looked at Rachel, who still appeared somewhat uneasy, which Baxter thought was odd because anyone as enchanting as she was should be much more confident. He found it charming. "Do you still have it in your bag, dear?" Alana quizzed her, giving a look that seemed to pull her out of herself and break her shyness.

"Oh, yes. My apologies. I have it right here." She reached into her bag, which was a little out of date, but still nice, and handed a wrapped package to Baxter. "I hope you like it," she said. She looked over to her mother and added, "I still have the other one, as well."

"Why, I had almost forgotten!" her mother said, putting the fingertips of one hand to her bottom lip. "William, I got this from a colleague. It is for you. A souvenir of the last project on which we collaborated. I think you will find it very interesting."

"Well thank you," his father said, reaching to take the small package from Alana. "I am sure that, whatever it is, I shall treasure it."

"So," Alana said, looking to Rachel, "We really should carry on, but it was very nice to meet you Baxter, and I extend my deepest congratulations to you and hope we will meet again soon."

"Thank you, Mrs Forester. It was nice to meet you," and then turning to look at Rachel he added, "It was an immense pleasure to meet you, as well."

Rachel broke eye contact, looking down again as Alana turned her attention back to Father. "You really should come to visit sometime soon."

"I will," Father said with a nod. "We will arrange it as soon as possible."

Rachel said goodbye, still glowing, and the two ladies left them, heading back to the exit to the street.

Baxter watched the fantastic creature he had just met moving through the crowd with the grace of one of the big jungle cats he had seen in holos. Her physical movements belied her meekness and Baxter became more deeply intrigued. She was focused and lithe, and he wondered why his father had never mentioned this Alana lady before, or spoken of her lovely daughter.

Baxter slowly turned to look up at his father, who was also watching them leave.

William seemed to feel Baxter's stare and looked back. "What?"

Baxter said nothing. He was too busy being overwhelmed by the coincidence of walking into a random place and meeting two remarkable people who just happened to have gifts for them in their bag.

LAENA SURVIVED THE previous day but had been stretched tighter than a funeral drum throughout it. She learned that guard 482 would be on for another four days, as was the sentry's duty rotation. 482 was often designated to other areas while on assignment, and Laena started a calendar running in her head that told her when his string of shifts would be finished, and then she waited to see if he showed up in her area or not.

Not that she was afraid of him, physically, because she was pretty sure she could handle him, but she was fearful of the possible repercussions of her actions. She had to continually repress anger when she was around him.

She knew that if she were reported for striking a guard, she wouldn't appreciate the possibilities for what followed. She had only been in the compound a short time but had already seen prisoners taken away, and hadn't seen them again.

The hardest part of all of this was keeping herself in check despite all the stress and the cajoling and the insinuations and the insults. Sometimes she just craved to rip that prick's head right off and throw it into a garbage disintegrator, hopeful that his brain and eyes would still register what was happening to him as his cranium disappeared into oblivion.

Damn. Laena knew that she couldn't follow through on the pleasing thought - not if she wanted to continue living without finding out what horrors befell those who were taken away. But it sure was fun to think about.

She trudged her way through her morning routine, preparing for another day of sorting recyclables out of the trash before it went into the disintegrator. She hated the job, as everyone did. No one got up in the morning thinking "God I hope I get to root through other people's stinky refuse looking for things that can be salvaged so I can help the Ascended". At least she didn't think anyone did. People were funny.

When she went out for the headcount, she was hopeful that 482 was not there, because he had not done the morning wake-up routine. Her spirit was lifted somewhat at that, but came crashing down once again when she saw him at roll call. He said nothing specific to her and seemed to be quieter, yet more stern than usual.

She had her breakfast - same shit as yesterday - before heading to her assigned garbage duty for the day.

She was one of the last to arrive for the daily work, and found an open spot along the conveyor belt near the opening to the disintegrator - not the most cherished place on the line. She worked there diligently until morning break, and afterwards she wound up on the line even closer to the disintegrator than she had been before.

482 had been rude to her all morning, but she didn't think his heart was in it. He was mean to everybody but mainly focused his shitty attitude on

her. She maintained her composure and said nothing in response to his jibing at her, and it wasn't until almost lunchtime that things got out of hand.

A big, awkward article was coming down the belt, and when a few of the workers near the start of the line got together to remove it, 482 barked at them to leave it alone. When one of them asked if they would let the object go through, he said that "Prisoner Reisatra would get it". Laena looked up from her work and saw the cumbersome article, now about a third of the way down the line, and told 482 that there was no way she was going to get that off the belt by herself.

482 drew his weapon from its holster and said, "You will get it off there, or you will simply 'get it'. Pick one!"

Laena looked and saw that the bulky article was now almost halfway down the line, and if she acted quickly, she might pull it off before it completed its journey to oblivion.

The other workers cleared out of the way as she leapt from her stool and ran to the object. She struggled to pull at it, and could make it move slightly, but she foresaw that she would never get it to clear the edge of the conveyor and off onto the floor. "I can't get a grip on it!" she yelled to 482 over her shoulder.

"Well then, you better get up there," he replied, still pointing his gun at her. "It's nearly at the disintegrator, and if it goes, you go too. Move it!"

The object was three-quarters of the way to its destination, and Laena jumped up onto the belt behind it. She grabbed it low and with both hands, crouching to increase her leverage on it. She rocked it up onto the edge of the conveyor, and it rotated with one corner caught on the stationary edging along the belt. She decided to use that to her advantage and pushed to turn it some more as it neared the opening to the disintegrator. As the article spun, she managed to get more and more of it off the conveyor.

It finally broke loose and fell, landing on the floor while she toppled onto her belly on the belt, staring straight into the smokeless fire of matter being converted into nothing. She pulled her knees in and rolled backwards, buying just enough time to vault to the floor before she arrived at the opening to the disintegrator.

There were relieved hoots and applause from her peers, but 482 told them to shut up, and they did.

He holstered his weapon again and said nothing more, but was laughing out loud as he turned and walked away.

A couple of recyclable goods made their way into the disintegrator as the prisoners returned to their stations, and Laena Reisatra sat on the floor with her arms cradling her knees, ready to kill that bastard no matter what the consequences might be.

DOYLE WAS NOT IMPRESSED. He sat in his medium-sized office, staring out the window and stewing about the whole aftermath of the committee meeting and the news he had overheard there.

Could it be true? Were those two lap dogs having some fun at his expense? Undoubtedly that was not the case. They weren't smart enough to come up with a ruse like that on their own. More likely they were merely spouting off at an improper place and time.

The words "Chancellor Burke" did not compute in his head, and he thought he might explode. If he were going to rupture violently, he might as well go downtown, do it there and blame it on the Sylvans. The thought caused him a sharp, grunting laugh.

What was he going to do? Was there any way he could prevent this absolute travesty from transpiring? Surely he could think of something.

He had put a great deal of effort into ascending. Everything that had been expected of him on the path upward had been accomplished competently - and a lot more. Way more.

Doyle had been told early in his career that moving up within the Ascendancy was a process, and he adhered to that exactingly.

He made his work the entire focus of his life, giving up everything he had ever known, and all he could have built for himself outside his job. He had put in more than anybody else, and he deserved credit for it.

Doyle knew that the computation for his points accumulation contained a buffer in the algorithm because of his history. But that notwithstanding, he still should have been running the damned place by now. He was confident that he must have moved past his shortcoming with the sheer numbers of hours he had put in and the substantial contributions he had made.

Maybe it wasn't enough. Perhaps he needed to do more.

And he certainly needed to see Michael Burke credited with less. If he couldn't ascend above Burke fairly, then he might as well descend Burke as much as he could. If both things were achieved simultaneously, the dust would settle and he would come out ahead of that miserable prick and get what he needed. What he deserved.

He knew that Michael couldn't stand him anyway, but as far as it concerned Doyle, there was no higher praise than the rejection of an idiot.

Burke didn't deserve this. Not even close.

Doyle had potential connections of his own who could be very helpful in this endeavour. He would direct his resources toward making contact with them.

Chancellor Burke, indeed.

Fuck him.

BAXTER, KENT AND LILA had met many times on the rooftop, a place where they were not supposed to go, but to which Kent had somehow gained access. So, it became a private place to get away from everyone and enjoy time detached from prying eyes and ears.

It was as high as a person could go within the city, at the top of the tallest building at its center, and as near to the plasma shield as one could get without being fried to a crisp. It hummed and crackled, and its smooth, even glow lit the area from all sides so that nothing there cast a shadow. The city was far below them, and the sounds it made were a drone that amalgamated with the hum from the shield, resulting in a soft white noise that permeated the open space.

Lila was not coming, and Baxter felt guilty that he was glad about that. He usually liked it when she joined them, though. They would talk about important issues, their personal lives, and their plans for the future, and she was stimulating and thoughtful.

Baxter had always just taken it for granted that they would be married someday. He was used to the idea of being paired with Lila, but when he called Kent and asked if he would like to meet at The Lookout, as they called their rooftop hideout, Baxter could think of only one thing he wanted to discuss with his closest male friend.

"I met a girl, and I cannot stop thinking about her," he said flatly to Kent once the greetings were over and they had settled in their favourite places to sit. "She was like no one I have ever met before." He turned to his long-time friend, who didn't seem startled or anything, as Baxter was sure Kent would be when he told him this.

Kent's face drew into his usual smirk, and he shifted slightly in Baxter's direction but did not face him directly, still looking off into the distance. "That took longer than I thought it was going to. What is her name, my lovelorn friend?"

It embarrassed Baxter, but he knew Kent wouldn't judge him. They had been through too much together for either of them to be judgemental about the other.

"Her name is Rachel. I met her while I was in the arcade with my father."

"Your father went to the arcade with you?"

"I know. But, anyway, we met this girl there, and her mother knew Father, and she was sweet and shy, but seemed a little dangerous at the same time, you know?"

"So you met a demure lioness and her mother in the arcade with your father? It all sounds a little outlandish to me. Are you sure you were not asleep at the time?"

"No, drone. We didn't talk much, but I felt like there was a connection. I wonder where she lives."

"I could track her down if you want. There is no place in the 12 cities she can hide from me. The huntress becomes the hunted." He growled and brought his hands up in curled claws, feigning a swipe at Baxter with one of them.

"Go dock, you moron. I'm just glad Lila wasn't with me at the time."

"That could have been problematic."

"Don't get me wrong. I love Lila, but I love her the same way I love other people who are special to me. There is no big flame there for her or anything like that. And I surely have never thought about her in the way I have been obsessing over Rachel." Saying her name out loud felt good.

Baxter didn't know what to say next, but Kent just sat there, looking somewhat displeased with him and patiently waiting for him. He wondered if Kent thought he was crazy, and he almost asked him but reconsidered at the last moment. He knew Kent well enough to know that whether he did or didn't, he would say he did and then give him a hard time about it.

"I do not know what to do," was all he could finally get out.

"Well, I know that you had best not let Lila find out about this. If you are serious about pursuing this, my friend, you should do it soon enough. It is less than a year from now that you are to be married. That means your time is limited if you want to apply for reassignment of your marriage partner."

"I know not how serious this is. I do not even know where she lives, or if she had similar feelings when we met. I mean, I think she did, but I cannot know for sure unless I see her again. Maybe this is just a passing phase. I should be with Lila." He put his head down, resting his head on the palm of his hand. "Ohhh Goodness," he said to himself.

Kent reached over and patted Baxter on the back, then stood up. "It sounds to me like you have some soul searching to do, my good man," he said before heading to the door that led into the building. "You had best get on this. And not just for yourself. Don't you dare make this all about you. Lila deserves to be treated respectfully, and you must ensure that no matter what else you do, you do that." Kent pulled the heavy manual door behind him, bidding Baxter good night. Baxter waved over his shoulder without looking as the large steel door clanked shut.

He remained there for a few more minutes on his own before he said, with no one around him to hear it, "Yeah. I know."

CANDACE WAITED UNTIL she heard Baxter leave to go out with Kent before she went looking for William. She didn't know how she would broach the subject with him, but she had been thinking about it for the better part of the evening, and she assumed that something would come to her.

She patrolled through the kitchen and living areas, shutting off the holo on her way through. She continued through the rest of her home until she arrived at the workshop. There was a light emanating from under the door, and she paused a moment to take a deep, slow breath. She knocked and then waved to open the door and stood frozen in the opening.

William glanced up from his table at her and then lowered his gaze once again to what he was doing. "Hello, dear," he said. "Do you need something?"

She did not answer right away, and after a second William looked back at her, seeming to take more notice of the expression she bore this time, and put his work aside and turned in his chair to face her.

"Who was the lady you met at the arcade with Baxter?" She interrogated, surprised to hear the question come out of her mouth. She hadn't intended to be so direct, and she cleared her throat and adjusted her stance slightly, waiting for him to answer.

"What?" he replied, looking puzzled. "The lady from the - oh, that was Alana from the Foundation. We did some work on practical applications after the first Gates were in place. Her daughter was with her, too. She says hello, and she is sorry that she could not attend the party."

"She wasn't invited to the party. I don't know anyone named Alana, so I could not have sent Alana an invitation. And I am fairly sure I knew all of your coworkers from the Foundation. I do not recall there being an 'Alana'. So, what did she give you?"

"What?"

"It does not suit you well to play dumb, William. Baxter said he met a young lady at the arcade with you today, and that her mother was with her, and that she gave you a gift. What was it?"

"Well, it is here somewhere; I'll show it to you. It must be buried under all of this mess." He looked up with panic and frustration painted on his face. "I will show you once I find it."

"And the arcade? What were you doing there?

"I took Baxter there. Look, I went out with Baxter to spend some quality time with my son, and I ran into an old colleague. There is no big mystery here, so please cease with the interrogation."

Candace took a couple of steps into the room and looked at her husband sternly. "No. You took Baxter for a reason, and you went to the arcade to meet some spy person there. And the gift was probably some spy thing, as well." Her voice rose in pitch and volume. "There is no need to think of me as stupid, William Clarke. I may not be as intelligent as you are, but I am not naive, either."

"I do not think you are stupid, dear, but I also do not know what you are talking about. Spy stuff? That is absurd." He wrinkled his brow and soured his features at her.

"Oh, William. I have known for some time that you are in cahoots with those Illuminating people, or whatever they are called. It took a long time to figure out what was wrong, but there were clues, and you did not always do a good job of hiding them. I found strange things around the house and odd patterns in your comings and goings. After a while, the truth I was hiding from became the obvious answer, and I could not hide anymore."

Her voice shook, and the first of what would be many tears rolled down her cheek and into the corner of her mouth, pausing before it continued its journey downward. "I could not bring myself to mention anything. But now that you have involved Baxter in it, I have to speak. I have to say something." The last of her words trailed off, replaced by low sobs. She hung her head, weeping softly.

William got up from where he was seated and crossed to where she stood in the middle of the room. He reached his arms around her in consolation, but she put her fists against his chest and held him back. "Get out of this, William. You could be incarcerated or shot or who knows what for what you do. Baxter and I would have no one here for us anymore. You are no good to us in jail, William."

She lowered her arms and allowed her husband to embrace her. "Maybe you would be better off in prison. At least you would be alive."

William stood there with his face in her hair, holding Candace tightly and not speaking. She opened her eyes and looked up at him, expecting some defensive reply. What she got instead was entirely unexpected.

"I cannot stop now. If you would let me explain to you why this is so important, I am sure you would come to share my views. I apologize for not having told you before, but you were so excited about your ascended status and position that I did not wish to diminish you. I hope you can understand."

Candace was formulating an answer when they turned in unison to look at the open door. From beyond it, they heard hastily retreating footsteps followed by the chime that indicated the opening and closing of the main door.

They looked again at one another, now bound by a common fear. Baxter had just left the flat, and likely had overheard them talking.

This was not good.

Chapter 5

RAISHANN WATCHED AS Timoth left the house, and she sometimes couldn't believe they were brother and sister. Whereas he was never content and always bored, she had a lust for life that allowed her to experience what she was doing fully most of the time, experiencing it profoundly and happily. She hoped for him that he would learn whatever he needed that would allow him some insight into the wonders of the world, so he might see it in a more meaningful way. She was grateful for the things she had in her life, despite her recent losses, and she saw every morning's waking as a new chance for adventure gifted to her with each new day.

The effects of the raid still weighed on her, and she thought a lot about Laena and her mother, but even in regard to that she found some solace in knowing that she was doing all she could to set things right. And she would continue to do more. Getting the device to Shadaar was a big step toward toward that, and had come with a secondary benefit that she had not foreseen.

Meeting the boy from the city was one of those cherished moments for which she was thankful. There was an indefinable quality that drew her to him instantly, but her logical processes kept coming up with reasons she should not feel as she did. She had known she would meet someone, somewhere along her journey, who made her feel this way, but she never suspected that it could be an Ascended. A city boy who lived in the zoo, working for materialism and comfort.

Raishann needed expert guidance, which was why she called her mother into the room after Timoth was gone. She'd have sooner spoken to Laena, but, of course, that was no longer an option. She put the thought out of her head as Aellana sat down on the bed, and Raishann regretted having summoned her already.

Maybe this was something that didn't really need to be discussed. Her bursting compulsion to talk to somebody about him won over her reasons for staying quiet. Raishann awkwardly settled in beside her mother and searched for a way to start.

How was she going to present this? Aellana was looking at her in a way that conveyed that her mom knew already. It made Raishann uncomfortable that her mom was on to her before she said a word, and she shifted slightly on the edge of the wooden-framed bed. She also knew that she was being waited on to say something. She hesitated, neither wanting to broach the intended subject nor launch into some phoney, fabricated one.

Thankfully, her mom got the conversation going. "You liked him, didn't you?", she asked.

"How do you know?", Raishann responded, looking at her mother with a sense of wonder and respect. "It's not like I've told anybody yet."

"Ah, you get older, and you know things, that's all. He was kind of cute, wasn't he?" Aellana smiled knowingly.

"Yeah, he was." Raishann twisted on the bed to face her mom more directly, and put one leg up on it, snuggling in. "But that's where I have a problem. Can you like a guy you don't even really know? Not just think he's cute, or whatever, but really like him. Feel something in your heart. It's confusing. When I think about him, I feel good, but when I look at the whole situation, it doesn't make sense somehow. I mean, he could be perfectly alright, or he could just be another Ascendancy no-mind with no goals other than achieving whatever so he can be all cozy. I don't know."

"Well, if his father is any indicator, Baxter Clarke is probably more than meets the eye. When I first met William, I was sure he was going to turn me into the authorities. Get the points, you know. But not only did he save my life, while risking his own I might add, but he came to be a valued Luminant, and a terrific friend to your dad and I. We trust and count on him, and from what I've seen and heard, Baxter is a lot like him. So there's that."

"But Baxter doesn't know about any of that stuff about his dad, right? He lives like the rest of them, doesn't he?"

"William brought Baxter along to meet us the other day to get a feel for his reaction to us. But honestly? I don't know. He might."

Raishann looked down and wrung her hands together nervously. "God, I hope not."

BAXTER WATCHED AND remained patient until he saw, on the smart-wall window he monitored in his room, his father looking around corners, checking, and attempting to leave the flat in a clumsy, yet clandestine manner. Now he would find out what was going on, though he already had his suspicions.

He had been watching Father closely the past few days, always trying to position himself within the house so he could see or hear him better and not get caught doing it. His father had made no unusual actions or said anything particularly striking, but since hearing the end of the conversation between him and Mother, Baxter had taken it upon himself to find out if what Mother said was correct. If it was valid, it would iron out some quirks of his life, and also answer a lot of questions he had about the bizarre encounter at the arcade.

He was glad that his parents hadn't questioned whether he overheard their discussion. Maybe they didn't want to know. He had decided that if they asked about it, he would play dumb, and say he had come back to his room to get something he had forgotten while Kent waited for him. He would say he had heard nothing at all.

Part of him had been itching to tell his parents the lie preemptively, but there had been no opportunities to slide it naturally into a conversation, and so he was able to resist using his excuse awkwardly or unnecessarily.

Baxter crept from his room and went to a corner where he could hide and yet see Father approaching the front door. It was late, and Baxter knew that his father would have no professional appointments or social calls. William took a small device out of an inside pocket and pointed it at the exit as he went out. Baxter stayed back after the door closed without chiming as it usually did when it opened or shut. He followed his father, who headed toward the elevators at the front of the building. Baxter used the ones at the rear and arrived on the main floor first, so he ran outside and concealed himself until he saw his father exit to the street. He stuck tightly enough to keep sight of Father, but far enough away, he thought, to remain undetected. The only illumination came from the dome overhead and the signs that beckoned shoppers from the sides of buildings. Baxter stayed hidden as well as he could while he stalked William along the street.

When he saw his father call for an aircar, Baxter drafted another one and had it follow along. The ride took them all the way out to a vicinage in Seventh Circle, only one ring away from the city wall.

William got out of his conveyance and walked from there all the way to the outer rim, and Baxter was becoming more concerned with every step that Mother had been right about all of this.

Baxter had never been this far away from the Core at night and was a little afraid, but his curiosity was driving him to go wherever his father may lead him. It was becoming clear that Father was doing something illegal, and it was burning inside him to find out exactly what that was.

Father went right out to the wall, with the plasma shield crackling above it, and he performed the same clumsy check he had done in the flat before opening a cover on one of the maintenance hatches and going inside, then pulling the door closed behind him.

Baxter delayed for what seemed an appropriate interval before doing the same. It was dark in the small tunnel that the door concealed, but there were no turns or branching channels within. He merely followed it to its end, removed a grated cover from the exit, and stepped into the grass and dirt beyond it. He replaced the grate and made a scrape mark in the soil with the heel of his shoe, and then he turned around.

Baxter was awestruck by the sheer vastness that lay before him. The sky was clear and incredibly far away, yet it appeared he could reach out and put his palm on the moon. It tempted him to try before his intellect stopped him from it. The never-ending darkness above him was dotted with a myriad of little lights he knew were stars, despite never having seen them before, except on a monitor or in a holo. One star, in particular, glowed brilliantly and flashed like none around it. After a quick survey, he discerned that it was the Avalon, reflecting sunlight off its immense structure as it orbited high above. He shivered in the damp breeze that enveloped him, which was more cheerful and invigorating than he imagined it might be.

He was standing somewhere he had never expected to be, and when he looked back over his shoulder, he had to turn all the way around and look up to see the broad arc of the shield glowing there like half of an immense electric ball. For the first time, he saw the opposite curvature to the one he was used to. It occurred to him that the dome looked more significant from the inside.

Baxter jerked back to reality and remembered the reason he was in this unfamiliar place. Looking again to the bright periphery of the forest nearby, he saw his father entering a shadow-spattered trail that opened at its edge.

He was terrified now, but decided that he would stay a little closer to his father so he didn't lose sight of him, and also for the security of being near someone who appeared to be used to doing this. Perhaps he should have brought some weapon with him. It was too late now. He was committed.

He tagged along on the path, being very careful to remain quiet as he stumbled onward, and wondered if there were any wild animals or Sylvan barbarians lurking in the harsh shadows of the forest, waiting to pounce on easy prey.

There were lots of twists and turns, and several other trails that led off in different directions. He found his walking continually hindered by the uneven ground and the myriad of tree roots and other small obstacles on the path.

Baxter began to worry. If he lost sight of his father, he might not make it back home. His anxiety lessened, however, when a glance over his shoulder reminded him that the familiar glow of the city was there in the distance, diminishing on the horizon. He would be able to see that for a long way. He would be fine.

He tailed his father for what seemed to be forever, and finally slowed himself and watched intently as father entered a large, moonlit clearing ahead on the trail.

When Baxter arrived at the opening to the clearing, his father was walking toward someone who was standing on the far side, motionless except for their long coat fluttering in the wind. A smaller silhouette accompanied the person but stood a little farther away in the background.

The figures took a few steps ahead and walked to meet his father in the middle, the larger of the two extending a greeting hand as they converged. His father took the hand and shook it, and Baxter heard him say 'hello'.

It surprised Baxter when a female voice responded. His father then put his hand on the shoulder of the smaller figure, and they all turned to face away from where Baxter was hiding and strolled into the distance.

Now there were even more questions racing through his mind. Why was Father meeting people in the woods instead of in the city? There must be Gates they could take to any place in the 12 cities that would suffice to do their business. Why come to the forest, with the animals and the Sylvans and all manner of danger?

The three of them left the clearing together, continuing away from the city. Baxter remained where he was, frozen in place for a moment, before remembering he should stay close to his father. He made his way around the edge of the clearing until he came to the opening he had seen them leave through and continued his pursuit.

When he got settled on the next section of the trail, he found that he could not see the trio ahead. He slowed down, scanning ahead for a side passage or somewhere else they could have gone. Seeing nothing that satisfied him, he turned around to gauge whether he had come in at the right place. To his dismay, everything there looked the same to him, and he decided it would be best to forge ahead a little farther to see if they would become visible from there.

He went along slowly, searching as well as he could along the edges of the trail for signs of openings or other paths that may have been taken. He listened intently for traces of them but heard nothing.

Then he stopped, and his heart skipped with the realization that he had lost them. He looked back for the glow of the plasma-dome and found that the dense branches and foliage had almost wholly obscured it. There was, however, a brighter spot between the trees, but it was now very far away. This had been a bad, bad idea.

There was a snap from behind him, and he spun around, raising his fist as though he were going to attack whatever he found there. Something hit him full force from the side and he went down with a solid thump, and his head bounced off of the earthen floor of the trail. The figure on top of him held him down tightly, restraining the one free hand he had and locking the rest of his body in place so he could not move.

Baxter yelled and squirmed, trying to kick or punch or bite or do something, but the assailant seemed to know exactly what to do to negate his efforts.

The looming figure commanded, "Stop it!", right in his face and then added softly, in an almost motherly tone, "I'm not gonna hurt you." The grip on him lessened.

Now he could place the voice. It was the lady he had met in the arcade - Rachel's mother. Was she tangled up in all of this, too? Oh, crap.

He stopped struggling, and the woman released him slowly. He sat up, rubbing his head while she crouched in front of him. She extended a hand to him, and he refused it while they both stood up.

Father exited from the bushes on the edge of the trail, with the smaller figure beside him. "What are you doing here?" his father demanded.

Baxter looked at his father angrily, and then spun around, relaxing somewhat when he met the familiar but now solemn eyes of Rachel. She turned away from him and walked toward her mother. Baxter's confusion and emotional reaction to the sensory overload congealed as rage.

It all came out in a focused verbal inferno directed at the man who had let him down. Let his family down. "Never mind what I am doing!" Father was stunned by the attack, and Baxter vented again. "So, Mother was telling the truth about all that stuff the other night?" He already knew that everything he had overheard was thoroughly accurate, but all his emotions could allow him to do right now was to lash out.

"Oh shit," William said before turning to look at Aellana. "Would you give us a minute?" he asked her, and she moved silently up the trail with Rachel beside her.

Baxter had not slowed in his rant, and when William turned back to face his boy, he was still going. "So, that lady is a Sylvan. And Rachel is a Sylvan, too? What are they doing to you? Are they..."

"Hey!" his father bellowed at him. "You need to calm down, right now!" Baxter was taken aback and stood silently while he collected himself. Father had never yelled at him like that before. In this context, it made him seem primitive and animalistic. They were both acting inhuman, and he didn't like it one bit. Even this brief sojourn into the woods had stripped them both of what was most important to the Ascended: civility.

William softened, continuing in subdued, but very deliberate tones. "Yes, they are both Sylvan. They are not doing anything bad. And yes, your mother was right the other night. We weren't sure if you heard us or not, so we thought it best not to say anything to you. But I didn't think you would do this." He spread his hands out at Baxter then swept them around to indicate their current surroundings. "You could've been killed out here. What were you thinking?"

That was it. Baxter had been through too much in the last while, and it was all at the surface now. It came bursting through him like a whale through thin Arctic ice.

"You lied to us!" he screamed, leaning ahead and challenging his father, looking squarely into his eyes. "You have been consorting with those animals, selling your people out to terrorists, and who knows what else. And you're asking me what I'm doing? You should be ashamed! They should descend you!" He pointed toward Aellana and Raishann. "And they should arrest you for what you're doing!" They said nothing, and he turned his attention back to the source of his disappointment. "These people are trying to kill us, Father, and you come out here in the middle of the night, leaving Mother and me behind, to help them?" He calmed a little and backed a step. "I cannot believe it. I cannot have this." He hung his head and shook it slowly from side to side as he continued backing away from his father. "I cannot handle this."

His father tried to approach him, spreading his arms out to his son as he moved, but Baxter wheeled around and went into a full run back toward the faint glow that could be seen intermittently between trunks and branches.

William turned to address Aellana, but didn't know what to say. She cupped her hands around her mouth and called out, "Go! We will talk again later! Go after him!"

He waved back, and then rushed off in pursuit of his son.

CANDACE SPENT A LOT of time preparing for what she was about to do.

Once William became immersed in his project, she went to him and said she was closing the workshop because the drones were being sent to give the house a once-over. William did not look up, but nodded and made a noise, and she shut the door before heading to where the bedrooms were.

Candace could tell that Baxter was out of sorts these last few days, and seemed to grow increasingly distant and quiet, but she had waited to see if he would bring any issues up with her. He had not, and she knew that there was only so much that the daily mood stabilizer they took could stave off.

She was reasonably sure he had overheard her discussion with William the other night, and he was probably somewhat perplexed and disenchanted right now. This had gone on long enough. William's private life had already become a cancer within the household just by them knowing about it.

She would not have her family dishonoured among the Ascended. She would not let all they had built topple into disarray. She would take care of this at once.

She went to Baxter's bedroom door without opening it and listened carefully. She knocked tentatively, not wanting to be heard by her husband, despite his being in a closed room and a state of creative reverie. "Baxter?" she beckoned in a low voice. She rapped again and was about to call out when the door opened.

Baxter did not look well. She felt sorry for him and deepened her resolve to protect him from all of this subversive nonsense. If she couldn't get through to William, she may at least be able to save her son.

"We need to talk," she said and then walked into his room and bid him close the door. She did not sit down.

He went back across the room, sitting in the chair at his desk. His studies were on his terminal with his neuroheadset laying next to it, and Candace asked him to shut it off. Baxter gestured to it, and it blinked out unceremoniously. She then told the house computer to turn off the distracting room scene he had playing, and once the room was quiet, she set about her business.

"I suppose you heard your father and I talking the other night."

"What? About what?" He sat there looking his mother in the eye, and she could tell he was not sincere. She changed tactics.

"You know about your father and what he does with his spare time. I know."

Baxter hesitated and then told her he had come in to get something while Kent waited, but she knew it was contrived. She spoke more firmly. "Baxter. You let on that you don't even know what conversation I am speaking of, and yet you are pinning down the time. You heard us talking, and it is alright. I want to keep you on track and away from it is all. You have too much to lose otherwise."

Baxter sat back and lowered his head, relenting to her. Good. She needed him to be subordinate and merely listen.

"You are not your father's keeper. Okay? You have nothing to do with all this nonsense, and you can still ascend. You are doing well in your studies and are already ahead of everyone else your age. You are to be married to a properly ascended young lady, and your future can still be dazzling. The Ascendancy will always look out for your best interests and keep you comfortable and safe. Do you understand that?"

Baxter nodded but said nothing.

Candace went on. "I do not agree with what your father is doing, but I agree that it needs to remain hidden. That is of utmost importance. Can you imagine what might happen to you and me if this were to get out? I cannot even fathom where to begin. You can tell no one of it, and, as a matter of fact, it would ultimately be best if it were not even discussed here. But, if you have questions or want to talk about this, you come to me. Are we clear?"

Baxter nodded again. Candace gave him an opportunity to speak his mind, but he silently shook his head.

She turned to leave but wanted to be sure she had indeed punctuated the primary purpose of this visit. "It would serve you well to remember that everything on the other side of that dome would kill you without hesitation or remorse. Those rebel people are a curse on the Ascendancy, and it's only a matter of time before they get what they have coming to them. Anyone who is associated with them is putting themselves at risk. Anyone. Your father needs to rethink his priorities, or he may end up facing the same justice they do." Baxter regarded her with wide eyes, and then could not hold the contact any longer. Candace thought he got the point.

"Are we clear about this Baxter? I want to be sure you fully understand the importance of this. We must never be descended. We have worked too hard to build what we have, and I will not lose it now. Are we clear? When the Ascendancy Day Rally comes, I want us to be front and center with the highest of the Ascended as we have always been."

Baxter looked up into her eyes and said, "Yes, Mother", and she left the room, stopping to look on him one more time, as he reached for his headset and restarted his terminal.

She closed the door behind her and, standing in the hallway, drew a breath and held it for an instant before she released it. *There*, she thought, *that takes care of that.*

Candace smoothed out the front of her dress and stood fully erect, taking another full breath before she drifted back into the flat and returned to her day.

She worried about her family, and it occurred to her that it might, in fact, be better for everyone - including her rebellious husband - if he *was* in jail.

RAISHANN WAS CRYING as she ran through the central area of the house. Shawan and Timoth looked away from the game they were playing as she passed, then back to each other in bewilderment. Timoth stood but did not follow her.

It had only been a short time ago that Raishann was infatuated with the young Ascended man, and now all hope of his exceptionality fell away, just as she fell limply from her high hopes.

Shawan got up when he saw Aellana come in and asked, "Where is Shadaar?" but Mom waved him off and said, "Not now," as she continued past him. "We're okay; I'll explain it to you later." She followed Raishann into her room and closed the wooden door.

Raishann was sitting on the edge of her bed with her hands in her face and wet hair in her mouth, crying inconsolably. Her mother sat beside her and rubbed her grieving daughter's back slowly.

"It's gonna be okay," Aellana said over and over softly, as she continued to caress Raishann's back.

"He's such an asshole," Raishann huffed out between sobs. "He was so mean. I hate him. I hate them all." She turned and put her face on her mom's shoulder and continued to huff while Mom said "It's gonna be okay" every once in a while until she regained her self-control.

She wiped her nose and eyes with the sleeve of her shirt, sniffling, and sat up again. "He's just another one of them, I guess," she suggested once she could breathe more slowly. "He's just a no-mind Ascendancy robot."

Mom removed the hair from Raishann's face and lifted her chin with the side of one finger so she could look her in the eye. "He doesn't know any different, Raish. And he just found out his dad has been hiding something that, you've gotta admit, is pretty damn big for all of his life."

"Yeah, I guess so, but he still said some really mean shit, Mom. He called us terrorists. He said we were animals." She choked a couple more times but was able to regain her composure quickly. "He hates us. They all hate us. Why do we even help them, Mom?"

"We do what we do for everybody. Sylvan or not. Just because it's right. They don't know us, Raish. And he sure as hell doesn't know you. That's for sure. But I saw the way he looked at you in the city, and I know that you were sweet on him, too. He's from another world, though, honey. He's not Sylvan; it's not like it would have been easy to pursue him." She shrugged her shoulders and looked into Raishann's glassy red eyes. "We may never even see him again." She glanced down and shook her head, shrugging again. "Time will tell, I suppose."

Raishann leaned in to put her head on her mom's chest again and took a deep breath. "I don't care if I never saw any of those people ever again, Mom." She put her face right into Aellana's shirt and said in a muffled tone, "They deserve whatever they get. I'm not helping them anymore."

"I know, sweetie." Aellana brushed back her hair again. "I know."

Aellana got up from the edge of the bed, and Raishann flopped back into it, pulled a pillow into herself and curled around it, exhausted.

Mom walked to the door and opened it. Timoth was there, and Mom raised a finger to her lips as she stepped out and gently shut the door behind her.

Raishann could hear beyond the door, though, and Timoth sounded annoyed when he asked if his sister was alright. Mom said she would be fine and just needed some time, and Timoth shot back that he was sick of all this without saying what he meant.

Raishann fell asleep with wet cheeks and a headache and slept until well after the sun was up in the morning.

Chapter 6

IT WAS HOT AND HUMID in Nylen, as usual, but Timoth found it to be especially uncomfortable. The warmth of the sun coupled with the heat of his anger was too much for him to bear.

He sat in a shaded spot just outside the house watching people and reflecting on his place in the world.

He seethed over what he had overheard between Raishann and Mom last night, and it upset him that the city boy had hurt Raish like that, but that wasn't the main thing that troubled him.

Timoth drank in his surroundings. People walked with their livestock in the street, taking them to pasture for the day. There was a constant crowding as old, noisy vehicles transported their cargos between the pedestrians. The neighboring buildings were in varying states, ranging from very well maintained to fit for condemnation.

What distressed him, he realized, was that a part of him agreed with the city boy. The Sylvans did live like animals. Comparatively, anyway.

There were no holos and no high society. They had video screens and some interactive games, but nothing as polished as in the cities. The streets were little more than well-travelled packed earth, and they built everything to be mobile, using old technologies. In the distance, he could hear and smell the evidence of agriculture. Children ran between the crowds of people and vehicles, and occasionally an adult would chastize them for being an impediment or doing something unsafe. Everyone raised the children of Sylvan towns collectively, and parents seldom took offence to another adult disciplining their little ones unless it was over the top or uncalled for.

Timoth heard a commotion down the street. Someone was either obstructing people or had caused an accident. His money was on there having been an accident.

He craned his neck around to get a better view, but he could not see past all the vehicles and people between him and the incident. He stood up and brushed off the back of his pants, still trying to understand what was going on, when a man burst out of the crowd, coming straight toward him.

He recognized the man as Rhodhall Carvyre, a friend of his parents and member of the Luminants. Even before arriving where Timoth stood, the man called to him. "Timoth, are your parents home?" Timoth nodded his head and stepped toward the door, which he opened to expedite the man's entrance and to keep him from yelling out anything more in a public space.

Rhodhall went past him into the cooler air inside, and Timoth followed, closing the door behind him.

As soon as he was inside, the man called out, "Shawan!"

"Yeah, yeah, I'm coming," Timoth heard from further inside the house. His father appeared, moving from the hallway into the main area. He was shirtless and towelling off his chest with one hand as he carried a shirt with the other, which was still bandaged. "Rhodhall, what's going on?" Shawan demanded.

Rhodhall requested that Dad sit at the kitchen table, and he pulled out a chair for himself and sat in it. Father said, "Timoth, get Mr Carvyre something cold to drink," and Timoth moved immediately to comply.

Dad pulled his shirt on with the practiced movements of someone who had nursed a fair share of injuries, though he was still not quite dry, and sat with his friend. Rhodhall got straight to the point. "I come from meeting with Leukas, who has received a message from his informant in Enswell. The Ascendancy is going to set off an explosive device in the city and blame it on us."

"Black flag operations?"

"Sounds like it. Leukas wanted to know what you think we should do about it. Personally, I think if the Ascendancy wants to blow up some of their own people, then fine."

"No, it's not fine. Not if they're gonna pin it on us, anyway. It means they're going on the offensive for some reason. It could lead to something bigger. Do we know when this is supposed to happen?"

"Apparently, the bomb will be readied outside the city and then taken in by a small squad of Ascendancy goons made up to look like us sometime in the next few days. Leukas says he will get details to us when his informant finds out more."

Timoth was awestruck. For as long as he could remember, they had been plotting and running and hiding, and railing against a system that had much more to offer than the one they fought to preserve. He had been around this for his whole life, but it was only hitting him now. From where he sat, he looked back and forth as the conversation went on between Dad and Rhodhall like he was watching two boys playing catch.

"So we have no idea as to the actual time of the attack?" his dad continued.

"No, only that it's gonna be soon. 'In the next few days', Leukas said."

"So we should get prepared now. Maybe we should have patrols   out watching for signs of Ascendancy movements."

"And take them out if we happen to see them? That leaves a lot to chance, don't ya think? I mean, what if we don't see them out there at all?"

"Well, we'll be getting more intel as it comes in. We can fine-tune the operation in the field as we know more. But we can't put a stop to anything if we do nothing, right?"

Rhodhall blew a raspberry. "Obviously. So, what should we do right now?"

"Organize a general meeting at the compound for this evening. I'll talk with the elders, and hopefully, we have something more from the informant to share at the meeting. Thanks, Rhodhall."

"Yeah, okay. I'll make sure the word gets around, and I guess I'll see you tonight."

Rhodhall got up from the table, polished off what was left in his glass and then set it back down. He thanked Timoth for the drink and then bid Shawan farewell. He put a hand on Timoth's shoulder briefly as he walked past him and left.

Timoth looked over at his dad, who was still at the table. He was going to say something to him. He wanted to know why they were fighting. He wanted to know what was so wrong that they had to do this. He knew that the Ascendancy patrols were mostly 'bots, but there were men out there, too. Destroying O-bots was okay, but killing men was not right. All of this confused and tore at him.

Timoth didn't feel that he could ask his dad about these things because he already knew what he would say. He had heard it all before, from both his dad and his mom. They had taught it to him and Raish since they were old enough to talk.

Part of him felt that the Ascendancy had to take some aggressive measures considering all the things he knew the Luminants had done to them. This plan they had found out about was more like a counter-attack than an unprovoked assault. But, of course, the Sylvans would have to defend themselves, too. It was all very complicated, and he didn't know how to respond. But he knew that it frustrated him to no end.

Timoth assumed that everyone accumulated shameful secrets that would never be shared with anyone else. But his list had grown to be extensive and mostly consisted of misgivings about the way the Sylvans lived.

He supposed that the most significant difference between him and those around him was that he refused to remain ashamed. The thoughts he had were only wrong because others told him they were wrong. He was done with living for their approval and ready to embrace his own truth.

He thought maybe Raishann might help him, but in the state she was in right now, she probably wasn't the person to ask, either.

Timoth wished he had someone he could talk to about this. Someone who could be objective about the whole thing.

But, there was no one he could think of, so he went back outside to his shady spot and watched the world go by, pondering what it would take to make his ideas of a better life into reality.

DOYLE'S PLAN HAD BORNE fruit much more quickly than he had expected. It was as though his newfound ally had been waiting for him to reach out.

He sat in the small office in his home, dressed in his night clothes and enjoying a glass of his favourite synthetic alcohol. Aggressive music with corresponding video was playing in the background as he stared at the holo-monitor before him.

He wasn't sure that such an invitation as he had extended would even be taken seriously. Doyle had ensured that it was untraceable and that the only way to reply was direct to the message, which came from an encrypted terminal he had secretly set up in his home, not knowing at the time it would be used for such nefarious purposes. He had stated that he was seeking knowledge that was not available through standard Ascendancy practices, with no questions asked as to how they would use the information and that he was offering a reward.

Within hours of posting his request, he had received a response. The message was anticlimactic insofar as it was very dull and straightforward. What appeared on his screen was just enough to let him know things were moving in the desired direction. It simply read:

-Interested in helping. -Payment is negotiable, but will not be currency. -Let's talk.

It was signed "Someone who will prove dedication to the Ascendancy." And that was it.

Doyle stared at the screen for a while before he shut the terminal down and went to the lounge, with his music following him, emanating from the interactive walls wherever he went. He sat on a large sofa and leaned into the soft cushions that surrounded him.

He wondered if he should wait to reply, or if he should do it right away, then reminded himself not to be overly hasty as he had often done in the past.

Doyle wondered what the person on the other end of the transmission wanted for payment. He would have to be careful on that point.

He was very curious to learn more about this person who had come when beckoned, ready to sell information for personal gain. Maybe the person wanted ascending points as a recompense; he couldn't do that. He could think of no way to give somebody a lot of points for no apparent reason. He would be caught immediately.

All in good time, he thought. He called out, "Holo. RoboMania Channel," and reclined further into the lounger, a sense of renewed confidence filling him.

He decided to connect with the mystery advisor tomorrow, and settled himself so he could savour his drink and watch robots rip each other apart.

SHE WAS AT THE END of her ability to restrain herself. Laena couldn't take any more.

The guards who witnessed what happened on the line had just turned away, and the prisoners who had seen it were powerless to do anything about it. If someone were to ask about it now, no one would attest to having noticed anything untoward having taken place in the recycling area.

It also pissed her off that she wasn't even in prison for any good reason. It wasn't like she was a criminal. She had been stolen from her home by an Ascendancy patrol and incarcerated with no other rationale than her having darker skin than city people and talking differently than they did.

Laena had been edgy all day, snapping at her fellow inmates, few of whom were any more guilty of crimes than she was, but could not stop herself from doing it. Once her peers came to understand her temperament, they had just given her a wide berth and did what they could to avoid her altogether. She was alright with that. She could use the space today, anyway.

Her comrades offered her a preferred place on the recycling line, about a third of the way between the area where the belt was loaded by a noisy machine and the other end, where the garbage went into the disintegrator. It was far enough from the disintegrator to be safe, but also far enough from the loading side that you were not in a terrible rush. Other workers would catch anything you missed before the refuse arrived at its ultimate destination.

Despite being in a position where she received a lot of support from further up the line, Laena worked as diligently as she could. She was grateful and didn't want to burden the others.

But her anger was compounded by everything the guards said to her. It was as if they were all 482 - all the same. Even 482 had given her a little extra space today, and if she could make it until the end of this shift, he would be off duty for a few days and then, hopefully, assigned to another area for his next tour.

She finished out her day without incident, but she was as mad as a wet cat by the time she went to the refresher room after work. She was looking forward to challenging someone to a game of Highball so she could blow off steam. Maybe Jorge would play her; he always gave her a good fight.

Laena was able to relax somewhat in the refresher, but she wished she could control the temperature of the spray to make it hotter. The smelly water ran full force for a while and then went down to about half pressure as a signal to get rinsed off quickly before the water was cut off altogether. She used up all of her time in the shower, not getting out before the water died as had become her new habit.

She grabbed her towel from over the bar and started to dry off in the stall. It was still warm in there, and she was enjoying it.

"Hello, Princess. Are you in there?" she heard from the change room. It was him.

Dammit! She was just starting to look forward to tonight. Now she had to deal with this prick again. Shit.

She reached past the curtain of the refresher stall and grabbed her onesie from the bench there. She pulled it on hurriedly and was zipping the front of it when a hand caught the drape and her together as one, breaking rings at the top of the curtain off as it came down.

She kicked out with her foot but was constrained by the curtain clinging to her. 482 wrapped the shroud around her and held it tightly, binding her arms, and pushed her against the back of the stall. More of the rings popped, and the curtain hung awkwardly, allowing her to see his face.

"You are not going to get vicious now, are you?" he needled with a stupid grin. "Because that would not be good for..."

He didn't see the head-butt coming. Laena lunged ahead, leading with the center of her forehead and catching 482 in the bridge of the nose.

The guard recoiled, putting some distance between them, and Laena used the opportunity to get out of the restricting stall that confined her.

She stepped ahead, and her feet became tangled in the curtain. Falling forward, the whole thing came down, along with the bar that held it in place, and it became wrapped around her again. She hit the floor in front of 482 with a thump, and as ungracefully as possible.

As she twisted to free herself and regain a fighting stance, 482 came at her again, with blood running from his nose and a new ferocity in his eyes. His lips curled into a vicious snarl, and he let out a growl as he attacked her.

She could not complete her recovery, and her adversary knocked her back onto the floor, standing over her in a strategically advantageous position. She struggled to hit him with her fists, but he readily blocked her attempts.

He continued to block as she repeatedly struck out at him with one hand. Her other hand searched, looking for a tool to change the dynamics of the encounter. She found the edge of a bench and pulled at it, but it was too heavy to handle. There was the shower curtain, and she couldn't use that either, but she remembered that the object at the end of the drapery was perfectly usable.

Turning onto her side, she used both hands to reel in the curtain until she reached the bar, now held in place by only one ring. She swung it upwards in an arc that ended at the side of 482's head.

The impact snapped his face backwards, and the rest of his body followed it. His bloodied head struck the bench behind him, and he was dazed when he looked back toward her. Laena stood over him with the shower bar, huffing deeply, an enraged look emblazoned across her face.

He did the only thing he could think of. Reaching out, he pleaded, "Hey, let's not do this, okay? You have no idea-"

He attempted to block the first blow, unsuccessfully. He didn't even feel the ones that followed.

Once her nemesis lacked any animation, Laena stopped, and the bar clanged to the floor as she fell to her knees.

She began to cry, and then she realized why.

She was so glad that bastard was dead that she had no words. The tears changed to laughter, and she went on laughing as three guards scurried into the room, restrained and cuffed her, and took her away.

DOYLE WAS AT WORK WHEN he received the next message from his new contact, but he could not risk opening it at the office to read it. He had come too far and put too much energy into setting all of this up to lose it because he was excited.

It distracted him and he was unfocused in his duties for the rest of the workday. Some of his colleagues had noticed and inquired if he was okay, but he wrote it off as being tired from watching holos until late the night before. He was impatient and stand-offish and left in a rush when office hours were finished, so he could get home and look at the note he had received.

Once he arrived at his apartment, he dropped his keys on the table inside the door and marched past them as they fell to the floor. He peeled off his jacket en route to his computer and threw it onto the chair next to his work station as he sat down.

The terminal came to life instantly, but he had to wait for his encryption protocols to load up before he could open the message. His heart pounded, and he wrung his hands as he waited.

When he finally read it, his body and spirit relaxed together with the realization that his patience and the measures he had taken were paying off.

His source had informed him that there would be a Luminant assault against the Black Op. They would attempt to stop it from happening. This was precious. Used to its most significant advantage, this information could lead to something good for him.

But even more valuable than the intel on the Luminants was the mention of a specific name. A man would be there, taking part in this act of terrorism, and that intelligence was worth more to Doyle than even preventing the planned counter-attack.

Doyle would be a hero to Marshall and everyone else when he turned over the traitor named William Clarke.

He had not yet finalized the terms of the contract with his new connection, but he would arrange whatever the person wanted.

Nothing was too good for his current best friend.

Doyle leaned back, relaxed for the first time all day, and took a moment to drink it in.

They would have to give him a shitload of points for this, wouldn't they? And, once he crossed the next threshold into his subsequent level, he would be on a par with the prestigious Mr Michael Burke, and a real contender for Marshall's position.

He would be unstoppable.

Chapter 7

WILLIAM HATED WHAT he knew he must do.

He hadn't seen Baxter since the night he was followed into Sylva, and he was not looking forward to the follow-up that was necessary. He would have to speak to Baxter about it.

He waited until he saw his son heading for the door, going out during the day for no apparent reason. William was already dressed for outside, and as Baxter was leaving, he caught up to his son and exited right behind him, trying to create the illusion of coincidence.

"Where are you off to?" he asked casually.

"Nowhere," came Baxter's reply. It was likely meant to be non-committal, but it was precisely what William wanted to hear. It suggested that he could follow along without having to stop in the middle of the proposed chat because Baxter had arrived at his destination. With no specific goal in mind, William could talk as they walked until he felt he had explained everything he wanted to.

"Me either," William said incidentally.

The ride down in the lift was quiet, but once they exited the building together, William decided that if he didn't start the conversation right away, he may lose his nerve and not do it at all.

"We have not discussed what happened the other night," he led off with as they walked, hoping Baxter would answer and reveal his thoughts on the matter.

"I am not sure what to think of it all, to be honest. I mean-" He dropped his voice to a whisper and looked around him before continuing. "You are a spy, Father. If anyone ever found out, they would punish you as a conspirator.

They would at the very least lock you up, and in the worst case they would have you executed. I do not fathom why you do it - why you take the risk."

This was a perfect place for William to begin. "The fact that I might get locked up or killed for expressing thoughts contrary to Ascendancy doctrine is a substantial part of the reason I do what I do. You see, Bax, if people even question them, it could lead to trouble, or at least being descended to a point where your privileges are taken away. We have to be allowed to think for ourselves, especially when everything they have built here-" He gestured around him, indicating the whole city, "is based on lies. Right from the beginning. None of it is true."

"What do you mean, 'right from the beginning'? The beginning of what?"

"The Ascendancy. Nobody knows that they caused the Great Cataclysm to reduce the global population to where they could control it."

Baxter stopped and turned to look at him. "What?" he shouted, then looked around and lowered his volume as he got closer to his father. "They saved humanity after the Cataclysm and built the cities so we could live in safety. The Sylvans wanted to - and even actively tried to - destroy us. This is in basic history, Father. Seven-year-olds know this."

"Maybe, but where does that history come from? Here, come in here and sit." William ushered Baxter to a table on a patio outside a bistro. They sat, and William was glad that Baxter at least seemed to be curious about a counter-argument and willing to listen to it. He had been a little afraid that Baxter would completely shut down and not hear a word of this. He took a deep breath and looked at his son lovingly before going on. "Our history is given to us by them. Just like all the information we get. They have control over everything you see, hear and read. What really happened - and there is proof of this that they do not want you to access - is that before the Cataclysm there was a war where they tried to dominate the people of the world by force. And when it looked like they would lose that war, they used a satellite to pull an asteroid onto a collision course with the Earth while they all went up to a space station to wait out the aftermath."

A serving drone came to the table, and William stopped and sat up straight. "What can I get for you?" their robotic host solicited, and William and Baxter both said "water" at the same time. The server said it would be right back with their order and moved silently back toward the bistro.

William looked around and leaned toward Baxter so he could speak in a bright but soft tone. "They stayed up there until the Dark Times were becoming less intense, and they already had drones and nanites building the outer walls of the cities. Once the walls were good enough that they could be safe inside them, and they had some basic infrastructure in place, they came back down and made it look as though they were survivors, too, and had built everything that was there with help from the robots. They brought people in and offer them shelter, and that's where the lies piled upon lies. The Sylvans were just a bunch of people who decided to risk living on their own rather than concede to the rule of the new government. The Ascendancy."

The server returned to the table and placed two glasses of water there, asking if they would need anything else. William said they were fine, and the drone went off to wait on other patrons. William gave Baxter a chance to say something, but nothing came out of the young man. He just sat wide-eyed and bewildered. When the server was far enough away, William took a drink, then inclined toward the confused young man to continue.

"They gave people who contributed the most to the cities places of privilege, and it went on from there."

"Well, what about the terrorist attacks?" Baxter finally interjected. "The Sylvans have been attacking us all along."

"Some of that is accurate, but only in cases where it is an assault against the government or a hack-job to send in messages or something like that. Most of what you hear about didn't even really happen or at least didn't happen the way they told us. Did you ever notice that in these alleged attacks, that you never know anyone, or even anyone who knows anyone, who experienced what we hear about in the news? With all the supposed attacks on us, you would think that you would at least know someone who had seen something, right?

Baxter looked down at the table, pondering for a moment. Then he leaned right into his father and looked him in the eye most seriously. "How can you prove any of this? Because of what the Sylvans tell you? They might be the ones who are lying."

"I have all kinds of unbiased proof I can show you, but it's not readily accessible. For now, you will have to take my word for it. But I will arrange for you to see the evidence for yourself."

William sat back in his chair and reached for his water glass. He held it in front of him, hesitantly, and decided that the discussion would have to end for now. He would take Baxter to the Nest sometime soon, even though it would ultimately damn him as a saboteur. It would also give him the opportunity to show Baxter things that might convince him that what he was doing was right.

He summed up. "Civilization is not as great as its leaders, but as great as the knowledge of the average person within that civilization. A government that keeps information from the people cannot be great - but if they shared true knowledge with the people to increase the understanding of the whole, they could make themselves great by making the people great. Does that make sense?"

Baxter nodded his agreement. "I agree with that statement, Father, but I do not know what to think of it all. I need some time, I suppose."

"Fair enough." William drank the last of his water and stood up. "Shall we?"

Baxter left his untouched glass on the table, and the two of them started off for the long, quiet walk back home.

LAENA SAT PASSIVELY in the new cell they assigned her. This one was smaller, and as much as the one she had occupied since she arrived didn't have much - this one had less. It wasn't even as clean as the other one - but the Ascendancy wasn't trying too hard to make her comfortable these days.

She had beaten 482 brutally, and she went on hitting him for quite some time after he was dead.

When she was interrogated about what happened in the refresher room, she replied, "I had a shower." And when they asked her if she was responsible for the death of 482, she shrugged and said, "Wasn't me."

Her sarcastic responses, and the fact that when they apprehended her she was whooping like a rabid squirrel, left the Ascendancy with revenge on their minds. Surely they would make an example of her, and she might even have her sentence carried out publicly, in front of the other prisoners.

Oh well, it was totally worth it, she thought while trying to suppress a smile that she knew would be recorded by the camera that looked into her tiny space. She already had enough trouble without appearing unremorseful. Sometimes she couldn't help herself, though. She wondered if it would make a difference at this point, anyway.

She laid back on her cot and went through it all in her mind yet again. She couldn't believe that she was being punished for defending herself. But she had a hard time with the fact that she was imprisoned at all. Nothing made sense. Had the world gone utterly crazy?

Here she was, waiting to have her fate dictated to her by a bunch of scoundrels who were only as good as the amount of butt-smooching they did. They had hauled her in for no reason, then treated her like shit, and now she would probably die because she wouldn't put up with it and play their ridiculous game. Assholes.

A guard appeared outside the crackling shield that sealed her cell. Laena could tell it was a woman - the shapes and stature were wrong for a man. "Get up. It is time to see the Warden."

Laena turned to face her as she dropped the plasma. "Oh, come on - just five more minutes."

The guard entered her cell and reached out to grab her. Laena shifted in her cot and sat up quickly, and it startled the woman.

Laena felt a smug sense of satisfaction, but then the guard slapped her face. The woman was fast - Laena had to give her that. She hadn't even seen it coming. Crap. She needed to be more aware of her surroundings, and not so certain in her assumptions of what would happen next.

She rubbed the red spot on her cheek and looked at the guard. Now she couldn't help but smile. "Not bad for a city girl," she said as she passed the escort who kept her distance. "Let's go see what they're gonna do with me."

BAXTER HADN'T CALLED Kent or Lila. They just showed up on the rooftop, knowing he'd be there. He supposed he was not too hard to figure out, and he wasn't hiding, anyway.

This was the place he always went to sort himself out, even though Kent had accessed it, and they all shared it. But it was on top of Baxter's building, and he felt a sense of ownership for it.

He didn't begrudge them being there now; he was just in a state where he didn't know what to say to them, and he was a little embarrassed. He couldn't tell them the details of what was going on in his life, but he supposed he could divulge enough to his closest friends that they may be helpful in bringing some light to bear on his bleak circumstances - although he wasn't terribly hopeful of that.

When he turned to look at them from where he sat, he was met with Lila's loving and concerned smile. He returned it to her half-heartedly, and when it dissolved from his face, he looked back down into his lap. "Hello," he said.

Lila said hello and Kent said nothing, and the two of them came to sit on either side of him.

"So, what has you beat up, my friend?" Kent opened with.

Lila continued. "We have seen little of you lately, Bax, and when we do, you are not acting like your usual self." She sat quietly next to him and waited for a response.

"My parents are fighting," Baxter replied. It wasn't a lie, but an awful lot was missing from that statement. He wanted to tell them about everything that had happened and holding back made him feel ill. "It is pretty bad, and most unsavoury. And they have me stuck in the middle of it all, as though they want me to choose which of them I believe is right."

"That is not fair," Kent said. Lila was probably thinking the same thing, but would never make a judgement call like that, so she remained silent. She reached over and put a hand on his knee.

"No, it is not fair," Baxter concurred. "Their points of view directly contradict each other, and I feel torn. I think one of them is right and mismanaging it, and the other is wrong but doing the right things. Does that even make sense? I don't know what to make of it."

Now that he had opened the floodgates, more and more came pouring out. He had to remind himself continually not to go too far. "I have a great concern for Father, and Mother only seems to be concerned with herself, as usual."

Now Lila chimed in. "What is the matter with your father?" she implored.

Baxter thought about how he would handle answering that. Then Kent asked if William was alright, and it gave Baxter the chance to respond by merely saying that his father was okay.

"So, what seems to be the problem, then?" Kent went on.

"Ah, Father is just confused about his work. He thinks he is on the right path, but he is not congruent with the expectations that are placed on him, especially for a man at his level. Mother believes he should do what is conventional and leave it at that."

"Your mother is quite the character," Kent piped in. "She would have no idea what to do with herself if she was not Enswell royalty." He made a circle with one hand as he bowed slightly. No one laughed. He sat up straight again and allowed the moment to pass before he went on. "But, I suppose your father must be pretty far off the beaten path to elicit such a response from her, even such as she is."

Lila added, "She can be a little unsavoury sometimes."

Baxter nodded, still looking down. "Yes, she can. She sure has it in for Father right now. She has even spoken of going to extremes and letting the Ascendancy punish him. She says it is for his protection, but I know she is more concerned with our status. But, on the other hand, she is often correct about such matters. She is where she is because she always knows what to do and say in any situation. I know not. Maybe it is her who is correct in this matter. Things are as they are for a reason. They do not mean for us to reinvent the wheel, just to keep it turning."

Now it was Kent's turn to be silent. Kent seldom said anything when politics or the system came up, even at times such as this.

"That is right," Lila said. "We each ascend so we might all ascend. The contributions we make as individuals help humanity as a whole."

Baxter pondered this in the new light of what Father had just told him. The Ascended weren't 'humanity as a whole'. The Ascended were only a part of humanity, and the rest were living like the ancients did - in the wilderness, exposed and crude in their existence. He shook it off. Not here. Not now.

"I just want to be left out of the whole thing. I wish I had not heard them discussing the issue at all."

"They do love you, Baxter," Lila consoled, "They are just going through something right now. These things work themselves out in time. Maybe you should try to stay out of it until they get past it. It does not sound like it is your problem."

"You are right, Lila. This is not my problem. Thank you. That is what I needed to hear. My parents are both being ridiculous and obstinate and I should not be allowing it to affect me like this." He stood up and brushed off the back of his pants while Kent and Lila looked up at him. "I will endeavour to go about my business and leave those two to work it out. Or not. I do not care anymore."

Lila stood up and hugged Baxter. "What will you do now?"

Baxter backed his face away from her so he could look at her, with his hands resting on her hips. "I will choose my implant, work at my studies, then play Holoball until my brain leaks from my skull." He froze briefly and pondered her. She was a good fit for him. Not as exciting as Rachel, or whatever her name was, but she was kind and attractive in her own way, and she was always there to get him back on track when he needed it.

"Thank you," he said as he pulled her back in for another hug. He held her close and closed his eyes. Yeah, this was good - the way things were supposed to be.

"Okay, that will be enough now, children," Kent said as he rose to join them. He clapped a hand on Baxter's shoulder as he released Lila, and they exchanged reassuring looks with one another. "We all have things to do, and I must go now. You two can stay here if you like, but I have to leave."

"No, no. I want to get started at letting go of all of this, but I am grateful for your input. If one of you misses hitting the nail on the head, the other usually gets it. Thanks, again."

"Are you going to be okay?" Lila beseeched, looking deeply into her future husband's eyes. "You scared me, and I want you to be savoury again, understand?"

"I will," Baxter said without looking away from her. "Do not worry about me. Then I will have to worry about you and, well, it gets out of hand fast."

Lila giggled and then noticed that Kent was already on his way to the door. "Goodnight, idiots," he called out to them as he opened the roof door. "I'll see you tomorrow."

Baxter called back to him, saying goodnight, and started off when Lila caught him by the arm, rotated him back to face her and kissed him. It was over quickly, but it was full and right on the lips, and Baxter was flabbergasted. Lila gave him one more look, said goodnight, and spun on her heel to follow Kent.

Baxter stood and watched her walking away before he pursued with a big grin plastered across his face. Maybe everything would be okay after all.

Chapter 8

THE LUMINANTS HAD BEEN hiding in the forest for two days. There was a steady stream of supplies coming in to meet their physical needs, but the soldiers grew impatient. They were ready for a fight, but what they got instead was cramped from sitting uncomfortably in the bushes of the woodlands.

William joined them from Enswell, as his expertise in Ascendancy tech would be required once they found the bomb. He was not faring nearly as well as the Sylvans with being in the woods, and he was more anxious than most to get up and move around.

Shawan had to hold William back from leaving with a scouting party, even though he had asked several times if he could. Shadaar was to be kept safe at all costs to diffuse the bomb once they secured it.

Going on patrol had become a preferred duty. Everyone wanted a chance to stretch their legs and maybe see some action. A couple of the scouts had even come back with rabbits they hunted while out scouting, and they were cleaned and sent back to the village with the next supply run.

When he first saw the bagged bunnies, Shawan was a little upset - the soldiers were supposed to be focused on the mission, after all - but he let it go. It kept morale up, happened while they were scouting anyway, and provided a meal for someone back home. No harm, no foul.

Timoth had decided he wanted to come with them, also, and as glad as Shawan was that Tim was showing an interest in the Luminants, he was hesitant to let him follow along. But when they received an intelligence update that said the Ascendancy forces would not be moving for another day or two, and knowing that his son could be sent home long before that, he allowed it.

Tim came out with troops that morning but was told that he would have to leave with the last supply run of the day, which was due to happen in twenty minutes or so. Timoth would have time to make it home before dark, and the Ascendancy forces weren't expected until at least first light tomorrow, and probably later than that.

Aellana was furious initially, but when Shawan reminded her of how distant Timoth had been lately, that this represented a chance to reconnect, and ensured her several times that her boy would be home before anything too exciting happened, she had relented.

So, Shawan was able to take his son out to show him the ropes and have some bonding time, and he was enjoying it. Also, it was good for Tim to see his father in charge of all these other men. Shawan loved it when things came together.

They had hunkered down in a brushy area that offered them some natural cover, and Shawan sat proudly on the ground with his son at his side. Timoth ate a sandwich and listened to the other soldiers murmuring amongst themselves.

Then someone in the group let out a barking laugh. Shawan turned in their direction, and said in a low voice, but firmly, "Hey! Lock that shit down. Half the forest is gonna hear us." He then shifted back to Timoth, who smiled at him nervously.

Timoth hadn't been himself on this trip. Shawan wasn't sure if it was because it was his first time out on patrol, or if he was uncomfortable seeing his dad in a command position, or something else. He ignored it and concentrated on the mission.

William had a pad with him, and he was doing some things on it that Shawan didn't understand. Shawan liked William even though he had been a little apprehensive when he first met him, because of the bond that was forming between him and Aellana. It hadn't taken Shawan very long, however, to figure out that he had nothing to be concerned about. William was a terrific guy, but he was also really dorky, and he knew Aellana had no interest in that. Perfect. The two had eventually become close, with each of them looking up to the other for different reasons.

One man who was sitting where the laugh had come from called out. "Incoming, someone's headed this way!" Shawan pushed Timoth behind him as he raised his weapon, an old projectile rifle that fired bullets instead of energy. William grabbed Timoth and pulled him down low, and they belly-crawled into some cover behind Shawan.

"It's one of ours," the voice proclaimed. "Repeat, it's one of ours."

"Stand down!" Shawan ordered as he lowered the rifle. Everyone William could see did the same. He could not see, but heard some chatter from the next opening in the trees where the other men were, and a man appeared from behind the bushes that obscured his view, running toward him. When the man arrived, he was huffing, and he took a minute before he spoke.

"Sir, there's an urgent message for you to report to these coordinates." He handed over a pad that showed a map with concentric circles converging on a point, and a series of numbers under it.

"Why, what's going on there?" Shawan demanded.

"I'm not sure, Sir. The coordinates aren't part of our mission parameters, but the coding all checks out - it's completely legit - and they said for you to get there quick. Sir."

Shawan glanced at Timoth, who was peeking out from the bushes he had cached himself behind. He turned back to address the messenger. "The coding is ours, so there must be something to it. We've got time before the attack. You, come with me, and we'll check this out." He called to the men in the next bush. "Carvyre, you make sure that Timoth goes back with the supply run. As a matter of fact, I want you to escort him, got it?"

Rhodhall Carvyre was going to protest, as he was one of their best fighters. Then he realized that was why Shawan wanted him with Timoth, and he thought better of it. "Yes, sir," he called back.

"Okay, let's move," Shawan said to the man with the pad, and they worked their way into the forest as Timoth and Rhodhall waited for the supply shipment to come.

I FUCKING KNEW IT, Laena thought as the gavel came down and they made the decree.

The Tribunal had sentenced her to execution, and it was to be carried out as soon as they could finalize arrangements. Usually, if a prisoner was condemned to death, they just disappeared and were never seen or heard from again.

This time, it would be put off slightly because they decided to perform the execution in a common area within the facility so the other inmates could witness it. The Warden and two others that made up the Tribunal had resolved that, due to the nature of the offence - and because other prisoners were aware of it - they were going to send a message that would resonate throughout Aldergate: this is what would happen to any prisoner who behaved as she had.

The Tribunal rose and left the lavish chamber, and two guards converged on Laena to take her away. She stood as they lifted her by the arms and was surprised at how calm she was being.

Carbon nanotube cables bound her hands together, then from there connected to her likewise restrained feet, and they became taut when she tried to stand fully erect. She had to remind herself to slump somewhat, so there was enough give in them to allow her to walk. She trundled off with her escorts and did not say a single word.

It was a go-to modality for Laena to be sarcastic, spit, yell, kick, or bite when she was perturbed, but the certainty of this verdict, along with the sense of futility she felt of late, had reduced her to a mousy waif who gave no further resistance.

She gave up. What could she do?

As the guards moved her from the Tribunal chambers back toward her new cell, she wondered what it would be like to die. She had heard various theories about it, but none of them gave her any solace in her current circumstances.

She didn't want to die. No - she would not die.

Her focus began to sharpen, and she was becoming more unclouded with each awkward step. She had resigned herself to this fate until now, but she was shaking it off and remembering who she was. She supposed she must have forgotten while she was so busy pitying herself.

To hell with this dying stuff, she thought. *I have never let anybody mess with me, and I'm not about to start now.*

She turned her head to look at the guard on her right, a tall, lanky fellow whose hair looked like it had been scribbled on with a pencil, and she imagined he looked like the embodiment of a child's portrait of him.

She laughed, and when the guard to her left gave a jerk on her arm, she twisted toward him and furrowed her brow, making sure that he could see it. "Hey! Knock it off you drone! If I wanted any crap, I'd go shopping in the restrooms." She turned back to the frizzy-haired guard on her right and said, "And what about you? What's your excuse for lookin' like that? Face caught on fire, and somebody put it out with a shovel?"

Pencil Hair kicked her in the back of the knee, and she buckled and went down. She laughed again and felt much more like her usual self.

Laena Reisatra wasn't going to die. Not at the hands of the likes of these people. Fuck that.

She was getting out of here. She just had to figure out how.

WILLIAM FELT UNEASY after Shawan left the group. He hadn't noticed how much he leaned on his old ally and found his presence reassuring.

Shawan was not only a trusted friend, but he was also an accomplished fighter and knew what to do in situations that William was unequipped for. It was getting dark, and he was glad that they were not expecting any action until morning. Hopefully, Shawan would be back by then, and he could breathe a little more comfortably.

Not that he didn't trust the other men who were watching out for him, he just had a brotherhood with Shawan that none of those other people had earned yet.

He hoped that Shawan had noticed him protecting Timoth when they thought the enemy was coming, but it hadn't been acknowledged it in any way.

Timoth had crawled into the bushes on his own, but once they were in there, he moved closer to William when he looked scared. William felt satisfaction knowing that the boy received a bolstering from his presence.

Maybe Tim would tell Shawan about it later, at home.

It was not long after Shawan left that the supplies arrived. There were some fruits and bread and some dried salted meat, and some weapons - handguns, extra ammunition and more grenades.

Two soldiers came from each of the squads, the loot was divided up evenly, and then it went out to the units to be further split among the men.

The supply crew left, mostly younger Luminants who were new to the game, and Timoth followed them, with a very focused Rhodhall Carvyre bringing up the rear.

When the squad reps from his unit returned from the supply cart, William received a handgun with a full clip and an extra clip of ammo. He already had a rifle, which he would return after the foray, but he likely would not have to use any of these things.

He was here to take care of the bomb, and the other men were to take care of him and ensure that he was given enough time to diffuse whatever they found. The guns were his last resort.

William went into his food bag to see what he had to eat, even though he was not especially hungry. When he got nervous like this, his appetite tended to be the first thing to go. He just needed something to do.

He found a ripe mango in there, and it looked inviting to him. He took it out of the bag and smelled it. The fresh fruit of Sylva was so much better than the overly processed garbage that was available in Enswell.

"Incoming! Go hot! Lock and load!" he heard from the next unit. All the soldiers raised their rifles, and there were a few places where he could not see a person, just the barrel of a gun sticking out of a bush or from behind a fallen tree.

A man in the squad closest to his was the first to fire a shot, and it was returned immediately from a distant, invisible source. An energy bolt from an ion blaster hit the man square in the chest, and he went down in a heap, giving no sign that he would get back up.

Then rifle fire erupted from what seemed to be all around him, and in the distance he saw the first Guardians coming out from the dense foliage. More appeared and some of the Luminants took positions behind trees and rocks and peeked out periodically to fire on the first wave of O-bots.

William remembered his rifle, and dropped his fruit to raise it but did not shoot, unsure of what he should do. A man from his unit put his hand on William's shoulder. "Stay back, Shadaar," the man directed. It was Leukas Merandish, whom he had met a few times before, and the guerilla stepped in front of William, knelt, and opened fire toward the bots.

The O-bots were advancing on them slowly, but relentlessly. Most were standing at their full height, but others were down on all fours, waiting to pounce when the opportunity arose. The Luminants' projectile weapons were somewhat effective against them, but they had to hit critical points to make a successful kill. A hit in the neck, or between the chest and stomach areas seemed to be most effective, but they were low-percentage shots.

A few of the Luminants had energy weapons they had taken from Ascendancy forces over the years, but many of those were old and unreliable. Altogether, it was not enough to stop the advance of a much larger battalion than they had expected.

They thought they would be dealing with a small cadre of specialized forces, but instead found themselves the target of an all-out assault. They were guilty of bringing a knife to a gunfight, and it wouldn't be long before they were overwhelmed.

It was as though the Ascendancy was prepared for this. There were more Guardians than were needed just to get some humans with a bomb into the city and accomplish their goal. There was also the fact that they had come early and caught them off guard.

It was lucky for Timoth that he had made it out in time. Shawan would not have been happy if his son was still around when the fighting started.

All around William, men were falling. Some were hurt but still firing on the oncoming forces, but others were yelling out in pain and trying to nurse terrible wounds. It seemed to William that a lot of the collapsed Luminants were staring into nothing and not moving.

Time slowed for William, and he watched as his comrades did their best, but were being met with more than they could handle. Those who were able continued to fire on the O-bots, and now they could see human officers bringing up the rear, also shooting at them. It was clear from the Luminants' preparations, or lack thereof, that they were not expecting this.

The rebel in front of him turned to look at William between shots at the oncoming force and told him that it was time to get up and open fire. He crawled up beside his squadmate and moved his rifle into a prone firing position.

William squeezed off a few rounds, and the smell of the burnt gunpowder awakened him wholly to what was transpiring around him. He focused his efforts, and his next shots were much more earnest in attempting to bring down Ascendancy soldiers, both robotic and human.

"Fall back!" he heard from a point far in the distance, and another voice much closer to him repeated it loudly. Then he was startled to hear Leukas yell out the order from right beside him, so that others, in the thicker brambles behind them, might get the message as well.

Leukas took William by the arm and helped him up, and the two of them turned and ran, looking for other Luminants so that they might re-group. They jumped over some smaller bushes but mostly tried to keep moving as fast as they could through places where there was less resistance.

"This way!" his comrade yelled at him as he twisted sharply to his left. William followed and, looking into the distance beyond the man in front of him he could see other Luminants also running into the thicker part of the forest.

William batted low-hanging branches out of his way with his rifle, but he was still getting hit and scratched a lot by the trees. It appeared that the entire forest was trying to hurt him.

They continued through the rough terrain until they joined with the other men they had observed, and a small group broke off, presumably the highest-ranking, while the rest of the soldiers turned once again to face the direction of the enemy, awaiting their inevitable approach.

Leukas waved William into the inner circle, and he moved in tentatively. He stood near them as they assessed remaining troops and resources. Once they knew what they had to work with, they discussed strategy and decided that a small unit, which was to include Shadaar, would go around the main Ascendancy forces and try to get at the bomb from the rear.

One of the circle questioned whether there even was a bomb, stating that it was clear to him that someone had sold them out. Leukas indicated that they had to assume that there was an explosive device, and they should complete their assigned mission.

The soldiers who were defending this position hadn't fired, so presumably the Guardians hadn't found them yet. A squad was chosen from the remaining forces, and they were told to take Shadaar and move immediately.

The new unit broke off from the group and made their way into the forest before taking a sharp right and circling off in that direction, keeping a keen eye to ensure that they stayed far enough away from the O-bots to avoid detection. They heard the men who were left behind open fire, reengaging the Ascendancy troops.

They went farther toward the city than William thought they needed to as the forest continued to accost him. Then they turned right again, slowing themselves as they moved toward the place where the Ascendancy troops had come from.

When they returned to the relative openness of the forest trail, there were no signs of the enemy. They swung to the right to come up behind the troops that were engaging their comrades.

After just a few steps, William stopped. He called out to Leukas, and the small unit came to a halt after Leukas raised a hand and then formed it into a fist.

"What?" Leukas blurted to William. He looked annoyed, and it made William hesitate for a second before he responded.

"What if the troops up there were just after our men, and the explosive is that way, closer to Enswell? Surely they will complete their mission just as we are trying to finish ours?"

Leukas pulled his head back slightly in contemplation of what he had just heard. He took out his comm device and radioed the other units. "Has anyone up there seen anything that looks like it could be the explosive device?" he petitioned into the keyed mic. He waited a moment and was about to repeat himself when a voice came back, staticy, and backgrounded with the sounds of gunfire. "We have not seen a device. Repeat, we have not seen the device."

Leukas responded. "If you see it, call for assistance - do you copy?" The garbled voice responded, "Copy that. Will call for assistance on visual confirmation of device, over."

Leukas put his comm away and addressed the unit. "We'll go back toward Enswell. Either we'll find the bomb or they will. We'll just hope it's us, because if they find it first, it's gonna take us extra time to get back to them. Gadan, you scout ahead. The rest of you, stay off the trail, but follow it and be sure to stay together. Shadaar, you stay close to me. Let's move."

Studaar Gadan jogged a bit up the trail in front of them before cutting into the woods. William stayed close to Leukas as they trudged off the path and then turned to move parallel to it, making their way toward the city.

William was getting more and more offended by the forest. It kept slapping and poking at him, scratching him here and there. He fell behind several times as they made their way, but Leukas always had the group stop while they waited for him.

They went for a long way before they saw Studaar crouched beside the trail. Studaar motioned for the group to get down, then put two fingers in front of his eyes before casting them out to a point farther up the pathway.

Leukas raised himself slightly, trying to identify what Studaar was looking at. Then he lowered himself and faced the unit, put a finger to his lips to indicate quiet, and then motioned for them to move slowly. He started off, and William followed, searching in the distance. He could see nothing until the squad arrived at Studaar's position.

Ahead, in a place where the trail opened into a clearing, there was a group of human soldiers with Guardians standing watch nearby. At the center of the team, there was a shiny, knee-high cube with handles on opposite ends and the top opened like a trunk lid.

Two of the men were fidgeting inside the box while the others looked on. The shining, curved forms of the O-bots stood stoically, scanning left and right, prepared to deal with any interlopers.

Leukas indicated to the ranks that they would encircle the Ascendancy platoon. He pointed to them and then made a circle to show the periphery of where they were. He then cut the team in half with his hand, indicating for each division to move in the opposite direction. He singled William out by pointing at him directly, then stabbed his finger downwards at the ground beside him. He looked William in the eyes and raised his eyebrows, waiting for a response. William nodded his acknowledgement. He would stay with Leukas.

They started out, and it wasn't long before the squad had silently taken up positions around the officers with the silver case. The human officers stood, having finished whatever they were doing, and the O-bots moved in. The mechanical officers closed the lid and latched it, and stood erect as they lifted it by its handles, one of them at each end, and then were motionless with the box suspended between them.

The human officers gathered and spoke to one another, and Leukas saw what might be his only chance.

He opened fire, taking down one human, and the rest of them ran for cover behind anything they could find. A few shots flung sparks off the O-bots as they set the box down and went for their weapons.

Gunshots erupted from all around the Ascendancy platoon, and some of those men found that the defensive position they had taken against Leukas' fire made them an easy target for the other Luminants behind them.

The bots advanced, firing confidently, and recreated the Luminant's circle on a smaller scale, facing outward. They continued in their assault and pushed forward.

William heard an occasional scream or grunt between the cracks of gunfire and the howls of ion rifles, and the number of Luminant gunshots grew smaller and smaller until they only came from him and directly beside him.

The Guardians broke their circle, and all of them came to bear on William and Leukas. William fired one more shot, and then Leukas put a hand on his rifle, pushing it down, while his other hand showed his gun to the O-bots before he dropped it. Leukas then raised both his hands and William followed suit.

The two of them were forced at gunpoint into the clearing and they made Leukas kneel close to where the explosive cube was. Two O-bots stood over him with their weapons on him and ready to fire. "You have been selected for relocation," one of them said to Leukas. Another bot stayed back, but paid the prisoner no attention, facing the forest.

They separated William from Leukas, and three O-bots marched him further up the path, away from the city, and apart from Leukas and the bomb.

Once they had walked for a while, William was struck across the back of his knees, and he fell to the ground, facing the explosive and Leukas in the distance. Two of the bots pointed their rifles at him, staying close, while the third took a lookout position. William closed his eyes, bowing his head.

On the other side of the bomb, he heard a rustling in the forest headed toward where Leukas was. The bots did not hesitate. They fired on Leukas, and he fell forward to the ground. The O-bots then turned their attention to the source of the commotion.

"No!" shouted a voice from the woods. It was Shawan, and hearing him was music to William's ears. He lifted his head and saw an object fly from his friend to the edge of the clearing, bounce, and come to rest between the grey box and Leukas' silent and twisted body.

There was a small explosion, quickly followed by a much more impressive one, and William fell back as the bots that stood over him shifted their weight against the shock wave that came.

Debris and dust flew past him, and he shielded his face with his arms until it stopped, then lowered them slowly, opening his eyes.

William saw Shawan coming into the clearing and felt his tension replaced by a familiar comfort. Shawan always came through for him. There was hope yet.

Two of the bots fired on William's friend, and Shawan dodged as he continued to advance, yelling like a savage.

But William's smile faded as the O-bot nearest him retrained its weapon, pointing it right between his eyes. William stared into the barrel, and his eyes widened as he saw the softened features of the bot's face tilt slightly and its trigger finger start to flex, and he opened his mouth to yell, but before anything could come out, it fired.

Chapter 9

SHE COULDN'T BELIEVE what she was hearing.

When her dad returned with some other Luminants limping along with him and shared what had transpired on the mission, Raishann could only listen in stunned silence. She sat across the infirmary from where Shawan and other surviving soldiers were having wounds tended to. Those with more severe injuries went to the main hospital, but they sent the people with minor wounds to this smaller facility.

The small medical building was round, like most modest structures in the village, and it had beds in partitioned stalls at the back, with an open front area that had some chairs, shelves of supplies along a curved wall, and an examination table. From her chair, she listened, fascinated, as she heard the most outrageous tale she'd ever been exposed to.

Had it not been for the corroboration of the other men, she may have thought he was being deceitful or perhaps dipping into his limitless supply of dark humour.

Most of the Luminant troops that went on the mission had been shot and killed along with William Clarke, the city-dweller known to the rebels as Shadaar.

Shawan had been called away from the site of the Ascendancy assault just before it started, only to find that the place he had been directed to was devoid of anything unusual. None of it made any sense, but one thing was agreed on and appeared to be quite clear: the Ascendancy had known the Luminants were coming, where they would be, and how to take them by surprise.

Tears flowed as Raishann listened, and she thought of people she knew who went out there and hadn't come back. Leukas Merandish, for one, had been a friend of the family for as long as she could remember.

Thankfully, Dad had come back, beat up and hurt again, and Timoth had returned with Rhodhall Carvyre and some other people from the supply run. If they had been caught out there, this could have been much worse for her. Her family was bruised and battered, but other families had not been as lucky, and they would have to mourn in a much more intimate way.

Dad made it out after escaping the bots that killed Leukas and Shadaar but not before catching some carbon-fiber shrapnel from a bomb in his chest, one side of his face, and in the same leg he had hurt before . Father's wounds were easily treatable for the most part, and the doctor didn't seem too worried about them, but they did make her father look awful. His previous injuries were still bothering him, and his body was abused beyond anything normal.

But that poor boy, Baxter, from the city, lost his dad and maybe didn't even know he was gone. Would he hear about this at all? Were the Ascendancy forces going to share this information? Surely they wouldn't just leave things like this, with William gone and no one in the city knowing what had happened to him.

Raishann remembered Baxter fondly from their first meeting, and the anger she had toward him for their subsequent interaction was diminished now. William had been brave, and perhaps Baxter had some of that in him. He would need that bravery now, as she thought he probably knew nothing of his father's passing or, even worse, had been fed a line of horseshit by the Ascendancy. Either way, she felt sorry for him and tried to project spiritual strength from herself to the young man.

Mr Saaberos, who taught Raishann hand-to-hand combat, startled her out of her thoughts. "Are you okay, Miss Forander?" he queried. He never called her by her first name even though he was informal with the other students. When he addressed her, it was always "Miss" or "Miss Forander".

She snapped her head up to look at him, and his long moustache hung out of place as he leaned forward to engage her. "Yeah, I'm alright," she responded and reached out to take the hand he offered her in condolence.

"Is it okay if I sit?" he asked, indicating the empty chair next to her with his unoccupied hand.

"Please," she said, nodding toward the chair.

He sat down beside her, still holding her hand. "Your father will heal. He always does, you know. He is strong of mind and body. And I know that you know that. So, is there something else that troubles you?"

"Yeah," she said bluntly. "I'm really pissed off that someone ratted out the mission, but what I can't stop thinking about is the city boy. Shadaar's son. I should hate him, you know, but I just can't. Is that weird?"

Mr Saaberos sat back and looked straight ahead. He gave the back of her hand a pat. "I've heard weirder."

Raishann looked at him for a second, trying to figure out what he meant by that. She presumed it was supposed to indicate that it was not that big of a deal.

She knew her teacher would not tell her anything outright. He often spoke in riddles and wanted his students discern for themselves how they should handle whatever situation they were in. He would offer guidance, but not answers. She joined her mentor in sitting back and looking straight ahead to where her father was having his cuts stitched closed, still holding the supportive hand of Mr Saaberos.

She would have to glean meaning in this herself, she asserted. She thought about the mass of new data she had to interpret and hoped it would not take too long. She was growing tired of not knowing what to do.

THE HOLO WAS ON MORE for background noise than anything, and Candace tried not to be annoyed while Baxter sat in the sitting area with his portable terminal in his lap and neuroheadset on, working on his studies. The volume of the holograph was low, and the image was in 3-D mode so characters roamed around the living room as they played out their dramas.

Baxter tapped away at his pad, not entirely relaxed, but not as tense as he had been in the past while, either.

She hoped that her little chat with him had taken root and that Baxter was following her advice to stay on the path to ascension. She was pleased with herself, and she was about to leave the room when the holo grabbed her attention.

She couldn't determine what the correspondent was saying when the news broadcast came on, but behind the reporter there was a picture of a man, and she had to look a second time to discern that it was, indeed, William.

She moved to stand behind Baxter, still immersed in his work, and tapped him on top of the head to get his attention. Baxter turned around as he removed his headset and, when he saw her staring past him, he twisted to face the holocast as well. "Holo, increase volume by 25 percent," she said blankly. The volume increased, and Baxter joined in her disbelief at what was being announced.

"-the bright blast was visible through the dome and even heard and felt by residents of Enswell's outer rim. Officers received an anonymous tip that enabled them to stop the attacker from getting the explosive device into the city, although several Ascendancy officers were slaughtered or wounded in the detonation. The tip also led to officers attempting to apprehend the perpetrator, William Clarke of Enswell Core. Clarke, however, resisted arrest and was shot and killed at the scene, just outside the city wall. Investigators are looking into the attack, and we will have more on this story as information becomes available. In other news, an accident in Caringport ended with citizens being startled yesterday as a-"

"Shut it off," Candace ordered. The holo continued, now showing another city and a small amount of smoke coming out of a building. "Holo off!" she yelled, leaning toward it as though to punctuate that she was addressing it in particular. The holo popped out of sight, and Candace sat on the back of the sofa behind Baxter.

The claytronic furniture responded to her weight and converted itself into an s-shape, with Baxter remaining where he was, and a new place created for Candace to sit facing the other way.

Baxter watched her silently, neither knowing what to say. Candace went through a list in her mind of things that she wanted to convey, but none of them sounded appropriate. "This was just a matter of time", and "See what happens when you go against the Ascendancy" topped the list, but she said neither of them.

She hung her head and cried, and her makeup adjusted itself accordingly.

"Is it true?" Baxter finally inquired, still staring at her.

"I told him that if he kept doing this, he would end up in jail, but I never thought that this would happen." She broke into huffing sobs, and Baxter leaned over to her, and the sofa reformed itself again to give him access to his mother. He put his arms around her and tilted his head into the back of her neck, and the two of them cried together.

Candace needed Baxter to ascend now more than ever. She took a slow breath and closed her eyes. She would have to nurture his understanding of the responsibility he now had toward her, and he would have to make good on following through. If he didn't, she had no one else to turn to.

The strength that she once possessed had all been used up on William, pretending that she didn't know what he was involved in, and trying to steer him toward a more honourable mindset. She had no plan for what was happening now. She never thought things would go this far.

There was a chime at the main door, and it opened without either her or Baxter saying that it was okay to do so.

She wheeled toward the door, as did Baxter, and they watched as two men in Ascendancy uniforms entered the house, accompanied by a pair of Guardians.

"What are you doing?" she yelled at them as she stood. Baxter rose also but said nothing.

"Madame, we are here to search the premises for evidence against the traitor, William Clarke."

"You mean alleged traitor, right?" Baxter corrected.

The uniformed men added nothing further and made indications to the O-bots to initiate a search. The lithe androids moved past the men, and then each of them headed in a different direction. One man reached into a chest pocket and handed Candace a folded paper while the other stood behind him with his fingers curled around the handle of his holstered energy weapon. "We have been commissioned to perform this duty, and any action on your part to obstruct us from doing it will be seen as guilt of conspiracy. Do you understand, Madame?" The uniform said to her.

"I- I will do whatever you need to help in the investigation," she said as Baxter looked on. She extended a hand toward her son. "We had no idea that William was involved in anything like this and only just now saw it on the holo." She took a sharp breath, adjusted her dress and stood tall. "We are loyal to the Ascendancy and will comply fully."

"Is my father dead?" Baxter asked. Candace looked at her boy and noticed that he was drained of any blood in his face, and she told him to sit down. He didn't even look at her as he settled on the sofa.

The men moved into the household with no further regard for her or Baxter and began looking through their things. One of the men started directly toward the back of the house where William's workshop was, as though he was going to it specifically. Baxter got up and followed him, and Candace told him not to but didn't cause a scene when he continued despite her objection.

Candace went to the kitchen area, and when an officer came through with his handheld scanner out in front of him, she offered a cup of coffee, but he refused.

Standing against the counter and being ignored by representatives of the establishment she had pledged her life to gave her the revelation that it was going to be very hard, indeed, to show her loyalty and the dedication of her brilliant son to the Ascendancy. She had already sacrificed deeply to prove herself, but it would take even more from now on. So be it. She would get Baxter on board, and the two of them would continue their ascension no matter what obstacles they encountered.

William's passing upset her, of course, but she had to make this work for the future of herself and her household. She would do anything for her family.

DOYLE WAS GLOWING WITH self-worth as he strode into Marshall's office. He closed the door behind him and took a seat in front of the large desk that occupied the space in front of the window. He smoothed his jacket and drank deeply of his confidence as he looked up to face his boss.

Marshall was sitting with his back to him, facing out the window as he often did when he knew someone would enter his sanctum. Doyle wondered if perhaps Marshall thought it made him look mysterious, but he felt it just caused the Chancellor to appear pompous and conceited.

Marshall turned slowly around to meet Doyle's grinning visage and then shocked him beyond all reason. "So, are you going to explain to me what went wrong?" he demanded as Doyle's smiling face withered into surprise and dismay.

"Wrong? They took the traitor into custody, and, and our returning troops say that the entire Sylvan hit-squad was terminated. What's wrong with that?"

"Only that the original intent of the operation was never actualized," Marshall sarcastically iterated as he leaned ahead putting his elbows up on the desk and his fingertips together. "The whole purpose of this was to have people in Sylvan garb be seen entering the city and setting off an explosion in the outer rim. And that never happened, did it?"

Doyle sat up straight and furrowed his brow as he retaliated. "No, that did not happen, but we gained something even better with my intel and altering the plan to achieve a greater goal-"

"Your goal, you mean. Yes, you were able to take a traitor out, but we had to go behind you cleaning up the mess you made with a last-minute cover story and broadcast. We were supposed to turn the people of Enswell against the entire Sylvan population, not have them angry at one of their own, a single man from within their city. The well-laid plans that Michael put into place were wiped out by your ego and your lack of respect for the hierarchy of this office. You placed your own needs before those of the Ascendancy, without clearing any of your ideas first, I might add, and now we have a predicament to sort."

It dumbfounded Doyle. He had not thought of things in the way they had just been presented to him, and he didn't agree with the skewed interpretation of events. There was some truth to it, he supposed, if looked at from a twisted perspective. He was astounded that Marshall had wrung all the negativity out of what had happened, and focused on only that rather than all the good that had come from it.

"I do not know what to say, Sir," was all he could get out when he noticed that the Chancellor was waiting for his response.

"Typical," said Marshall as he picked up a pad on his desk and tapped at it. "I will deduct 2000 points from your account." Doyle began to protest, but Marshall overspoke him as he continued. "You will have to learn a few more things before you can move ahead in this organization. Rules must be followed, and there is a chain of command that likewise must be adhered to. Do you understand?"

"Yes, Sir, I have always understood. Things were laid out very clearly for me when I was brought into the fold. And I am very grateful for that - please do not take it otherwise - but I feel like I have accomplished everything I was asked to do, and followed every rule, and done more than what was needed at any time. I mean, shit, I've done more than most anybody else around here, and-"

"That barbaric speech that you resort to using periodically is one of the many reasons why you do not ascend to your potential. The bottom line, Mr Morgan," Marshall sneered, leaning ahead to punctuate what he was about to say, "is that your base instincts will always be there, rearing their ugliness when it is unwelcome. You will always be a brute, no matter what you do." He sat back again and rotated toward the window. "I have nothing further to add right now. But we will discuss this again once the horrid business you have brought into my office is sorted out."

Doyle got up and walked to the door. He stood there with his hand on the old-fashioned handle, trying to decide what he should say upon his exit. As much as he was furious with Marshall and the organization, and he wanted to let His Worship know what he thought of the whole arrangement, finally he decided on saying "Yes, sir," through his teeth and exited the room.

He would have to find another way. If properly navigating the system wasn't going to work for him, then he supposed he'd have to go around it.

Okay, fine. Whatever would get results.

Fuck Marshall and his sanctimonious shit. And fuck Burke, too.

BAXTER HAD BEEN LAYING on his bed for hours, and though his eyes were closed the entire time, he could not fall asleep.

His head swam with visions of his trip to Sylva with Father, the talk with his mother, the nature of the Ascendancy, Lila's comments about it, and everything he learned from school and the network.

He thought about the meeting with Rachel and her mother, and all the lying and secret-keeping that had occurred, all of which ultimately led to where things were now.

His father was dead, and he was sad and angry and hurt and alone. Mother was still here, but she had become engulfed in self-pity and trying to figure out how she would maintain her Level of Ascendance now that her husband was not only gone, but labelled as a traitor. Very few of her high-level friends had so much as sent a note offering their condolences. Most were silent, choosing to keep themselves distanced from the Clarke family and any potential repercussions on being sympathetic to the household of a subversive radical.

It was especially important to her now that the search of the house had resulted in the Officers walking away with what they claimed was conclusive evidence of a conspiracy against the Ascendancy and involvement in terrorist activities.

A knock at the door startled Baxter into lucidity. Probably mother looking to give him a speech about how he should toe the line and ascend for her benefit. "Open door," he grumbled.

The door opened, and Lila was standing at the threshold. Baxter sat up and spun his legs over the edge of the bed, twisting the sheets under him. He stared, not expecting to see anyone other than immediate family. Not even his aunt and uncle had visited, but at least they had sent a virtual card.

"Can I come in?" Lila requested after standing awkwardly longer than she should have.

"Oh. Yes, of course. I am very pleased to see you, Lila."

Lila drifted toward him with her hands clasped together at the waist. "I was not sure that you would want to see anyone yet, but I thought I would come anyway. To see if you are okay."

"No, thank you. You are the first non-mother person I have seen since we found out."

Lila meekly took a seat beside him on the edge of the bed. "Is it true?" she asked without looking at him.

"I am not sure. I mean, it could be true. I cannot help but feel that at least some of what they said in the reports was right, but I think that they have stated the most important details wrong. It could not possibly be everything that they say it is."

"Is this what your parents were fighting about?"

Baxter had to make himself collect his thoughts. He nodded noncommittally and let his head hang.

Lila put an arm around his back and pulled him close to her. Baxter turned and put his arms around her, burying his face in her hair.

He breathed in short, stilted gasps, and after a few repetitions, tears flowed, and Baxter held his sobs in his chest so Mother wouldn't hear them. "Close door," Lila said, and the bedroom door shut itself. She cradled his head with one hand while she rubbed his back with the other. "It will be okay," she whispered, looking past him.

It relieved Baxter to hear her say it, but when he was brutally honest with himself, he didn't think things would be okay. He huffed harder as he cried into his proposed mate's shoulder. "It hurts so much, Lila," he got out between heaving breaths. "I do not know what to do."

"For right now, you go ahead and let it out. I am here for you." She shushed him quietly and rocked Baxter slightly as she tightened her hold on him. "I am here."

Once Baxter regained his composure, he told Lila about the trip to the arcade, and the conversation between his parents he had overheard, and the journey to Sylva. He didn't realize until he was nearly through it all that he never mentioned Rachel.

That was something for another day, he surmised. He realized he would never see the Sylvan girl again, anyway. There was no need to embarrass himself to Lila by mentioning the savage that had captivated him briefly.

"So, are you saying that he did do it? The bomb and all that?" Lila gently implored.

"I have my doubts," Baxter responded. "Some men were here just after the first holo broadcast about it, and I followed one of them to Father's shop. He was deliberately trying to be nonchalant about going through everything and acting casual but, suffice it to say he will never be a Holo-Star. I swear, Lila, that I saw him reach into a pocket and pull something out that he was keeping hidden. Then he reached into the back of a workbench, opened his hand, and came out with the object. Then he called the other man and showed it to him. They talked and nodded a lot, and they put it in a sealed bag and marked something on the outside. It was all very bizarre. They questioned Mother and me, and then they left. I think they put something in the workshop so they could say they had evidence against Father. So, as much as he was involved in something, I do not believe that he built a bomb, snuck it out of the city, and then was caught trying to bring it back in. There are too many obvious questions that are not even being asked by the reporters on the holo, and they keep saying the same things over and over, as though repeating them often enough will make us believe them."

Lila absorbed the whole story attentively, not interrupting until she thought Baxter was done. She had never in all her life heard such a tale, but what was most interesting about it was that she believed Baxter and agreed with every word. "Do you sincerely think the Ascendancy could do something like that?" she finally got out.

"It does mesh nicely with what Father told me about them. But at the same time, I feel like I should be able to have faith in them. They are our leaders. They are supposed to represent everything that we aspire to become. Are they not?"

Baxter didn't expect a response from Lila to his query; he assumed that she must be trying to digest all of this much like he had when he first learned of it.

They sat silently for a while, and then Lila stood and bent at the waist to give him a soft kiss on the forehead. She told him that she was there for him if he needed anything, and then she left.

Baxter thought about how she was a stabilizing influence on him, and he felt much better now that he had spoken to her. She was perfectly lovely, and a good match for him.

Rachel was undoubtedly alluring, and exciting and mysterious and a lot of other things, but he reminded himself that she was not an option. That card had to be removed from play.

Chapter 10

WHEN HE REGAINED CONSCIOUSNESS, his head was so sore he was sure he must be bleeding out of every orifice in it.

William slowly opened his eyes, and even though he could make out some vague shapes throbbing in and out of focus, nothing seemed familiar. Despite being sore through and through and his brain pounding like never before, the one thing he was sure of was that he did not know where he was.

"Chief, he is awake," stated a voice that sounded as though it was emanating from somewhere not too distant from him.

William turned to locate the disembodied voice, but stopped instantly, as the small movement only amplified the pain in his skull.

He winced and closed his eyes again, having discovered that the only relief he could get came from stillness and darkness.

"Hello, Mr Clarke," a different voice said, coming from much closer. He could probably find this person if he cared at all to try. "You are presumably confused about your whereabouts and current condition. First, let me assure you that you are not in the afterlife. As much as you have been a thorn in the Ascendancy's side, we have recognized your potential and your life has been pardoned based on those merits. Tell me, William, what is the last thing you remember?"

William opened his mouth and tried to force air past his vocal chords, but all that came out was more pain. He swallowed hard and thought of the best way to get the message across in the least number of words. "Dead," he said weakly and cleared his throat.

"You recall being shot, then. So, you must certainly be wondering why you are alive. You had a tracking device on you, put there by someone you know, that caused any weapons pointed at you to fire a non-lethal but still quite debilitating burst. They spared you your life, but I would wager that you are not exactly comfortable right now, are you?"

William opened his lips, then closed them and shook his head as little as he could while conveying his answer.

"Here is what is happening. We have been waiting for you to awaken so you can be transferred to the Aldergate facility, so as not to damage this." William felt a slap to the side of his face and then found it within himself to vocalize fully, but what came out was not pleasant, and closer to inhuman than any noise a man would ever make. He closed his eyes tighter and tilted his head down, away from the lights.

"At Aldergate, you will continue your studies into single-portal transport. And you will make progress. We know you will make progress, because if you do not, then horrible things will happen to your family. There are fates worse than death, especially in a society where your standing determines your life. We will descend your wife and son so low they will have to look up to tie their own shoes." Another man behind William laughed.

"And if that is not enough, we will implant them with things that will render them helpless, useless, and further destitute than you can even imagine. We would exile them, but then your friends in the forest might take them in and give them reasons to live. That will never happen." The voice moved to directly in front of his face, shadowing his eyes and filling his nostrils with foul breath. "If you do not produce for us, your family will be so broken they will want desperately to die, but we will do everything we can to ensure they become the oldest citizens in the 12 cities. Is that clear?"

William nodded as tears broke loose and rolled down his cheeks.

"You will be moved to the facility presently, and there, you will make us all very proud."

William bobbed his head as he tried to stay attentive, but his agony overwhelmed him and he slipped once again into the oblivion of unconsciousness, only slightly aware that he had ever been awake.

THE DAY OF THE FUNERAL came faster than Baxter expected. Though he thought he had mentally prepared himself for the experience, he found himself as much a wreck as he had been on day one, after hearing the bitter news for the first time.

His mother had requested that the services be held in a central location, but they denied her request, and Father's life was to be honoured in a vicinage that was a three-minute aircar ride from the outer rim. Mother was not pleased.

Lila and Kent escorted Baxter into the funeral parlour, and it surprised him to see more people there than he expected. They turned their heads to see him as he entered behind his Mother, with his closest friends on either arm.

People rose from their seats, and some offered handshakes or other acknowledgements as the family made their way to the places designated for them at the front.

Most in attendance were people from upper-mid levels, and there were very few who were highly ascended. There were even some people there that Baxter did not know, and they stood silently as his family walked up the brightly carpeted aisle.

Baxter did his best to convey inner strength to everyone as Lila and Kent ushered him to his seat, and Kent moved around to the far side of his mother so Baxter could sit next to her.

He was able to maintain his composure through the services, but as the funeral director spoke, Baxter could hear the undertones of condemnation and pangs of pro-Ascendancy propaganda the speech was seasoned with, and it offended him. He seemed to recognize more things all the time that punctuated the integrity of what his father had shared with him.

He noticed Kent a couple of times through the sermon, leaning past Mother and looking at him when questionable things were said, possibly trying to get a read on what he thought of it. Kent didn't talk politics much, but he sure seemed to have a head for it.

When the services were finished, the empty casket that substituted for a corpse was moved down a belt and out through a hole in the wall to go somewhere, but nobody knew where that was, and few even cared to ask.

He left the building with Kent, Lila and his mother as a nameplate dedicated to Father was being placed on the Wall of The Departed outside. Baxter noted that it was being put in an out-of-the-way corner where a person would have to search extensively to find it. He thought Kent caught it too, but neither of them said anything to one another.

His mother left them to socialize with some of the attendees; not those who were being kind to her, but those with the most accumulated points, as usual. Baxter stood with Lila and Kent while some people came past, shaking Baxter's hand and sharing kind words. Baxter politely accepted each of their offerings, and then he fell silent as an unexpected face looked into his and offered a hand to shake.

He looked into her eyes, staring, and not knowing what he should say to Rachel. Or to her mother, who stood close behind her.

Baxter took the Sylvan girl's hand and shook it, and she said that she was sorry for his loss. Baxter stood there, still staring and shaking her hand, wondering if he shouldn't yell out for an officer or tell his mother who these people were. Mother would have them strung up in a heartbeat.

Then Lila stepped up and offered her hand to the unknown guest. "Hello, I'm Lila. And you are?" She was smiling, but she looked defiantly into Rachel's eyes as she waited for a response.

"My name is Rachel Forester. It is nice to meet you." Rachel indicated the woman who stood behind her, who Baxter had barely noticed until then. "And this is my mother, Alana."

Alana and Lila exchanged pleasantries, then Lila turned her attention back to Rachel. "We have not met before. How do you know Baxter?"

"Oh. My mother worked with his father some time ago, and we met at a function the workplace put on for families of the staff. We have not seen one another for a long time. I am surprised that he even remembers me."

"Sorry, it took me a minute to recognize you," Baxter interjected, taking the opportunity to cover himself. "Hello, Mrs Forester. It is nice to see you again."

"You also, Baxter," Mrs Forester expressed. "Although I do wish we could have met again under better circumstances. Your father was a brilliant man, and it was a privilege to have served alongside him."

"Thank you," came Baxter's gratitude. Of all the people who had offered similar platitudes to him today, she was probably the one who meant it the most.

Alana stepped up beside Rachel and looked at Baxter very seriously. "We were wondering if we could take a moment of your time, Baxter." She looked over at a stern Lila and amused Kent, then back to him again. "Alone, preferably."

"Yes, that will be fine," Baxter complied. He excused himself from the group, and the three of them moved to the bottom of the stairs to the parlour, away from the other guests.

Baxter looked up to where they had just been and could see Lila interrogating Kent, and Kent doing his best to keep her temperate.

He looked back at Rachel, and, recalling the deception that had been perpetrated against him that had caused so much confusion of late, his expression hardened. "Is there one good reason why I should not turn you over to the authorities?"

"I can give you more than one fantastic reason," Rachel retorted.

Alana intervened before things got too heated. There was a significant reason they had risked coming into the city - and to a public function, at that - and it would not do to drive the object of that reason away before they did their business. "Baxter, we came here because of Shad-, uh, because William wanted us to. We have something vital to give you. It is from him, and he wanted you to have it if, well, if anything like this happened." She held out her closed hand, and when she opened it, there was a small box laying there. It was about as long as her palm, half as wide, and half again as thick as that.

"What is it?" Baxter questioned. He made no motion to accept it.

"It's a gift from your father. Something he wanted you to have." She reached out with her empty hand and took him by the wrist, bringing his hand alongside hers. "Take it," she said as she turned her hand over, spilling the box into his. "You'll figure it out."

Baxter looked at the container and then, realizing where he was, he scanned around quickly and put it into his jacket's inside pocket. "I do not know what to say. Were you there when it happened?"

"No," Rachel interjected, "But my dad was. He was trying to stop the Ascend-holes from setting off a bomb in your precious city, and he nearly died, too. Right now he's out of his mind on pain medication in a medical clinic, and it'll be a long time before he gets better." She had leaned in toward Baxter and was speaking harshly.

Her mother put a hand in front of her and prompted her to stand upright. Rachel did what she was instructed to but still had her brow knitted tightly. Her mother took over, speaking in much less emotionally charged tones. "Someone let the Ascendancy know that we would try to stop them from setting off a bomb in the city and they ambushed our people. A lot of men and women died that day, Baxter," Alana continued. "I was lucky that my husband made it home, but there are many services, much like this one, happening in Sylva for those who didn't."

Baxter looked at Rachel, and he could see that sadness had softened her face somewhat. "I'm sorry, Rachel," he offered. "I did not mean what I said before. I am still bewildered by this whole thing, and I do not quite know what to do or think. And I certainly have no idea what comes next for me, but I had no right to speak that way. I'm sorry."

Rachel nodded her head and said it was alright, and that she was sorry, too.

Alana summed up. "We are terribly sad for your loss, Baxter, but the truth of the matter is that we both lost a lot because people were willing to risk their lives trying to prevent something even more horrific. We will honour the spirit of your father in our services later, and we hope that you will bring honour to his memory, too." She nodded, indicating where he had put the box. "Use that."

Baxter looked down at the lines of his jacket to ensure that the gift didn't show too much, and it seemed okay. "I am sorry for your losses, as well. But I should get back to my family now."

"We should get out of here, too," Alana declared, "before we overstay our welcome here."

They both shook hands with Baxter, and Rachel lingered when her turn came. She looked Baxter in the eye intently, trying to send an unspoken message to him. Baxter took her hand in both of his and nodded.

"By the way," Rachel added, "My name is Raishann. And hers," she indicated her mother, "is Aellana Forander." Baxter released her hand and stepped back from them.

They said goodbye to one another, and when Baxter turned to go back, Kent was there waiting for him, but Lila was not.

MAYBE I HAVE BEEN GOING about this in the wrong way, Chancellor Marshall thought as he stood before the window of his office with his hands clasped behind his back. *There has to be a better approach to resolving this issue.*

Marshall had seen the benefits of what Doyle Morgan had done, but he could not acknowledge it. Not officially, at any rate. He had to ensure that Burke remained the front-runner for the position of Chancellor, even though he fully realized that Michael was not the best man for the job.

Michael made his share of mistakes (and maybe even a portion of someone else's mistakes), but the bottom line was that Michael Burke's family was ascended into the 13th city. And that was where Joseph Marshall wanted to be.

To keep balance in his strategy, however, he told Doyle that he would be the successor to the Chancellorship to ensure things were done proficiently. Meanwhile, he had sent Michael to a facility outside the city where the potential for him messing anything up would be minimized. It was a necessary tactic to ensure his ascension by playing both sides. But, in the end, Michael Burke would get the mantle of Chancellor once he secured his admission to the 13th. Handling Doyle would be his problem then.

The 13th city was a place kept from general citizens, and it was only even known within the 12 cities by those in the most ascended positions, and had potential, through achievement and the correct attitude, had a chance of being admitted.

It was not as large as the other cities, but its population was also much smaller, measured in hundreds of thousands rather than millions.

Anyone who ascended to the point where they were given access to the hidden city was granted "Level Infinite", and there was no higher a person could go.

Medical science made available to the Level Infinites was far superior to that provided to the general population, which only granted about 150 years of quality life, at which time people were allowed to die. The Level Infinites could potentially live for 250 years or more and were likely to be tired *of* living before they were exhausted *from* living.

There was so much the people of Enswell did not know. They did not understand who ruled over them or even where their ultimate leaders were.

They didn't know the truth about the Great Cataclysm, the origins of the cities, the censorship of the information that was made available to them, or how they were slaves from the day they were born, living in servitude to the upper echelon.

The people who had created the Great Cataclysm and, later, the Ascendancy itself, came to know during their hiatus in space that humanity was far too fragile to rely solely on the Earth as a home. Humankind had to move beyond their little blue orb to survive in the long-term. That was why the Avalon Project had been started, and why people who developed the most helpful technology to bring people to the stars were given the right to ascend. Bringing people to the stars meant, by extension, bringing the Ascendancy to the stars.

If Joseph could be helpful to Michael and the Burke family, with all the power that came with their lives in the 13th city, not to mention being Level Infinite, they might see fit to help Marshall to ascend into the paradise of the 13th.

But the obstacle lay in his way had to be overcome before he went anywhere. The President, infinitely ascended herself, was not happy with his performance and wanted Enswell brought to a more manageable level.

He had tried doing it by appealing to the citizens, through propaganda, increasing their comfort, and even through fear. But nothing seemed to be working.

It was those damnable Sylvans. They occasionally hacked Ascendancy broadcasts and let out truths that were troublesome to those in power; the ones who knew that the 'barbarians' were correct. They also sometimes hit strategic targets that hurt the upper echelon and made them have to backpedal somewhat to clean up the messes they created. And, as with William Clarke, they occasionally even convinced citizens as ascended as he was to act against the government. If Mr Clarke was a Luminant, how many more were there out there, walking around and plotting against him?

No, motivating the people was a dead-end avenue.

He would have to hit the Sylvans directly, and hard enough to wipe them and all of their meddling out for good. They would have to keep some of them alive, of course, to continue working in the facilities, keeping the cities running and the citizens comfortable.

But no more than that.

The rest of them would have to die. And there was no better time than the present.

Facility workers could come from some other source, he supposed.

WHEN THEY ARRIVED HOME after the funeral, Baxter's thoughts were racing with the things that Aellana and Raishann had told him.

Those facts, combined with what his mother said to Father during their quarrel, led his mind to dark places. But, they meshed together cleanly enough that he at least had to consider the possibility.

It may have been Mother who contacted the Ascendancy regarding Father. It might be her who, ultimately, was culpable for what had happened.

He had to know, and he could think of no better way to find out than via the direct approach.

Baxter asked the home computer where she was, and it responded that she was in the sitting room.

He took his time crossing the house to confront her, and when he arrived, she was in a chair with her back to him, and he considered leaving before they discussed any unpleasantness. Maybe he didn't have to do this.

But he steeled himself and very deliberately walked to the center of the area before turning to face her.

Mother greeted him, but he didn't respond to it. He knew that unless he forced himself to do this immediately he would lose his nerve. "Mother, did you report Father to the Ascendancy?" he asked flatly.

She kept her eyes on him but set her glass down on the side table beside the chair without even looking. "Why would you ask such a thing?" she threw out.

Baxter wanted to keep the focus on her, and not allow his mother to turn the conversation into an argument against him. He had dealt with her prowess in this for too long to be distracted by her tactics while discussing something that bothered him so much. "Mother, it is a straightforward and simple question that requires a one-word answer. Was it you who told the Ascendancy about Father?" He adjusted his stance confidently, his posture demanding a response.

"No, Baxter. I did not notify the Ascendancy. I did not turn him in. But thank you for that glimpse into what you must think of me. Are you happy now?"

Baxter sought to decipher her expression and body language, but she put up an effective front against such readings. Nobody really knew what she was thinking, ever.

"Okay. I just felt I had to ask. It seemed odd to me. The story of what happened, I mean. It doesn't make sense. But I did hear you telling Father that he should be in prison for what he did."

Mother went on the offensive. "And he should have been, Baxter. His actions put all of us at risk and undermined everything we built. And look at what it got him, Baxter. And what it did to us. What are we going to do now? How will we continue to ascend with this stain on our records? He was selfish, and he did not consider for one minute what he was doing to us. Or what he was doing to the vicinage, or to Enswell, or to the whole of the 12 cities. What he was doing was wrong, and in the end, it was his downfall. That is what happens to traitors."

Baxter stood dumbfounded. He knew Mother was a staunch supporter of the Ascendancy, but he hadn't realized that she had such contempt for speaking or acting against it. He hated himself for mentioning the visit to the arcade to her. He wished he could take it back, but it was too late now.

He collected himself and relaxed his posture. "Alright, Mother. I just wanted to know. Thank you."

He walked past her as naturally as he could as she picked up her glass from the table.

Once he passed her, he widened his eyes, and his chest became tight with the air inside, and a shiver drove its way up his spine.

He was more certain now than ever that she handed Father over. She protested far more than was warranted, and she was clearly enraged by what Father had been doing and loyal to the Ascendancy beyond all questioning. She may not have thought that turning him in would result in his death, but she was still as guilty as could be.

Chapter 11

LAENA REISATRA MARCHED across the courtyard in her carbon nanotube bracelets and matching anklets, escorted by Aldergate staff. She didn't feel very stylish, though, hunched over by the short cable that connected her upper and lower accessories. Two guards and two Guardians brought her to a point near the outer wall and secured her ankle restraints to a steel peg in the ground, and then took positions around her, maintaining distance between her and those who came to look at the exhibit.

Arrangements for her execution were completed in the morning, and it was scheduled for later, but not until she spent some time in the courtyard on display for all to see.

Some prisoners had come as close as they were allowed, and a couple of them had even shouted their support to her. The guards shooed them away, and they backed off somewhat, but she remained the most popular attraction in the yard. Prisoners in red jumpsuits, on breaks from their duties or on a rest day, continued to come from all around the yard.

After some time, a substantial group had coalesced around them, and the two human guards were visibly getting nervous. One of them called on a comm for assistance while the O-bots circled Laena, opposite one another, weapons at the ready.

The convicts were getting louder, and this drew even more jumpsuits in, which again added to the volume of prisoners around her. There were shouts of "Free Laena" and "Let Laena go" and other slogans. Laena had to smile. She didn't realize that she was so well-known. It was a little overwhelming.

As much as the inmates were supporting her, she knew that the prisoners were scornful of the guards, and that was also a contributing factor to the noise. But Laena was not going to allow a detail to interfere with her enjoyment of the moment. It might be one of her last, after all.

The crowd constricted on the guards and bots, and Laena felt a shitstorm brewing.

The chanting and yelling continued, and then a rock came flying out of the middle of the throng, narrowly missing a guard. He pulled his gun up and put the stock against his shoulder, and looked down the length of the barrel, but his partner pushed it back down while remaining focused on the encroaching crowd. He said, "If you shoot one, they will all come at us," just loud enough for the other soldier and Laena to hear. "Reinforcements are coming. Stay calm."

The guard then addressed the crowd. "Back away, or we will be forced to open fire." The prisoners kept coming. He upped his volume. "Back away, or we will-"

The next rock caught him squarely in the jaw, rocking his head back and causing him to discharge his weapon into the air. The other Ascendancy guard fired into the crowd, and the Guardians copied their human counterparts. "Halt, halt," came the O-bots' voices as they dropped prisoner after prisoner.

Laena crouched down, unable to do anything else while confined by her restraints. She covered her head but kept watching as the riot grew in intensity.

The crowd split the four guards up. Though all Ascendancy agents, human and machine, were slowly losing ground, the bots were faring much better than the human soldiers were. It appeared that the bots might maintain their defence until more troops arrived on the scene.

Then the man who was hit with the rock was beaten to the ground, and it was not long before a prisoner - a mean-looking Sylvan man - came up from the scuffle with the guard's gun and charged toward Laena. "Open 'em up!" He barked when he got close. She rose as high as she was able, and put as much distance between her hands and feet as her restraints would allow. The Sylvan man fired downward, and Laena felt her stance widen as the restraints there came apart.

She lifted her hands over her head, with the short connecting cable dangling in front of her, and closed her eyes, turning her face away from the gun. But there was no second shot.

When she opened her eyes again, the Sylvan was being pummeled by an O-bot. A strike to the head knocked the guy down, and the bot raised its weapon to deliver another blow with the butt of its rifle. The man cried, "Laena!" and threw the gun he had taken in her direction. It hit the ground in front of her as the O-bot brought its weapon down, and an arc of blood left the Sylvan's head as he twisted to the ground.

Laena scrambled to pick the rifle up, quickly made sure it was active and then put a shot right on the Guardian's back. Electricity sparked in the spaces between its joints. It convulsed all the way down to the ground and continued until its circuitry fried, its eyes dimmed, and it became still. She looked around for the other unfriendly forces, but it appeared that the crowd had overcome them.

A siren blared from the main building, and Laena could see whole squads of soldiers and Guardians coming out of it in combat formation. Most of them were moving directly toward the riot, but a smaller battalion broke off and headed toward the wall, farther down from where she was.

She looked around at the crowd until she locked eyes with another woman in a red jumpsuit. "Go!" the woman yelled at her, and when Laena hesitated, she followed up with "Run, dammit!"

Laena took off, making her way through the crowd at a jerky pace, following the high outer wall away from the building as much as the raucous crowd would allow.

She finally broke free of the swarm of prisoners and opened up to full speed as she progressed along the edge of the wall toward the gatekeepers' building.

Laena fired a few shots at the unit that had diverged from the main force of soldiers. They appeared to be converging on the same point along the wall that she was approaching.

Dammit, where in the hell am I supposed to go?, she thought as she sprinted across the yard.

Then, ahead, she saw tangible evidence that the Universe was watching over her.

The main gate in the outer wall was opening.

BAXTER HAD NOT YET opened the box Aellana had given him. It was stashed away in his room and untouched since he arrived home from the funeral.

He wasn't ready for it at the time, but now his curiosity was burning, compelling him to know what was inside.

He fished it out of its hiding place and sat on the side of his bed facing away from the door. "Computer, door lock," he ordered, and a faint hiss followed by a click told him that it had complied.

He held the box in his lap, looking at it, wondering if its contents were something he really wanted to see. Then he furrowed his brow, caught the top and bottom in opposing hands, and pulled them apart.

The lid came away, and he observed for the first time what was so important that it made Raishann and Aellana risk being caught in the city.

It was a replica of an old-fashioned key, the kind you only saw in museums or as part of corporate logos. It was a dull, brassy colour, and the end that would enter a lock had no notches in it.

He checked the box for a note or some instructions as to what he should do with the item but found nothing. The empty container went into the waste disposal, and with a whoosh of air, it was gone.

He examined the key further and found no markings at all, and he wondered why Father would leave this for him. What was it meant to unlock?

It occurred to him that he might find some clue in the workshop. The room had been left as it was, except for the things the officer shuffled when he put the "evidence" from his pocket onto the table.

He went from his room toward the shop quietly, and on the way, he saw that Mother was sitting in her chair, with a half-empty glass on the table beside her.

When he entered his father's sanctum, he quietly called for the door to be locked and ensured that he heard the telltale sounds that followed.

He looked around and saw nothing significant. He sat in his father's chair and surveyed from there, but could find nothing with a keyhole, or anything else that looked like it might receive the key.

He spun the chair around and around, watching the room go by as he pivoted. Workbench, tools, desk with a terminal, blank wall, wall with pictures, door, repeat.

After a few revolutions, one of the hanging pictures caught his attention. He stopped the chair and went to it. It was a picture of him, and Mother and Father, taken a few years ago at a science competition. Baxter had won first place that day, and his parents were very proud. Well, Father was proud. Mother had been pleased - there was an immense difference.

He touched the image of his father and, feeling connected to him, relaxed his body into the corner of the room. The cool wall pressed against the bare skin of his arm as he fondly remembered his father.

The wall beside him shifted, a claytronic section dilated into an opening. Was this what the key opened? It must transmit a signal that the transforming wall received.

He stood up straight and backed away a step, and it closed again. He reached out to see if he could hold the aperture open, and as soon as he contacted it, the hole grew larger once again, until it reached its full size - a little shorter than he was, and barely wide enough to get through.

Baxter bent to look into the hole in the wall, and he could see from the outdated apparatus around the perimeter that there was a Gate in there.

Is this what Father wanted him to find? It must be.

Not knowing where he would find himself when he came out on the other side, Baxter stepped into the portal, and once he was gone, the wall sealed itself behind him.

FROM THE BACK SEAT of the armoured aircar he was in, William could see that they were approaching a large complex. There was a tall wall around its periphery, and above that there were posts at intervals with plasma crackling between them. He knew this would surely keep any jungle animals out, but he also knew that was not the intent of the security measure.

He watched a gate in the immense barrier widening, and the vehicle slowed as they approached. A soldier appeared in the expanding opening, waving for the aircar driver to enter. Then the man arched backwards as an ion bolt hit him, and he fell into the middle of the widening entrance.

"What do I do?", the driver implored of her male counterpart, who sat in the front passenger's seat.

"We need to get in there, so go over him I guess," came the response. The driver was hesitant and continued to slow the vehicle.

A young woman appeared next to the body of the fallen gatekeeper. She had an energy rifle in one hand, and she bent to grab one of the straps of the lifeless man's backpack, then rolled him over and pulled the whole bag from him. Ion blasts ripped past her, impacting the gate and ground. She threw the pack over her shoulder, then kneeled and picked up the collapsed guard's ion pistol. She stayed down for an instant and fired at unseen targets.

Then she tucked the smaller firearm into her belt, returned her rifle to a ready position, and was already running when she turned toward the open gate. When she saw the military aircar approaching, she opened fire on it, still moving fast as she came out of the gap.

The officer in the passenger seat instinctively covered his face with his arm, but the shots that hit the vehicle deflected off the rugged front window. The blasts kept coming, some connecting and some whizzing by, and the man in the front seat went for his sidearm. It was a sleek ion weapon that looked different from any William had seen Ascended officers carrying.

"Window open!" the soldier commanded, and the tempered glass on his side of the vehicle slid downward. He stuck his hand out the window and started shooting. Massive bolts of energy came out of the specialized weapon. The running woman turned toward the driver's side of the car, cutting down the angle and the officer's ability to shoot at her.

He pulled his arm back in and pointed the gun away from himself and the driver, angrily watching the crimson-clad woman running away from the complex.

"Do I pursue?" the driver questioned.

"No, our orders are to get this one in, not to stop that one from getting out. Plus, I think we should get in there before they shut that gate."

William looked out the side window at the young woman sprinting past in the opposite direction, and she turned and looked directly at him. Her mouth was open and, for a moment, William thought she was panting, but then he recognized that was not the case.

The woman was running at top speed. And laughing her fool head off.

IT WAS DARK AND COLD, and the air didn't feel right. It was unnatural.

Baxter panicked and turned to step back into the Gate when a light on the ceiling came on. A desk lamp followed it and the sound of a terminal starting.

It smelled funny, a variation on the essence of the forest from the night he pursued Father out of the city. There were shelves along two sides of the room filled with all manner of articles. Baxter could identify some of them, but there were also a lot of things he could not.

He stepped toward the terminal, and a thread of red light came out of the top of the screen and found its way into his eye. Baxter flinched and turned his head away, but then looked back, remembering that the area was his father's, and allowed the laser to search the recesses of his retina.

The beam winked out, and the desktop on the terminal changed, and an image of his father appeared. It remained static for a second before the attached video started. Then the familiar figure spoke.

"Baxter, you have found your way into my inner sanctum." The figure spread its hands out and indicated the surroundings. "I call this my Nest, and it is where I have kept all the artifacts that have come into my possession - ones that the Ascendancy would not want me to have. Contraband, I guess. Anyway, the things in this room will prove beyond any doubt the intentions of the Ascendancy, as well as its brutal origins and their crimes against everyone: the people of the 12 cities, the Sylvans, you, me, and every living creature on this Earth."

Baxter approached the desk with the terminal on it and pulled out the old chair next to it, sat down, and scootched himself up to the counter.

His father continued. "Have a look at these artifacts. Examine them closely. You will notice that each article has a number on the shelf in front of it. Those are my registration numbers, and if you have any questions about any of them, find the corresponding numbered video file on this terminal's home screen, and I will give a detailed explanation for each of them. I hope that you are well, my son, and I hope this place and the objects you find herein will serve to illuminate you as they did me. Well, I guess that's all for now. Just take a look around. I'm sure you'll find many things that will interest you." The figure on the screen leaned ahead to shut off the camera, then hesitated. "I love you, Baxter," he added before the picture blinked out.

Baxter sat back and wiped his eyes, looking for something to wash his face with, but he found nothing that looked clean enough to rub on his skin. He stood up and stretched, and paced around the small open area for a few laps then moved to one of the racks.

He went to the far left side, and the first article on the top row had a note stuck to the shelf in front of it: Number One.

Baxter lifted it down, and rolled it over in his hands, struggling to identify it. Unable to discern what it was, he brought it with him to the desk and set it down there while he relaxed in the chair again.

"Okay," he said to the article, "Let's find out what you are."

TIMOTH RECEIVED A MESSAGE from his contact in the Ascendancy asking for a face-to-face meeting. He was very nervous about it but agreed to the conference.

He assumed that the accomplishment of the task he had been given meant that he would be granted the payment he had requested for his services - citizenship in an Ascendancy city.

He was tired of life being little more than survival, when all the trappings of modern living were so close and yet entirely out of his reach. He had always been jealous of the Ascended, but never had the incentive to act on his rebellious feelings.

But hearing what the city boy said to Raish pushed him off the fence he had been sitting on for so long.

Who was that guy to judge them like that? He obviously thought of himself as being better than the Sylvans, and Timoth was tired of being considered a lower being. He wanted to spend the rest of his life elevated and looking down on others. He wanted to be among the powerful and superior for a change. He wanted to live in the ultra-clean, super-modern world he had seen in surveillance footage that came home with Luminant spies.

What right did the Sylvans have to say that the Ascendancy was wrong? As far as he could tell, the Ascendancy was taking better care of their people and providing them what they needed.

Timoth had been pacing up and down a small open patch just outside the wall of Enswell and cleared most of the debris from the area, kicking and shuffling through it as he performed his caged animal impression.

This was as close as he had been to the city in a long time, and he loved the crackling plasma that extended beyond the top of the barrier, separating the people within from the jungle outside.

The last time he was this near, he had put a tracker on the man the Sylvans called Shadaar - a traitor to the Ascendancy. He had also set a timer to send a false signal that ensured that his dad was not there when the Ascendancy troops arrived to catch the Sylvans off their guard. Dad got pretty beat up, but he was still alive.

A sound from up the trail caught his attention, and he turned to face it. A man appeared, and he was not what Timoth expected.

He knew his contact was a man, and that he was Ascended, and he had envisioned that he would be dressed in beautiful clothes and maybe even carrying a briefcase for some reason.

Instead, the man looked like a Sylvan, wearing grubby pants and a simple cotton shirt, and his hair was scruffy and uncombed. Perhaps he came like this to make Timoth feel at ease. Maybe he was mocking Sylvans.

Timoth called out to him. "Who are you?"

"My name is Doyle Morgan, and you must be Timoth."

"I am," Timoth said as he straightened himself and tried his best to look confident.

He stood unflinching as Doyle walked up to him. "I am very pleased to meet you," the man said happily.

"I'm pleased to meet you, too," Timoth repeated.

"You, my good man, have done me a great service, and I will grant you what you asked for."

Timoth beamed but did not interrupt. The man continued. "I will bring you into the Ascendancy under the guise of a youth program, and we will say you are a transfer student from another city. We will give you a false identity and background. You must memorize those. But before I can set this in motion for you, I need you to do one more thing for me."

"Anything," Tim said enthusiastically. "You name it, and consider it done."

Doyle looked pleased and pointed at the blue-white dome behind him as he lied straight into the young man's eyes. "You are going to love it in there."

Chapter 12

BAXTER WENT TO THE Nest at every available opportunity. He stayed there for a few hours his first time, and was reluctant to return home, but he forced himself to because he did not want to awaken any suspicions in his mother.

The things he discovered there astounded him, and he became more convinced with every visit that Father had been right. There was hard evidence that demonstrated clearly that the Ascendancy had caused the Great Cataclysm in order to maintain its power. There were ancient books that spoke of the way things were, in direct contradiction to what Ascended students learned in their lessons.

Ascendancy-approved history classes spoke of a decadent and dying world filled with famine, disease, and endless wars. Baxter discovered that some of that was true as he studied the artifacts and books his father left for him. But there was also much more autonomy than was allowed within the 12 cities. Art, literature and music were not policed. People protested against things they did not believe in, and most of the world maintained a comfortable standard of living.

There were no walls, no domes, and no limits. There was no pressure to ascend so the agenda of the government was fulfilled.

Baxter kept all of this well hidden from his mother and only went to his newfound sanctuary when he knew that she would be gone for protracted amounts of time. She had been out a lot lately, trying to maintain or rebuild the relationships that kept her status high. Everything worked out nicely, providing Baxter with the opportunities he craved to further his new awareness.

There were no signs of the Ascendancy reducing their status yet - maybe a show of benevolence to other highly ascended citizens. But the possibility lingered, and Baxter had already thought about what he would do if they were forced to move, and how he would retain his access to the Nest.

Between sessions in the hidden room and keeping up his regular life, he began looking for a way to clone the portal that led to his recent passion. He could not lose touch with that.

He had seen Kent only a couple of times since the funeral, as he was busy investigating a spatial feature he had discovered in his work. But Lila had been visiting regularly and, as much as he appreciated the time they spent together, he frequently felt guilty about thinking of the Nest while he was with her. It wasn't an issue while Mother was home anyway, but when he would have been alone otherwise, he sometimes anticipated Lila's departure so he could study.

At the same time, though, he had to admit that he was growing more infatuated with Lila's company. She had always been a source of comfort to him, and she had been there for him lately more than anyone else, helping him to maintain a modicum of sanity and keeping him grounded in reality. He was grateful for her companionship.

But still, as much as he trusted her, and even though he was dying to get it off his chest, he could not bring himself to share his newfound knowledge or the place it came from with her.

The only place he would be truly understood and get the opportunity to vent the new passion building within him was beyond the city and through a long stretch of dangerous forest. He wanted to speak with people who could answer his questions and assist him in learning even more. But, he also had to consider that the people who were most capable of supporting him might just decide to kill him.

THE FOREST GREW COLDER as the sun went down, and after several hours of switching between jogging and walking, Laena stopped to take her first rest.

The human guards would not have followed her this far into the woods. Not at the pace she had maintained. She was still worried about O-bots, but she thought if any were pursuing her, she probably would have dealt with them by now, one way or the other. There was an ion rifle over her shoulder and a pistol within quick-draw range, and it comforted her somewhat that either of them could disable a Guardian if one showed up.

Branches pulled at her as she searched for somewhere to hide and rest, and her adrenaline kept her eyes and ears open and her mind alert.

She was in decent shape, all things considered, and the running hadn't tired her out completely. Laena still had more in her, but she was likely far enough ahead of any pursuers to stop, and knew that she needed to find water to stay hydrated, or she would be in trouble soon.

She was also very curious to see the contents of the pack she had taken on her way out of Aldergate. She remembered that here was a combat knife strapped to the front of it. That was promising.

Laena sat on a fallen tree and removed the backpack. When she set it down beside her and opened the top, her anticipation quickly turned to disappointment. There was a data pad inside, three bottles of pills (none of which she could identify), some documents, a pair of strange-looking glasses, and a partial bottle of contraband alcohol.

At least once she emptied the vessel, probably into herself, she could use it as a water bottle. Assuming she ever found water, that is.

The rifle and handgun would keep her protected. And fed, too, because she had every intention of eating any animal that attacked her, and she would also hunt as she continued to make her way through the forest.

The thing that troubled her the most, though, was the one problem for which she had no solution. Her skillset would allow her to live in the woodlands indefinitely, but there was no way for her to know where she was and no means of calculating her current position. Which meant she had no idea which direction she would have to go to get to a village, or even if there was one in these parts. She looked up from her collection of junk and surveyed the surrounding area.

Laena had made it out of the frying pan alright, and she hoped that the only fires she had to deal with were ones that she started.

Judging by the fading light, she discerned that there was about an hour of daylight remaining. She repacked the bag, except for the knife, and slung it on her back. There was not much time left, and job number one was to build a shelter to protect her from the cold night air. She'd deal with lower priorities later.

She hadn't come this far just to make it this far, and after everything she'd been through, Laena figured that she might as well live to suffer another day.

BAXTER HEADED TOWARD Nylen, guided by maps his father had left in the Nest. He was pleased that he was able to find the village, but as he got closer, it occurred to him that he probably should have sent a message letting the Sylvans know he was coming.

About a kilometer from the small hamlet, he was captured by two sentries - a man and a woman - and he walked the rest of the way to Nylen with their rifles pointed at his back. They had searched him for weapons, and after finding none, they didn't bother to bind him. They just kept their distance and used their guns to maintain the upper hand.

They never threatened him, but Baxter wondered if they might be leading him to his death.

When they reached the edge of the village, one of the sentries took him by the back of his collar and steered him where he was supposed to go.

People who were working or relaxing outside took notice, and a small crowd began to form. Some people even followed as he was led deeper into the rustic town.

A group of children who had been playing in the worn earthen street jumped around him, and when they got too close, the escorts told them to get away. They stayed back but continued to taunt him, making jokes about his light skin and strange attire.

As they made their way into what appeared to be the center of the village, people were poking their heads out of windows and doors, curious about and entertained by the spectacle. Some of the locals seemed frightened of him, and one lady even pulled her child into their home by the arm and hastily closed the door.

Baxter thought it best to wait until they arrived at whatever their destination was before he made any arguments supporting his case, but he was given an early opportunity.

"Let him go," he heard from beyond the congregation. He gagged as the sentry behind him yanked on his collar, bringing him to a halt.

The crowd looked to the voice's source and created an opening there. Aellana Forander and Raishann approached Baxter through the gap, and Aellana restated her directive. "Let him go. He is the son of Shadaar and known to my family."

Baxter felt the tension around his neck subside as the fist that had been controlling him released, and he ran a finger inside his collar to return it to its usual state.

"What are you doing here?" Raishann demanded as she passed her mother. "Are you crazy?"

"I came here to see you," Baxter responded.

"Me? What do you need from me?"

"Well, you and your family, actually," he corrected. "I used the key, and I want to talk with Shawan about what happens next."

The crowd broke up, going back to their routine activities, and Baxter walked with Raishann and Aellana to their home. It was small and modest, but it was also cozy and warm, and a positive energy seemed to radiate from the walls and floorboards.

They offered Baxter a seat at the table in the front room, which was open from the kitchen through to the open room opposite. There were smells of cooking and coffee, and Raishann placed a cup of the latter before him. Aellana had disappeared down the hallway that marked the separation of the kitchen from the sitting room upon their entering the house, and now she returned, looking back over her shoulder, and pausing as she entered the room. Baxter heard another set of footsteps coming, along with a rhythmic clunking that coincided with the footfalls. Then a muscular man, bandaged in various places, limped into the room with them, and Aellana came ahead of him to pull out another chair at the table.

Baxter stood out of respect for the stern-looking figure that approached him. The man waved for him to sit back down, and he did. Then the man was helped slowly and carefully into the seat at the head of the table by Aellana, and he straightened up stiffly as another cup of hot coffee was placed on the table.

"I am Shawan Forander. I'm sorry we haven't met before, but every opportunity I've had to connect with you was interrupted by injury." He chuckled. "It seems this encounter was not meant to happen until now."

Raishann and Aellana joined them at the small round table, each with their own steaming cup.

"It is an honour to meet you, Sir," Baxter said as he reached out an open hand.

"It shouldn't be," Shawan corrected. "I'm the one who let myself get sent on a wild goose chase when I should have been there with your father. Might not have made any difference, but I'm sorry for your loss, at any rate."

"Thank you."

"I know you received the key. My wife and daughter told me they gave it to you. So, you must have found Shadaar's Nest by now. Is the memory module there?"

Baxter wanted to answer correctly but did not fully understand the question. "There are a lot of modules there, sir. Which one do you mean?"

Shawan finished the sip he was taking and returned his cup to the table as he swallowed tightly. "This one is bigger than most, and it has an interface that doesn't fit into a standard terminal. It's silver and about the size of my fist." Baxter watched the man's hand curl into a ball, and it occurred to him that getting hit with that thing would be like getting hit with a stone. He tried not to stare and looked back into the man's face. "I do not know. I have gone through many of the things there, but I have not yet found anything that fits that description." He looked from Shawan to Raishann, who seemed to be sizing him up.

When he looked back at the intimidating man across the table from him, he saw Shawan examining his wife's face with a look of concern, and she put a hand on his giant fist. "It's okay, Shawan. It must be there."

"It had better be. I didn't go through all this to not have it."

"What is it, Sir?" Baxter queried.

"What is on that module can bring the Ascendancy to its knees and save all of humanity, city people and Sylvan alike."

"Just that. No biggie," Raishann added, shrugging. Her mother told her not to be so sarcastic, and Raishann smirked at Baxter and folded her hands in her lap. "Sorry. Nervous habit."

Baxter tried not to look amused. Shawan ignored it and continued with the matter at hand. "We don't even know what's on it, but we do know that it would take specialized Ascendancy tech even to connect it, let alone open it and decode it."

Baxter thought he might be able to help with that, but he said nothing. He did not wish to be as deeply embroiled in this as his father had been. He knew that he was in it, and that from here on in it was merely a matter of degrees, but he did not want to obligate himself to anything too risky. Not yet, anyway.

Baxter said he would check the Nest to see if he could find the object they were talking about. He would reconnect to let them know, one way or the other.

Aellana interjected. "Which brings us back to Raishann's first question. Why did you come here?"

Baxter took a minute to think. It was a good question, and he felt it deserved a concise answer.

"I have learned a lot in my father's hidden place. I see the truth of what he said about the Ascendancy, and I guess I came here because I'm not sure what to do about it, and there was nowhere else I could go."

Aellana reached out to him and set her hand on the table, as though proximity increased understanding. "You should only do what you believe you should do, Baxter. There will never be pressure from us to do anything more. It's your choice. I guess you'll have to decide what you are willing to do to free yourself. And your people."

Baxter looked at his lap and nodded his head. "Thank you," he said sincerely. He lifted his head and found all eyes on him. "I will come back and let you know about the module. I will follow through on that."

"That's enough for now," Aellana assured him, and she stood up, pushing her chair back with her knees. "Raishann will take you out of the village to ensure no harm comes to you." She addressed Raishann, asking her to get

Baxter something to protect himself with, as she crossed the kitchen with empty cups from the table.

Raishann nodded obediently and rose from her seat, heading for the front door. "Yes, Mom," she said as she exited.

Baxter stood and watched Raishann going out the door. He noticed her sure-footed grace again.

When he looked back, Shawan was finishing the last of his coffee. Aellana was staring at Baxter, apparently appraising him. It made him uneasy. He felt like she could see right through him.

"You go with Raish, and come back when you can," she concluded matter-of-factly.

Baxter thanked them for their help and the coffee, and followed Raishann out the open door. He was a few steps out of the house before he heard it shut, and he could see Raishann going into a small building nearby.

When he caught up with her, she was coming back out of the hut with a long knife and a leather sleeve. She gingerly slid the knife into the sheath and handed it to him as he arrived. "Here," she said, "Try not to kill yourself with it."

Baxter thanked her sheepishly, and then questioned, "Where am I supposed to keep this thing?"

"Just stash it outside the city somewhere before you go back in," she replied. "Now come with me. I'd tell you to try not to look too conspicuous, but dressed like that there's nothing you could do to avoid standing out. I'll get you some regular clothes to take back with you for the next time you come." She walked confidently beside him, and he thanked her.

He wanted to say something savoury to her, but his mind drew a blank. He never had trouble talking to anyone before, no matter what level they were, or male or female, or whatever. All he could think to say was to ask the question that repeated in his head. "Why are you being so nice to me? I mean I've been harsh and acted like a, like-"

"A jackass," she finished.

"I do not know what that is, but if it means I was being a child and speaking out of turn, then, yes, I was a jackass." He smiled at her, and she responded in kind.

She stopped and regarded him carefully. "Listen, we're helping you because we could use a new contact in Enswell."

"Oh." His smile diminished.

"I'm helping you because you're not as much of a no-mind as I thought you were." She giggled. "And because you're kind of cute." She walked again, and Baxter followed.

"No, I'm not," Baxter humbly stated.

"Yeah, you're right. You're not that great I guess, but the jealous girl from the funeral thinks you are." She didn't look to see his reaction.

"Oh, her, she's just a, a-"

"Whatever she is, she's lucky to have you."

On the way to the edge of the village, Raishann showed him how to handle the knife and gave him some pointers about being in the forest. When they arrived, she stopped. "You're on your own from here," she said. "Don't be a stranger."

"I will visit again," Baxter said.

They waved to each other and went off in opposite directions, and when Baxter turned to look at her one last time, she was gone.

Chapter 13

WILLIAM'S LAB AT ALDERGATE was smaller and not as sophisticated as the rich environment he was used to, but he found that he was given any piece of equipment he requested in short order. He had everything he needed to work toward the goal of augmenting the Gates within the prison facility.

The guards seemed to treat him more gently than the other prisoners, and although he had never seen where they lived, he assumed his small apartment with its kitchenette, sitting room and bedroom with a separate bathroom was more than any of them had.

He was able to move freely, but only within the lab, and when he had to go anywhere else, escorts went with him. When he needed anything done, the guards ordered one of the other convicts to do it for him.

Some prisoners seemed to actively dislike him, but most were cordial, and he even heard one of them telling another to be more sympathetic because, after all, they were collectively in the same predicament.

One of the lab workers, a Sylvan man named Nalin, had been particularly kind to him and would engage in conversations whenever an opportunity arose. William enjoyed those talks, and they gave him a temporary feeling that he was still in his old life, and that when he finished chatting, he would go home. Talking to Nalin was a welcomed distraction while it lasted, but it always ended in disappointment and the realization that Aldergate was his home now.

They talked about what they had done before their incarcerations, and the families they left behind. They discussed prison survival and the best ways to manage being locked up.

But they had one particularly fascinating conversation; a discussion of the young lady who was leaving while William came in.

Her name was Laena, and Nalin said she was a real firecracker. She refused to tolerate things that other prisoners accepted as part of life in Aldergate.

William told Nalin what he had seen from his unique perspective as he entered the facility. He explained to him about the escapee shooting the guard and taking the pack and gun, and about how she had laughed as she ran past the aircar. Nalin had a good chuckle over it, saying that the story sounded exactly like something Laena would do.

William asked why she would bother to take the pack, and his Sylvan friend said that anything was better than nothing when you were on the run. William had no basis for comparison but thought that to be a reasonable assumption. He picked the man's brain as to what might be in the backpack, and the dark-skinned man replied there was probably nothing that would help her to survive for very long. She would get farther and last longer on her wits than she would because of anything she found in the bag.

There would be a pad in there because all the guards carried one, but that was of no use to her at all. She would likely abandon it as excess baggage. If she were lucky, there would be a water bottle or something to eat inside.

The man added that no one knew where they were, in geographic terms. Aldergate could be pretty much anywhere in the world, and being in the forest without proper tools - even having grown up in Sylva - it was just a matter of time before the girl died. That was why the Warden had sent no one, either man or machine, after her.

The main reason that no one had escaped Aldergate was that no one had ever tried. An escaped convict would die of exposure out there, and so, in the long run, it was generally accepted that a person was better off inside.

William investigated what 'proper tools' would look like, and the man mentioned a lot of things that William did not understand. Wilderness survival gear, he supposed. But there was one thing that Nalin said was more important than any other, and, if the girl still had a datapad, it might even be something that William could help with.

No one would survive for long in the harsh conditions of the forest with-out a map. An escapee would have to make it to a Sylvan settlement if they wanted to live beyond survival, and that couldn't be done unless they knew where they were and where they should go.

A map, William pondered. Yes, a map would be beneficial to her, indeed.

HE RETURNED TO THE Nest after talking to the Foranders and found the module that Shawan asked about. It was the last article on the bottom shelf, as the items there seemed to be displayed in the order they were found. It would have been one of the last things Baxter studied if he had continued going through the objects sequentially. He was glad it was there, though, and he would get the information to the Luminants soon.

But the module was not at the forefront of his thoughts. He had been thinking a lot about what Raishann had said, and that perhaps she had been right. Lila did care for him, and he felt guilty that he needed someone to remind him of that fact, and found that he wanted to spend time with his assigned mate. Raishann turned out to be as astute as she was intriguing. She had reduced his confusion over his romantic options, but heightened his frustration that he had not actively pursued either of them.

Baxter was still reeling after his trip to Sylva, and hearing that Lila was coming to call on him was a welcomed distraction.

When the chime rang, Baxter called for the door to open as he approached it, and when it did he found himself utterly unprepared for what he saw.

If Lila had taken extra care to look nice, she had been entirely successful. Her hair colour switched slowly from blonde to red, then back again. Her makeup shifted to highlight her delicate features when she smiled. Baxter liked what he saw, and he invited her in.

Mother was not home, and Baxter hung Lila's jacket where his mother's would typically rest. They went and sat together in the sitting room, Baxter on the sofa, and Lila across from him in Mother's chair. A drone brought them drinks, and they talked easily while Baxter drank in her beauty.

Baxter forgot about the Nest and the module, and even about Sylva for a while, and was relaxing for the first time in a long while.

After some pleasant conversation, Lila rose from her chair and crossed over to join Baxter on the sofa.

He moved against the arm to give her some space, the settee altered itself to accommodate the shift, and she set her drink on the table in front of them. They talked some more, and then Lila moved closer. Baxter was a little confused, but his familiarity with Lila and the smell of her hair kept him comfortable. She smiled at him in a way he liked, but did not remember seeing before. It was an exploration beyond their usual interactions, and he was enjoying it.

Then she surprised him by moving right up next to him. His heart beat quickened, and he couldn't help but be captivated by her eyes and the style of her hair and the soft scent emanating from her.

Without thinking, he leaned over and kissed her softly, and then backed up to gauge her reaction. She reached out and caught him by the back of the neck and pulled him in again, and the lips that met him were full of passion and enthusiasm.

Baxter closed his eyes and kissed her thoroughly, twisting on the sofa so he could get his arms around her better.

She embraced him, and her hands swept over his back and shoulders. He could feel her soft breasts against his chest, and he shifted again to maximize the contact between them.

With his eyes still closed, he backed up slightly to catch his breath, smiling like a sweepstake winner.

Then he opened his eyes and studied her again, and his smile diminished. Lila looked great, smelled fantastic and felt beautiful in his arms, but looking at her again, he found himself disappointed that her skin was not darker and her arms were not more firmly muscled. He wanted her eyes to be deep brown and her hair to be long and naturally dark.

He wanted her to be Raishann.

Lila noticed the change in his face and body and asked if he was okay.

Baxter said that he would be alright, but he needed a minute.

He let Lila go and sat back on the sofa.

She asked if she had been too aggressive, and Baxter told her that she had done nothing wrong and that it was him. Maybe, he added, he was not ready for this.

That was a lie. He was ready for it, all right, but the incident had shocked him into the realization that he wanted to share the experience with someone else.

Oh boy.

MAYBE I HAVE GONE TOO far, Doyle thought.

He spent the entire morning in his office. It was now past lunchtime and he had accomplished nothing significant.

All he had done was ruminate over whether asking the boy to give up his people was over the top. And this forced him to remember that he had peddled his own people, as well. Old guilt found its way into his current state, and he couldn't make it go away.

He sold himself to the Ascendancy when he was not much older than Timoth was now.

He knew that the Sylvans moved their villages from time to time and that the lay of the land had undoubtedly changed in the many years since he was a member of the rebel movement himself.

So, he charged Timoth with giving the current locations of as many villages as he knew. The boy had turned so pale he could almost have passed for an Ascended.

It tore Doyle. A portion of him felt sorry for the young man, and for the Sylvans he would be sacrificing. But he was able to repress that because the more significant part of him would use this to a fantastic advantage.

It would expose Burke as an incompetent - which alone made it reason enough to follow through - but it would also show his undeniable loyalty and deserved ascendance. He would finally be the front-runner for the title of Chancellor, and his ascent would be realized.

The boy would have to make his way within the Ascendancy and learn to navigate the system as he once had to.

As for the Sylvans; well, they were just on the wrong side of the whole dispute.

Maybe he would go a little easier on them once he was running the place.

BAXTER WAS EAGER TO get back to the village.

He consoled Lila as she left the house, but as soon as she was gone, Baxter started making preparations to leave the city.

It was raining when he got beyond the wall, and Baxter had never seen or experienced anything like it in his life. It was warm, and he took comfort in it until it weighed down his clothes and his skin and bones as he made his way along the trails of the forest.

He was disappointed when he arrived at the Forander home to find that Raishann was out and would not be back until later, but at least the locals had not accosted him when he walked into town. There was some consolation in that.

Aellana gave him a towel and the change of clothes that Raish had promised him. He took off his wet clothing and dried himself in Raishann's vacant room, and he could smell her as he got dressed. He tried not to be too nosy, but he could not help but take stock of the articles she had on display. There were pictures of family and other people, and some things Baxter could not identify but must be important to her. It revealed a little more of who she was, and endeared her more profoundly to him.

When he was finished changing and grooming himself, he went into the hallway, gave his wet clothes to Mrs Forander and thanked her, and she took them to be dried.

He found himself again at the kitchen table, steaming coffee before him, with the anxious faces of Mr and Mrs Forander eagerly awaiting his report.

"I found the memory module," he announced. His ears almost popped from the added pressure in the room from two of the most prominent sighs of relief he ever witnessed.

"Good," said Shawan. "Now, we need a computer to connect to it."

"Yes," Baxter continued, "I have done some looking into that, and I think I have a solution."

"Did William have anything in the Nest that might work?" inquired Aellana. "It seemed like that man could handle any technical problem that was given to him."

Baxter took a sip from his cup and set it back down. He was feeling more relaxed with the Forander family than he did in his own home. He shook his head as he swallowed. "No. I mean, there is nothing there that can interface with the module. It looks as though Father was putting something together for that purpose, but it is very preliminary and I do not have the computer expertise to finish it."

The front door opened, and Baxter turned to face it. He held his breath for a moment, and when Raishann walked in a sigh fell from him like rain from the heavens.

"Hello, Raishann," he greeted.

"Hi," she returned, not looking as she shook rainwater from her hair and clothes.

"Baxter found the module," Aellana reported as she rose and headed to the kitchen counter and retrieved another mug.

"Great!" she said, glancing at him for the first time. Her auburn hair was wet and clung to her face in streaks, alternately hiding and revealing her features as she removed her jacket and boots.

She came to join them at the table as a cup of coffee was presented to her by Aellana.

"So, what do we do with the module, then?" Shawan continued. "Is it useless to us?"

"No," Baxter corrected, "We must find a terminal with a corresponding connector and get it to a place where we can use it. I think I know where there is one, and someone who can help us to get it." Baxter was sitting straight and tall, and doing his best to convey confidence, especially to one of them in particular.

"Wait," Aellana chimed in. "It might not be a good idea to bring in anyone else. We don't know who we can trust. You don't know who to trust. It would be best to do this on our own if at all possible."

"Agreed," confirmed Shawan.

Baxter conceded that he would look into the matter further before he committed to anything, and that he would discuss any prospective plans with them before he acted.

Raishann removed a comb from a pocket and began running it through her hair. Every stroke ended with water dripping into her lap, and she turned her head as she needed to access it all.

It hypnotized Baxter, but Shawan's voice prompted him from his reverie. "I guess you had best be getting home, then," the strapping man said as he stood.

Baxter looked up to face the imposing figure that towered beside him in very close proximity.

"Yes, I suppose I should," Baxter stammered without moving.

"I'll get your clothes. They should be dry by now," Aellana added, breaking the tension. She stood, and Shawan backed up to accommodate his departure.

Raishann got up, too, and her father said that he should be able to find his way out of the village on his own. She cleared the hair from her face and sat back down.

Aellana returned with his clothing in a waterproof satchel and instructed him to wear the clothes he now had on until he was inside the city before changing.

Baxter thanked her, and shook hands with Shawan, who was sizing him up, but kind at the same time.

Baxter walked to the exit and put on his shoes. Raishann waved and said that she would see him next time. Baxter returned the gesture and headed out the door.

He had jogged the last of the way into the village when he was arriving, but now he walked slowly and casually, allowing the warm rain to streak over him.

He thought he might have to see a doctor once he got back to Enswell to find out if he could have his idiotic grin removed.

CANDACE HAD OUTDONE herself. She reconnected with some highly ascended people, and as time went on it looked more like William's transgressions against the Ascendancy would not be held against either her or Baxter. Her son could still ascend to match his potential.

She had done some questionable things to achieve this, and she hoped that Baxter would appreciate that she did it all for them. For him.

Baxter was aware of the pending Ascendancy Day Rally, a new opportunity she was preparing for, and he expressed limited interest. She expected more from him, but she also had to consider the complete picture of her son's life, including all that he had been through lately.

She knew that Baxter saw Kent from time to time, and had been spending a lot of time with Lila, but she wondered if he may not yet be ready for such a large crowd. Oh well. Despite everything that had happened, he was going to have to do his best to show enthusiasm.

The Rally was upon them, and their presence among the hoards of people celebrating their beloved society would help to repair more of the damage that William had done.

She called Lila and Kent, both of whom were solid citizens and came from good families, to ask if they would accompany Baxter. Kent was available, but Lila said that she was going with her family, and maybe they would see each other there.

As they arrived in the Midtown Square, about halfway between the fringes of the city and its center, Candace was confident. They were dressed in their most elegant clothes and making noise along with the rest of the crowd. They must be seen, heard, and recognized.

"Is this not grand?" She shouted at Baxter over the din. She clapped her hands hard enough that it hurt.

"Yes," Baxter responded. He looked at Kent, and the two of them feigned smiling and applauded likewise. Candace thought Kent was not being as supportive as he could have been.

Candace urged them, "Come on, boys, liven up a little will you? Your futures begin now, you know."

"Yes, quite right, Mrs Clarke," Kent said, raising the height and volume of his clapping. Baxter followed Kent's lead.

Candace raised her hands and yelled "Bravo" a few times, then went to work scanning the crowd, looking for people she wanted to be seen with.

She moved through the celebration, singing loudly and beaming, ensuring that everyone noticed her. She had to sell the notion of her undying allegiance.

Candace saw Lila and her family through the mass of people, and she beamed as she waved at them. Baxter seemed somewhat sheepish as he gestured to Lila, and his mate-to-be motioned back, but they did not speak to one another. Candace exchanged pleasant looks with Lila's father, and he turned his attention back to the ceremony.

Candace lead Baxter and Kent through the crowds and up to the front, and she waved to the dignitaries on the main stage.

She knew some of the Ascended up there personally, but she was aware of all their social standings, even if she didn't. They were smiling and waving to the crowds of people in the square, and great holos of them were floating above the stage, mimicking their every action. One of the officials looked down and caught her eye, and in a moment of recognition, turned her gaze elsewhere.

Candace had to push her resentment down and remind herself that reestablishing the Clarke family would take some time. She remembered that, in many social situations, the people who pay the least mind to you are the ones on whom you must focus your efforts. So, she locked on to the face of the scornful woman on the stage and cheered even more enthusiastically.

She was increasingly confident in her continued ascension with each passing second. She and Baxter were doing all the right things, being seen in the right places, and connecting with the right people. Their continued prosperity was ensured.

She turned to share the moment with her son, and Kent was there, still applauding and focused on the stage. Behind him, Baxter stood with his hands at his sides, looking at the ground.

Candace's applause slowed, and any excitement she had left her face and her heart. She had tried to deny it and stop it from happening, but it was glaringly apparent to her now.

Baxter was gone. She had lost him.

Chapter 14

WILLIAM APPEARED, TO the unknowing eyes that followed him, to be working on the projector portals, and he used the fact that no one could be sure of what he was doing to his advantage.

The guards and other prisoners who worked in the lab had seen him doing all manner of things, from tinkering with equipment and assembling devices to sitting and thinking while he stared out the window.

Being seated in front of his terminal and doing research was something they expected. There, he looked up various scientific principles, found equations that he needed, and poured over his designs for the gates. He was always scribbling notes onto his datapad, and the first couple of times people had come to see what he was doing, they walked away in complete bewilderment and never went back.

Even though everything appeared to be business as usual, William was not working on his proposed assignment.

He had launched a personal project under the noses of the sentries watching him, including Michael Burke, whom he had met socially on several occasions at functions with Candace. Michael observed him obliviously as William put together something that would be most useful - just not to the Ascendancy.

He knew that Laena, the girl who escaped while he was coming in, had a datapad - assuming she had not discarded it. He was also aware that she needed a map. He developed an unauthorized hack that allowed him access to her pad, and discerned from her position that he needed to work quickly.

William had ascertained the position of the Aldergate prison from astronomical data, overlayed that onto a current map of the world, and then used information from the Gates to put the 12 cities in their proper places. If he could get her from where she was to the Gate nearest her, he could then lead her through a series of portals that would provide the shortest possible route to Nylen.

Using his access to high levels of the computer network, he created an accurate map that he was proud of. It detailed the trip from Aldergate to the closest Gate, which was at an Ascendancy depot to the north. Laena would jump to Stableton, and from there she would go through some other cities before arriving in Enswell, where one last jump would get her to a point near the secret exit through the city wall. Then she could easily walk to her home in Sylva.

He had reduced a hopeless journey spanning thousands of kilometers to one she could do on foot in a couple of days.

He grinned and searched the lab from where he sat, looking for admiration. Michael meandered around the room as William worked, somewhat closer to him now.

Mr Burke was scrutinizing him, and William had to remind himself that no one realized what he was doing. And, that if anyone did catch on to him, it surely would not be Michael Burke, based on what he knew of the man.

The smile drifted from his face, and he went back to what he was doing.

He hoped he had done all of this soon enough, before the young woman made it too far from the compound. If she still had a pad and were presumably headed away from them, it would not be long before she was outside of the broadcast range of Aldergate's equipment. After that, she would indeed be on her own.

He scanned for pads and devices connected to the Aldergate network and then ordered them from the weakest signal to the strongest.

There she was. The first hit on the list was very weak already and appeared to be losing strength.

He would have to get this done quickly.

William assembled the geographic map to the initial jump point, and all the successive jumps that led to the village outside Enswell, into a single file and sent it from his terminal to her pad.

Under normal circumstances, transfers such as this would happen across the network instantly, but her distance and the weakness of the signal caused an upload progress bar to come up on his monitor.

He watched the progress bar increasing on one side of the screen and the signal strength diminishing on the other, and it was a race to see which would end first.

Burke approached and looked over his shoulder. "What are you doing?" he demanded. "Where is that upload actually going?"

"I am sending mapping schematics to myself so that I can access them later on a pad. In my room. You know, to work on this evening."

Burke scanned the surface of the desk and saw William's pad there with its screen blank and showing no sign of activity.

The progress bar reached 100 percent, and William checked the signal strength. The girl's device was still connected. The file was gone.

"Shouldn't your pad be acknowledging receipt of the transfer?" Burke said, reaching for his holstered sidearm.

William struggled to find an explanation. "I don't know what is-"

"Put your hands in the air and stand up slowly," Burke commanded with his weapon held in both fists and extended in William's direction. "You are coming with me."

Michael kept his distance from William, who complied with the directives, then ushered him toward the door.

A guard joined Burke, and the two of them led William to a passive Gate at the far end of the room that two serious-looking sentries guarded. "Open it," Burke barked at them. One of the stern men wheeled around and allowed his eye to be scanned, and the ominous Gate came to life.

"Step inside, Mr Clarke," Burke commanded, motioning with his gun where he wanted the prisoner to go.

I don't think I will care for this portal's destination, William thought as he blinked out of sight, closely followed by Burke and the guard.

THE WALK TO SYLVA WAS easier and drier than the last, and even though Baxter had important news to share, that was not his primary reason for going.

He needed to see her again.

She had not given him much to go on during his last visit - Raishann was hard to get a read from - and he was keen to find out, one way or the other, if she liked him. Not as a useful tool to the Luminants, or a comrade, or a friend.

He needed to know if she was interested in a relationship with him so he could clear his head. Otherwise he was stuck, with no hope of moving in any direction until he knew her feelings toward him.

If she were savoury, he would commit. If she were not, then he would drop it. Maybe he could patch things up with Lila.

But he had to know.

He was no longer accosted when he entered the village, and some locals even greeted him kindly. He said hello to the people as he walked along the familiar street that went from the edge of Nylen to the Forander residence.

When he arrived at the circular house, Raishann was there but preparing to leave.

Baxter quickly told Shawan about a computer that would allow access to the module, but he could not get to the terminal without help.

The Forander patriarch again cautioned him to be wary of bringing anyone else into the fold. Baxter was reminded of the risk to himself and the Luminants, but Mr Forander also clarified that nearly all the Ascended were so deeply ingrained in the system that it became difficult to convince them of anything that disagreed with information that came through official channels.

Baxter agreed and reassured Shawan that he would seek counsel before he made any further decisions or took action. He would approach someone he trusted to ask for help and then come back to discuss what would happen next.

Having taken care of business, he turned his attention to Raishann. "Where are you going?" Baxter elicited.

"Nowhere, I guess. Just out. Do you have time to go for a walk before you leave?"

"Yes. I'd like that," he enthused.

They left the house together and went through the village perpendicular to the only street he was familiar with. Lots of people said hello to Raishann, and some girls giggled and pointed as they walked past. Raishann waved to them, but said "fucking bitches" quietly through her smile. Baxter didn't know what that meant, but he was sure it was not a compliment.

They made their way to the edge of the village, and the road deteriorated into a well-beaten path with two evenly spaced ruts continuing out of town.

They followed those tracks until they became overgrown with grass and bushes, then kept moving through the scrub.

Baxter was fascinated as he waded through the waist-deep greenery, and he splayed his fingers out to maximize his contact with the various plants.

Raishann laughed, and Baxter asked, "What?"

"I'm sorry, I've just never seen anyone experiencing this for the first time. I guess I've kind of taken it all for granted, but it seems new to me again. Thanks, I guess."

"I'm glad you can live vicariously through me," Baxter said. It made her laugh a little, which he took as a good sign. "I'm delighted to be getting to know you, Raishann," he squeezed out.

"Me, too," she said. "Look ahead. At the edge of the river. Can you see anything?" She pointed straight ahead at a place in the distance.

Baxter scanned the area carefully. "No, I see nothing," he stated.

"Well, trust me, there's something there, and I hope you will enjoy it." She ran ahead of him, and he broke into a jog to keep up.

She trotted off down the hill and crossed to the shoreline, not caring how far behind he was. They made their way along the river for a short distance, then Raishann went up the bank and stopped to reach down into the grass. Baxter slowed to a walk again, and his short breaths struggled to keep his oxygen levels up.

"Get over here, you out of shape old man," she called to him, "I have a dead grandma who can move faster than you." Baxter smiled and picked up his pace.

She opened a door that led into the ground, and between panting breaths, he asked what it was.

"You'll see," she said as she lowered herself into the hole and climbed down.

She disappeared into the darkness, and Baxter chided himself for following her into a strange hole, but couldn't stop himself from doing it. The light grew dimmer as he descended, and by the time he reached the bottom, he could barely see. His eyes were not adjusted, and he just about jumped out of his skin when the light came on. His reaction even startled Raishann.

"Holy shit," she exclaimed, laughing.

"I'm sorry, I didn't mean to scare you."

She went to him and put a hand on his shoulder, still chuckling.

"You seem to be having a lot of fun at my expense today," Baxter stated while Raishann repressed a giggle. "No, that's okay, laugh it up. Someday I'll take you places you have never experienced, and we'll see how you like it."

Raishann told him that they were in a survival bunker from before the Cataclysm. It had been one of the first places she scavenged with her dad when the village was farther to the south. When Nylen moved to its current location, she began using the forgotten stronghold to get time to herself. She had not shared it with anyone else, except her best friend, who was not around anymore. She got quiet for a minute, then added that her dad knew of it, too, but never came.

They sat and talked for a while, sharing things about themselves and discussing their lives. Raishann had a lot of questions about living under the Ascendancy, and he told her about growing up in Enswell, and the Lookout, and his friends, and even about Lila.

Raishann continued calling Lila "Jealous Girl", and Baxter said nothing to correct her.

When he noticed the time and assessed that it must be getting dark outside, he reluctantly said that he would have to go.

Raishann let him go up the ladder ahead of her before shutting off the light and following to meet him in the grass above.

She pointed out to Baxter where the trail that led to the city was, and she went down the trail they had come in on, returning to the village.

After going a short distance, Baxter heard Raishann call out to him. He turned and took a couple steps toward her.

"This was fun," she yelled to him. "Let's do it again, okay?"

Baxter bellowed his agreement and waved to her, and she was still watching him when he continued into the forest.

He liked where things was going.

LAENA HAD NOT PROGRESSED very far in her first few days out. She just put more distance between herself and Aldergate every day, focusing on survival.

She travelled five or six kilometers daily, then set up a new campsite before going to hunt and forage for water. It had crossed her mind that once she found a suitable spot, she might build a semi-permanent camp, but she wasn't ready for that quite yet.

Laena had taken a rabbit the day before, and the blast from the ion rifle had killed it, cleaned it, and cooked it in one shot. There wasn't a lot of it left, and she made a mental note that the pistol was a better choice for small game. There was enough meat to have some food, but she would have to hunt larger game if she wanted any real sustenance.

She had also found some fruit, which was good because clean water was scarce. Every night she collected some by knotting a piece of plastic from the backpack around some leafy branches, and it guided the condensation that built up there into her bottle, which was affixed to the bottom of the apparatus.

She was living, but only in the most minimalist fashion, which was why she just about fell over dead when the most useless item in the pack became her godsend.

The screen of the pad flashed a notification while she searched the backpack again, and she poked at the device until it responded. Someone had sent a note that contained a map showing the way to Nylen. She studied it and found that if she made her way north, she would find an outpost from which a series of Ascendancy Gates would lead to her homeland. The note also gave instructions for connecting the glasses she had seen in the bag to the datapad. Laena zoomed the map out to see more area and was stunned at how far from home she was. She hadn't known or even guessed that Nylen was so distant, and she almost cried when she first saw the tremendous distance. There would have been no way she'd have gotten anywhere near it if not for the gifts she'd received.

Gates would shorten the trip, but following the path offered by the map also meant spending time in Ascended cities along the way. She wasn't sure how she would handle that, but she would figure something out as she moved.

First things first - she must get to the outpost and complete the first jump.

She did nothing with the campsite from the previous night and instead made preparations to leave as soon as she could.

Laena was excited, but it was going to be a long day.

She would start by travelling west, which was not where the outpost was, but the map showed that there was a river she had not been aware of. It would be two birds with one stone for her, as it would give her a source of water and a path to the north.

Following it would lead her to a very prominent bend away from her destination, at which point she would head east again and arrive at her objective. She would have to watch for animals who used the river to drink from, but she figured she was just as likely to see a game animal as she was to encounter a predator. It would be worth the risk.

She gathered up the few things she had and checked the remaining charge on the pad. It was at 48 percent, and she decided that she would only glance at it when she absolutely needed to.

Then, with everything in her pack, she found the morning sun, turned to put it at her back, and drew a full breath as she set out to go home.

THIS WAS GOING TO BE hard.

Baxter had only spoken to Lila once since they kissed, but that had been very brief.

Lila had assured him that everything was okay between them, but added that she was having some trouble reconciling the experience.

She asked if she done something wrong. Baxter told her that he was solely responsible. He had a lot going on after his father died and he was not ready for the encounter when it happened. Okay, good.

The conversation had been awkward, but necessary.

Baxter knew that much more foundational rebuilding would be required before they could fully revive their long-time friendship.

And now he stood at the Lookout, waiting to tell her that he needed her to risk herself and help him to betray the Ascendancy.

He would have to admit that his father had been a traitor - but not a terrorist - and that he had since become involved up to his neck, too. Maybe he would try talking to her instead about what had happened in that heated moment. Perhaps he should speak about reestablishing their friendship and then ask for help with the computer later.

He ran out of time to decide how he would handle the situation when the door to the roof opened, and Lila appeared there.

Baxter greeted her meekly, and she closed the door and covered the distance between them slowly.

He should have taken more time to think about this. He should have planned it out more carefully. It was too late now.

"You are involved with the rebels, am I right?", she charged.

It caught him off guard and he could not even begin formulating a response. He opened his mouth, and nothing came out.

"I know you better than anybody, Baxter, and after what happened to your father, I wasn't sure which way you would go. But, fundamentally, you only really had two choices - you could reject everything Mr Clarke did, or come to embrace it. Based on how you've been acting and piecing it all together, I figure you have chosen the latter. And with that in place even more things explained themselves. Like the fact that the lady and the pretty girl from the funeral must be part of it, too. And you like the girl, and that is why you would not kiss me."

Baxter did a self-check and caught himself standing there with his mouth open. He closed it.

Lila was one of the brightest people he had ever met, and she did know him better than anyone else did, and in hindsight, it made sense that she was on to him. He wanted to explain to her why he had done what he had done, but he thought that, at this point, it would just be disrespectful. There was nothing he could say that would fix this.

Actually, there was one way to handle this, and it was needed right now for the good of both of them. "Yes," he admitted. "How did you know?"

Lila shrugged her shoulders and then sat down in her usual spot and patted the empty place next to her, inviting him to join her.

He shuffled over and sat, but found that he could not look at her. "So? What now?" was all he could get out.

Lila took a deep breath. "Look, you may be a techno-geek extraordinaire, but I want you to remember that I am smarter than you. And I always will be." Her eyes sparkled within her coy expression.

Baxter chuckled nervously and shrugged his shoulders, but said nothing. "It was the simplest explanation that covered the most observable phenomena. Occam's Razor. Works for science, and equally well when applied to strange human behaviour."

Baxter looked at her, and she was studying him knowingly. "And I followed you after I left your house. I was outside the building having a little moment when I saw you come out the exit. So I stayed behind you, well, up to the point where you went to the machinery at the rim, anyway. Once I saw you go in that hole, I knew where you were going. I just want you to be careful, okay?" Baxter nodded his acknowledgement as he diverted his gaze. "I keep thinking about this girl, Kari, who used to work in the Martens building. She was escorted out of the building one day for accessing systems above her security level, and I have never seen her again - I think no one has. But, shortly after that, they moved one of her close coworkers - a lady named Westerman, I think - to a much higher position. The point is that there can be adverse consequences to what you are doing. Especially if someone finds out about it and then decides they can use the information to advance themselves."

Baxter stood frozen, unsure of what to say next.

"Do not worry yourself," Lila added, "I did not, and I will not, report you. As far as I am concerned, if this was important to your father, one of the most brilliant men I have ever known, and now it has become important to you, then it must be important in general. As for the girl, well, we shall see what happens. For now, let us say that I have not completely given up."

Baxter was in awe. He remembered how savoury Lila could be, and he felt both horrible and relieved. "Thank you," he stammered. "I suppose I am indebted to you. Which makes this even harder to ask, but easier at the same time. Anyway, your access to the computer labs?"

"Yes, what of it?"

"Well, there is a specialized piece of equipment there that I need to have access to."

"I thought when you called that this might go in some such direction. Carry on."

Baxter felt pressure behind his eyes as he drew his next breath. He was lucky to have Lila in his life. He felt as though he didn't deserve this from her, but there was a need for her abilities and access that was greater than him.

"There is this computer memory module…"

Chapter 15

CANDACE COULD NOT REMEMBER a time when she was as angry and upset as she was now.

How could Baxter not show any interest in his future? In their future? She was his mother, for the love of God, and had dedicated her life to the continued prosperity of her family.

Baxter was being ungrateful, and she would not stand for it.

This was all because of his father. Everything was fine until William went too far with his extracurriculars. She should have reacted sooner. She should have nipped this nonsense in the bud.

There was no way, she resolved, that she would make the same mistake again. This was coming to a conclusion. Now.

Baxter was not at home, and even if he had been, she probably would not have acted any differently.

She marched through the house, and into the room that William had used as his workshop. The place that she had seen Baxter coming and going from all too often since William's passing.

Everything was as she remembered it. There did not appear to be anything that was of such great interest that it would make Baxter want to spend hours upon hours inside.

She felt the heat of anger rising in her. All of this stuff had sent her husband over the edge, and now her boy was being pulled into that caustic world.

What was it about these things that drove the men in her life to senselessness? She hated William for what he brought into their home. Looking around the room revealed the taunting artifacts of a former life. She detested all of it - his 'work'.

She picked up the object nearest her and threw it at the terminal on the desk. The screen shattered and the shrill noise and visual stimulation of its passage into uselessness gave her a thrill of satisfaction.

Candace shoved things off the table and counter, flailing wildly, enjoying the wanton carnage until the chaos she created surrounded her.

She stood heaving and drinking in the destruction around her. She liked it.

Kyla appeared on the wall, asking if she should send a cleaning drone to the utility room. "Better send them all," Candace commanded. She stood in the open area of the room, with her arms and her disposition crossed, until a squad of robots flanked her on either side.

"Everything in here is garbage. Clean it up."

She walked out between the cleaning units as they bustled into compliance. For a moment, it seemed to Candace that the drones were trying to escape the fate of their fallen cousins - the half-finished electronic devices that William had made. *Smart move*, she thought.

She did not know what the things in the shop had been, but she knew what they represented, and she would not have them in her house any longer.

All signs of the stupid rebellion would be wiped from her home, and from the building, and the vicinage, Enswell, and all of the 12 cities.

She dragged her favourite chair from the sitting area down the hall and placed it near the entrance to the utility room. Then she had a drink brought to her, and she sipped it slowly while she watched her robotic minions taking the first steps toward cleaning up her life.

She would succeed in her new mission. There could be no place for doubt in her mind. She would ascend.

Candace drew a deep breath and exhaled through pursed lips as she envisioned a brighter future.

MARSHALL HAD INVITED Doyle to his office, and it was just as well because Doyle was going to set up a meeting with him, anyway.

The information he needed from the young Sylvan about the locations of the villages had been given. The boy had simply circled them on a hand-drawn map, but there were enough geographic landmarks included to ensure they could all be found without a lot of hassle.

With that intelligence, drones could be sent out on specific vectors, and when they encountered a village, its location would be reported to the police and a strike team would neutralize the people within it.

The Sylvans could not possibly run far enough to get beyond their grasp.

Once Marshall was done shitting himself, he would probably offer Doyle the Big Chair on the spot.

Doyle sat in his usual place in the empty office while he waited for the virtual image of the Chancellor to appear. He contemplated going around the desk to rest in His Worship's chair, but he was glad he hadn't done that when the holo crackled to life.

Marshall's virtual presence twisted into view and solidified between the desk and the window, and Doyle sat up straight and readied himself for greatness.

He stifled his enthusiasm and waited for Marshall to start, not wishing to appear as though he was begging for accolades.

He remained resolute but relaxed, and Marshall began.

"So, Mr Morgan, it appears that you are taking advantage of your unique position."

"In what way, Sir?"

"I'm referring to your insight into the ways of the low people. You have even convinced one of the woodland barbarians to conspire with you. You must be pleased with yourself. Turning a handicap into an asset, and all."

Doyle could no longer hide his satisfaction. Finally! The credit he had been waiting for! "Why, yes, your Worship. I do my best to make the most of any situation."

Marshall scowled. "And that is why you put the Ascendancy at risk by bringing this savage boy into the fold, I suppose."

Doyle recoiled and felt his face redden. His ears went hot, and he could hear his heart beating in them.

"Despite efforts to the contrary, you always seem to retain the notion that you know better than us, don't you, Mr Morgan? Do you think   your point of reference is so far removed that it gives you clairvoyance into what the administration should do?"

Doyle started to answer and was cut short. "I do not want to hear anything from you. I need you to listen. You continue to wreak havoc in the name of progress, undermining all that we have built. You do not follow procedure, you do not attend to advisement, and you do not belong in this office."

Doyle fumed as he awaited what he feared was coming next.

Marshall's virtual form straightened itself and paused, as though the Chancellor was savouring a moment he had long anticipated. "Doyle Morgan, effective immediately, you are demerited twenty thousand points and are no longer a member of this staff. You will await reassignment to a post where your shortcomings will not be a detriment to the Ascendancy."

Doyle sat silently, knowing that anything he said at this point could only make things worse.

"What? You have nothing to say now, Mr Morgan?"

"No, sir," Doyle grunted.

"Fine. You are dismissed." The holo image flickered out, leaving Doyle alone in the room again.

He felt ashamed. Not for being fired or demerited, but for not recognizing from the start that there was no place for him in this world.

He should never have betrayed his people. He should never have involved that kid, and he should never have thought that he could rise from the rim to be accepted in a system characterized by differentiation and prejudice.

He would remind the Ascendancy of who he really was.

He would give them exactly what they expected from him. They were *not* going to like it.

LAENA ARRIVED AT THE river's edge in the afternoon and followed against its current as far north as she could before making camp for the night.

She had seen a deer earlier, and she went for her gun, but then realized that she didn't want to take such a big animal now that she was planning to continue moving. Even though scavengers and other animals would finish off what she could not eat, it would be better to hunt smaller game as she made her way.

She hated to stop, having travelled a considerable distance that day, but she also knew that moving at night was not a good idea.

Laena went into the trees, away from the banks of the gurgling river, and scouted for an appropriate location to bed down.

She begrudgingly cut branches to make a small shelter and bed and gathered some dead wood for a fire. The ion pistol started her kindling burning, then she added larger pieces at intervals until she nursed her heat source to strong flames. She then headed back down to the river to fill her bottle with water.

The water from the river was not placed directly into the vessel even though it appeared to be clean. She took off the outer shirt she wore, tied one of the sleeve ends into a knot, and then filled it with alternate layers of sand, gravel, and some charcoal she had kept from yesterday's fire. The whole assembly was propped against some rocks on the shore so the makeshift filter hung suspended over the mouth of the bottle. She scooped water from the slow current with her hands and poured it into the open end of the shirt sleeve.

It wasn't the best setup, but without a container to boil the water in, this would have to do.

She brought the full bottle back to the campsite and drank a little as she sat warming herself by the fire for a while. It was the first peace she had felt in a long time. She almost didn't know what to do with it.

Laena thought of where life had taken her, from free and lively to incarcerated and surly. From being a child of nature to being a cog in a machine. And from having no limits, except those she imposed on herself, to living in a box when she was not busy being a slave.

Though she had only been imprisoned for a relatively short time, it was strange not looking at the world through the bars of her cell as she prepared for sleep.

She couldn't believe a chain of events that started with being kidnapped and continued through the act of killing a man had led her to this point. She had never given up hope - well, maybe once for a couple of minutes - and now everything she required was falling into place for her.

It was as though she was being driven in a specific direction by forces outside herself, but channelled through her. She needed this, and something out there must need her, too.

It was unbelievable.

She was going to make it.

THE DRONES HAD DONE a thorough job of cleaning the mess on the floor of the utility room, but they left all the articles on the desk and counter where they were.

Not good enough, Candace thought. *I want all of it gone!*

She paced the room while a hatred expanded within her for what William had become, for what he had subjected Baxter to, and for what he put her through even now.

A sense of guilt washed over her briefly as she remembered that he was gone, but then she recalled the buildup to the end of his life.

Yes, William had initially brought her ascension, but later he gave her worry and deceit. Now, in death, he brought her pain. And, he was also hurting Baxter from beyond the grave, even though her son may not realize it yet. That was too much. She would not have it.

With that, she picked up an article from the top of the desk and threw it. There was a thump when it connected with the wall, and then another when it hit the floor.

She followed that with another randomly chosen object, but this time there was almost no sound as it hit the wall, even though a crash issued from its impact with the floor.

Her anger subsided, replaced by curiosity as she approached the place where her second projectile impacted the wall. She knocked there tentatively, and the wall seemed to absorb her efforts. She hit it again, harder this time, and got the same result.

She went across to the counter and chose a long steel object from the remaining things there. She gripped the bar tightly and tried it for weight, stabbing the air with it several times.

Then she crossed the room to the questionable spot in the wall and jabbed one end of the impromptu pry bar into the surface while she put the other end on her hip and pushed with all her weight and both hands.

Slowly, the wall gave way, and once she had the object through it, she must have triggered an override, because the hole opened fully.

She dropped the bar and retreated a step as it clanged to the floor, awestruck at what lay within.

There was a Gate, but not like the ones they had in the malls or out at the Gate terminals. This one was smaller and looked like it might be handmade. She could hear its gentle hum, and she surmised that it must be active. She took a step, hesitated, and then walked through.

What she saw on the other side she could not bear.

She tried to control her breathing, but the tears broke past her efforts to hold them in and streamed down her face.

In the name of all things sacred, does this nightmare never end?

RAISHANN SAT IN THE soft glow of the solar and battery powered light that illuminated the inside of the bunker.

Usually, she would read or listen to music or watch something while she was in her sanctum, but today she just sat, drumming her fingers on the table in front of her.

Her thoughts were filled with the future, and who she would include in it.

She had no shortage of admirers within the village, but they were generic and boring, and Raishann thought of them as almost being clones of one another.

But there was something about the city boy that made her heart swell despite her best efforts. Maybe it was just because he was different, or seemed genuine, or because he was turning out to be something other than what she initially expected.

She liked him when they first met, then she hated him, then tolerated him, and now, she didn't know what to think.

She put her head down in her arms, pondering how she would quiet her internal conflict, and within minutes she was fast asleep.

THE TINY ROOM BEYOND the homemade Gate had William's touch, to be sure.

Even though there were shelves and tables and a desk, and it had the potential to be an organized space, the chamber was mostly in disarray. Any signs of a system in place were haphazard at best, and probably the result of absolute necessity.

Candace flinched when a laser from above the monitor on the desk tried to read her eye. Recognizing what was happening, she turned to face it, allowing the beam to invade her.

Once it had done its duty, it blinked out and the screen of the terminal powered down. Apparently, anything on the device was not meant to be shared with her.

She huffed her disapproval and sat in the uncomfortable chair at the small desk. How much was one woman supposed to take? Is this what Baxter had been doing all those times he came and went from the utility room? Of course it was.

She surveyed the area. It was a collection of odds and ends, most of which were unidentifiable, and all of them were incomprehensible. What would drive a person to this?

All the secrets and lies, and who knew what else, had stripped her of her dignity, taken her husband from her, and now threatened to ruin Baxter.

Well, Baxter could not rebel if there were no rebellion. She would take the entire counter-culture down, even if she had to do it alone. And she could start right here.

Candace looked for a tool to destroy the place. It frustrated her to find nothing, and she thought that she would go back through the Gate to get her wall-whacker from the other side.

Then, her muscles relaxed, and in a moment of clarity, she recognized her short-sightedness. Taking down the Sylvans meant taking them all down, not just removing an appendage.

She decided that it would be better to leave the room intact. Baxter would continue to spend time in the secret cave, unaware of her intrusion, and perhaps she could glean some insights from things left in the small space that would be helpful to her.

Information taken from here could be passed on to the Ascendancy, and she could wipe out the rebellion, reclaim her son, and ascend beyond all ascension, all in one move.

She would restore the utility room to its original condition and hope that Baxter would not notice the difference as he passed through it. If she played it smart and stayed patient, Baxter would use the room without knowing that she had access to it, and everything would come together for her.

She would have her life back.

She would get her boy back.

THEY HAD ASSEMBLED all of Enswell's top advisors, with the notable exception of one, in the boardroom.

The doors were closed, and Marshall paced at the head of the giant table in the oversized room, taking time to reassure himself that he was pursuing the correct course of action.

He thought about the sequence of events that had brought them to this point, and what the president wanted from him, and what they faced from the Sylvans.

He even included some of what Doyle Morgan had presented to him as he made his calculation. Doyle hadn't been entirely wrong.

The attendees were patient and said nothing as they waited, but looked on with anticipation.

Marshall had kept them in suspense long enough. It was time.

"Ladies and gentlemen, I have called you here to announce that on this day, the Administration of the City of Enswell is declaring war against Sylva." Murmurs filled the room, and he gave the people time to get the shock out of their systems before he continued. "They are a plague on us and have adversely affected our society and our way of life for too long. And now, with the recent bombing attempt and the apprehension of one of our own citizens, someone who was infected by those villains, I say that they have brought the fight to us. But they will not intimidate us. We will not allow them to guide our destiny. We will respond in kind, and remove this threat from our lives, the lives of our children, and all who live under the protection of the Ascendancy." Clapping and words of agreement filled the chamber.

Marshall scanned the attendees, looking for signs of dissent, but saw none. Perfect. He would have his war.

Many of the people in the room were unaware of the vital role the Sylvans played in their lives by keeping the city's infrastructure up and running; Sylvan slaves did all the grunt work in everything from freshwater provision to waste management. Those few who were aware said nothing, and knowingly saved any questions they had for a time when lower Ascension Levels were not intermingled.

"So then. I will meet with some of you further - each of you should have before you a duty roster and scheduled appointments to make this noble effort a reality - and all of you will need to begin immediately to carry out preparations for this, our finest hour." Applause erupted around the room, and Marshall waved them to quiet. "Go now. The next time we meet will be under dire circumstances, and we must be at our best. Thank you."

People rose from their seats, and some of them congratulated Marshall as they left the room. "Excellent, your Worship." "The time has come to end our suffering, sir." Marshall thanked them again and bid them well for the upcoming task.

When he saw Burke leaving, he called to him and asked him to stay. There was one more detail that needed attention. The others left the room, and Marshall prompted the last of them to please close the door on her way out. She smiled compliantly through the shrinking opening until it sealed.

"Yes, your Worship," Burke acknowledged.

Marshall directed Burke to take a seat near him as he returned to his chair at the head of the long table. "Doyle Morgan, as you are aware, has been descended into the police force," he stated.

"Yes, sir."

"He will be on the ground in the first raids. And so will you."

"Me, sir?"

"Yes. You will oversee deployment at the front, and will report to me directly."

"Thank you, sir," Burke said shakily.

"Quite. It is a dangerous mission, and I am convinced that you can handle it, but it will be hazardous, and some of the men will not make it back. Do you understand?"

Michael did not appreciate the order, but he knew better than to contradict the Chancellor. "Yes, sir."

"Good." Marshall leaned ahead, crossing his arms on the table as he closed the distance. "Doyle Morgan will not make it back." He raised an eyebrow at Michael, and it took Burke a moment before he got the message.

"Oh. Yes, sir. Doyle will not make it back." Michael was stammering as he spoke. Marshall had never asked him to take a life before, but he knew that Burke would do anything he was tasked with. He had a high level of Ascension to maintain, and Marshall thought that even as surprisingly dense as Michael could be at times, he must know that his family connections made it possible for him to get as far as he had. He undoubtedly also realized that he had to, occasionally, come through in a pinch to preserve his good standing in his job and with his lofty relatives.

"Very well. You will see to it that Mr Morgan comes to an unfortunate end. Nothing fancy or dramatic; just get it done. Making good on this will bode well for you when the dust settles, and we return to our regular business. Thank you, Mr Burke. Keep me apprised of your results. That is all."

Michael got up from his chair and smoothed the front of his suit coat, and said nothing further as he exited the room.

Alone and smiling, Marshall breathed deeply of his masterful handiwork.

The 13th city was going to be splendid.

Chapter 16

CANDACE WAS BOTH PATIENT and correct.

Leaving the hidden room intact paid off, as Baxter left drawings and notes on the desk outlining a plan to break into the Martens building to steal a computer.

She hoped that it was coincidental that the target of the robbery was Lila's place of business, and that her son had not drawn his future wife into this tangle of treachery with him.

Although it was ultimately Lila's decision to be part of it or not, the possibility strengthened Candace's resolve to stop this. Rebellion, it seemed, was a disease that spread rapidly.

Baxter was at home, and she knew that he would wait until he thought he had the flat to himself before he went through the utility room Gate, as per his usual pattern.

She had devised a plan of her own. She had even tested her proposed actions to be sure they would work when the time came. It was all very intrepid, and she congratulated herself on her cleverness.

"Baxter," she called, leaning around the corner of his open bedroom doorway, "I am going out for a while. Do you want anything?"

"No, thank you," he replied, not looking up from his terminal.

She feigned leaving the room, then quickly turned around again. "I am going to do something special for you, anyway."

"You do not have to do that," Baxter said. "You have already done more than enough. Enjoy your shopping. When will you be back?"

"I think I should be back for dinner around eight," she lied, giving a time that would lead him to believe he had three hours of autonomy. "Okay, I will see you later, then," she cooed.

"Yeah, bye," Baxter returned, looking at his screen for the place he had left off in his studies.

Candace walked down the hall and made a production of leaving, including being more noisy than usual. She approached the door, and it gave its sing-song chime as it opened, but she did not exit the flat as it closed.

She hid near the door, hoping that her son would not choose to leave the house. Explaining her presence in a cramped corner of the entrance would require creativity beyond her capacity.

It wasn't long before she heard some scuttling in the back of the flat. She tiptoed to the salon, staying close to the walls, and from there continued to the kitchen. She crouched down behind the counter and listened intently.

Baxter was in the utility room. The door whooshed shut, but she knew that she wouldn't hear the wall opening or the Gate activating from her position, so she allotted what she felt was an adequate amount of time before moving again.

When she crept to the utility room door and listened, there was no sound. She waved a hand in front of the door. It was sealed. Baxter was gone.

"Kyla, cut the power to the utility room. Code One," she commanded.

"Right away," Kyla responded, and the lights in the workshop went dark. Through the virtual assistant's knowledge of their home, and Candace sharing what was found in the utility room - which William had blocked from the system - they had together discovered that the power for the Gate depended on the electricity for the utility room. With that shut off, everything in there, including the private portal, stopped functioning.

And, even though she hadn't understood all of what William tried to tell her about the Gates and what they could do, there was one principle she remembered that had become pertinent in the development of her scheme.

Baxter couldn't rob anybody if he were stuck in the hole with no way out and furthermore, without an active Gate to allow wireless transmissions, no communication.

RAISHANN HAD ENTERED the city in her disguise as Rachel and made her way to the Martens building, and Lila appeared at the meeting point shortly after that. The plan was in motion.

She grew impatient as they waited outside the building where Lila worked as a computer tech and programmer. It was nearly time to go in.

The timing of this had all been set and calculated, and their window of opportunity was shrinking like thin plastic in a fire. Everything had been thoroughly planned out, and even Jealous Girl had arrived on time.

So where in the hell was Baxter?

Raishann looked at her watch, and less than a minute had elapsed since the last time she checked. She shook it off and turned to face Lila.

"Are you sure he didn't try to get a message to you?" Raishann beseeched. "I recognize that you don't live as we do, but we always have a comm with us. Our numbers are assigned at birth, and I have known him nearly that long, so barring some serious head injury, I think he would know how to contact me. He has not. And I have not been able to reach him."

"Okay, fine. We'll have to call this off."

"No!" Lila blurted. Then, remembering that she was taking part in a criminal act, she quieted herself. "If we do not use this opportunity wisely, we may never get another chance as we have right now. That was why we planned this for tonight, was it not?"

Raishann found it cute when Baxter talked in city-speak, but coming from Lila, it was just annoying.

"Yes. You are quite correct," she mocked. "We will have to do this without him."

"Okay, then," Lila said, convincing herself that this was a good idea.

"You studied the plan?" Raishann interrogated. She had gone over every aspect of it several times with her father and knew each detail by rote. She needed to know that her impromptu partner was equally prepared.

"Yes, thoroughly. I understand you only intended for me to provide information while you and Baxter went inside, but I made sure that I was intimately familiar with all aspects of the stratagem. It may have been too much, but I have done nothing like this before, and I was nervous."

"Good," Raishann stated. "So, we should get moving then."

Lila nodded her consent, and the two of them rose from where they were crouched in hiding and started toward the entrance point. Raishann lead them, and they advanced confidently to the main doors and walked in as though they owned the place.

There was no one at the front desk after regular working hours, but Raishann knew cameras were watching them. She tried to remain inconspicuous, fighting an urge to turn her face away from any lenses she saw pointed in her direction. Lila would fix that issue once they got up to her workspace, anyway.

They made their way to the lift, and Raishann was impatient as they rode up to the floor that included Lila's lab. The slight increase in gravity from the acceleration only added to her discomfort. The walls started to close in slightly, and then there was a chime, and the doors opened.

Lila took the lead, and they turned left when they exited the elevator and moved down a corridor that alternated windows and doors down one side. Raishann scanned each of them in turn as they passed, trying not to be nonchalant, but she saw no one.

Raishann had a handgun, and extra clips of bullets, in her bag. Lila was not aware of its presence, and Raish would only use it in the direst of conditions.

Near the end of the hallway, they stopped at an unmarked door, and Lila opened it. It was not locked - presumably, none of them were - and they entered without any impediment.

The room was a technological nightmare. Raishann had never seen such an altar to the Techno-Gods as this. Everywhere around the periphery there were screens and readouts and blinking lights from floor to ceiling. In the middle, there were chairs and desks with more displays on them, and machines throughout the space with wires hanging out and tools left beside them. Raishann thought they looked like they had been tortured to the point where they were half-dead.

"Come with me," Lila beckoned. "What we need is over there."

"What exactly do you do here?" Raishann queried as she followed.

"I am helping to create advanced AI. You know, artificial intelligence. It will help with running several of our city systems. A lot of them are run by AI now, but the advances we make here will make them better at it."

"So, it's not even people who call the shots around here? Machines do all that?"

"Well, yes and no," Lila reported as she fiddled with some wires and connections behind one of the computers. "People still make the big decisions, I suppose, but they leave all the little decisions to AI, so we are not bothered with them. We handle pretty much everything in here, except for the police force. They are upper-level only. But the Guardians are not very smart at all, and they can sometimes be very literal."

"Oh," Raishann agreed, although most of what Lila had just said made no sense to her.

Lila pulled the piece of equipment she had been fiddling with away from the wall, apparently finished whatever she had been doing. "Help me with this," she requested, and Raishann moved in to assist her.

The machine wasn't cumbersome - Raishann could easily have carried it herself - and they set it on a table nearby. Lila called for her backpack to move to her chest and removed the object that Raishann had heard described so many times. "Is that the memory module?" she asked.

"Yes, it is," Lila confirmed. "I am ensuring that it fits into the receptacle before we remove this equipment." She fitted the module into a space in the back of the computer and seemed satisfied with the results. "Okay, that is done, so I will now take care of the cameras."

Lila sat at a desktop terminal and poked at the holographic touchscreen before her.

"Come on," Raishann prompted. "We should get moving. Our window is closing."

"Almost done," responded Lila, and after a few more keystrokes, she stood and dusted herself off. "Done," she said with satisfaction. "There is no record of what happened here, and no way to tell anything was altered."

Raishann picked up the computer and started toward the door.

"Do you want help with that?" Lila offered, following.

"Nope. I've got it."

Raishann carried their prize toward the door, and once she could see out the window to the hallway, she barked at Lila to stop and hide.

"No one knows we are here," Lila protested, but Raishann told her to do it anyway.

Lila cached herself in a space under a desk, and Raishann just stood there, holding the computer in both hands, as Officers and O-bots passed the window and opened the door.

"Drop to the floor!" an officer bellowed, and Raishann complied immediately. She was careful with the computer, though, remembering that the precious module was still attached to it. Dammit, they should have put that back into Lila's bag. Too late now. It would be best to not call any attention to it.

She thought about going for the gun in her bag, but the police had her. They had caught her with her hands full, and if she attempted to go for it now, they would probably kill her. Compliance was the only thing that would keep her alive. And even that was not a guarantee.

The Guardians closed in on her and rolled her roughly onto her belly and yanked her hands behind her back while the officers covered her with their guns. "You have been selected for relocation," one of the soft-voiced bots said as it put restraints on her hands and feet. The bot then stood her upright and pulled a cable from between her feet, attaching it to the space between her wrists.

The android grabbed her restraints where the cable was attached, and the pressure on her hands increased suddenly.

"Hey, that hurts, you asshole!" she said to the unimpressed Guardian as it led her out of the room.

One of the officers commanded the other O-bot to bring the computer. He said it was evidence and needed to be processed.

Through the window in the hallway, Raishann saw the bot retrieving the hardware from the floor, and they kept her surrounded as they went down in the lift, and from there out to an awaiting aircar.

Baxter was going to be pissed.

Where the hell was he, anyway?

DOYLE WAS SO FAR PAST the point of no return that it would take the light from that point a thousand years to reach the Earth. But Timoth was still salvageable. There was no further need for the young man to go down this path, now that Doyle could tell the callow youth where it led.

He waited at the rendezvous site outside the city, thinking about what he had done, and how it had all been for nothing. He was relieved that he had not given the locations and codes to Marshall, who descended him to a position as a Captain with the Officer Corps before he could 'do any more damage'.

Timoth came over a rise in the distance, and Doyle prepared himself for the first decent thing he had chosen to do in a long time.

Timoth greeted him formally as he approached, and Doyle indicated a fallen tree where they could sit together.

Doyle didn't know where to start, so he backtracked to the beginning. "Listen, Timoth. You think the grass is greener in there," he said, jamming a thumb over his shoulder at the dome behind him, "But I am here to tell you that it's not."

Timoth looked perplexed. "Are you reneging on our deal? Did I do something-"

"No, no," Doyle interrupted. "You have done nothing wrong. Nothing that can't be fixed."

Timoth regarded him with a puzzled face, and Doyle knew he had to repair what he had broken. "I appreciate what you are feeling because I felt the same way when I betrayed my people, much like you are planning to do now." He gave Timoth a moment to digest.

Tim started to speak, but Doyle saved him the breath. "I gave them my people, even some who were family, and they took everything and everyone from me." He looked down and drew a breath before he carried on. "There's no place for us in there, Tim. They will use us if it suits their purposes, but when we need them, they'll cut us loose and leave us to rot. I'm telling you all of this now before you make the mistakes that I once made."

Tim listened silently with amazement spread over his face.

"What I'm getting at here, Tim, is that you need to get out of this. Go back to our people. Forget ascending. Ultimately, it would never have happened anyway, deal or no deal."

Doyle looked supportively into Tim's face. He wished someone had done this for him years ago when he was in the young man's place.

He studied the boy and wondered what was going through his head. Probably, he was confused and as disillusioned as hell. That was to be expected under the circumstances. He would get over this in time. What the youth needed now was a bone that he could throw to the dogs he had betrayed.

Doyle's new role in the police force was far removed from his former administrative position, but it gave him access to privileged information before other people became aware of it. The Ascended man shared what he had learned about his people's plans for the Sylvans, partly hoping it might buy the boy some much-needed forgiveness when he went home, but mostly to stick it to Marshall. He was long past recovering from what he had become, but there was still hope for the boy.

When he was done, Doyle rose and dusted himself off as he bid Timoth goodbye and sent him toward the village.

He lingered for a while longer, pondering the forces that guided the directions of his life.

Maybe he should give up.

THE GATE WAS NOT FUNCTIONING, and the problem seemed to originate on the other side. Baxter could not leave.

He had been stuck for a considerable amount of time, and he sat in the Nest wondering how long it would be before he would have to find an alternate way out. There was plenty of air thanks to the ventilation system, but there was no food or water in the secret space.

He was cut off from Raishann and Lila, and it was time for the plan to be carried out, and they were alone.

He hoped they would not go through with it, but part of him realized the importance of the timing of the robbery (he hated that word, but knew it was correct), and the impact it would have on the future of the rebellion. He was torn, and he wished he had some way to connect with them.

The only method that made any sense right now was to get a message to Lila over her comm. There was communication equipment in the

Nest, but it all relied on the assumption that the Gate was open, allowing information to pass through it.

No transmission could penetrate the plasma-dome. Signals could be sent within it, or between two points outside it, but nothing could get from one side to the other.

If he broke out and tunnelled to the surface, he would be in the forest - that much he knew from his father's notes - but he would not know which way to travel to get to Enswell. By the time he accomplished that it would be too late, anyway, as the girls would have either acted or not, long before he would be able to meet them.

He sat at the desk and dropped his head into his hands.

The light flickered, and he snapped to attention. Power outages were rare in Enswell - there hadn't been one in decades - but it was the only explanation for what was happening.

He crossed the small space and checked. The Gate was issuing its usual sounds and appeared to be functioning normally.

There was still a chance to get to Raish and Lila before it was too late.

He stepped anxiously through the Gate and came to an abrupt halt once he exited.

Mother sat in the utility room, looking at him smugly.

"Hello," she said.

Baxter stood frozen as he tried to come up with an explanation for what he was doing.

"I've known about this for a while now, Bax. I locked you in there to keep you safe."

"Safe from what?" Baxter grilled.

Candace was full of adrenaline, and it came out in her tone and canter. "Save you from what? Baxter, I'm trying to save you from your father, and yourself, and from the ridiculous, traitorous ideas that seem to be filling your head! I'm saving you from you!"

Baxter leaned into her and released his defence. "Mother, you don't know what I've learned! Terrible things are happening all around us, and no one wants to see them."

"Nonsense!" she interrupted.

"No. The people here go about their lives, sleepwalking through their existence, and devoting themselves to something that takes what they have to offer and uses it for their own gains. They lie to us, Mom, and take our whole lives away so they can increase their power!" He hesitated, then added, "It doesn't have to be this way, but someone needs to stand up to them."

Candace raised her voice, contesting her son's defence. "You know nothing except what those liars have told you! And now you have Lila wrapped up in this, too. It has become too much, Baxter. I hope for your sake and hers that she did not participate in tonight's insanity, because if she did, she would find herself in the same state as that Sylvan trollop from the funeral. Yes, that is correct; I know about all of it. But it is ending as we speak. The Ascendancy is likely arresting her right now."

"What? You reported them?"

"I did what needed to be done so that we could live in peace and prosperity, Baxter. Sacrificing her means they will give you a second chance. That was the deal I made. That is what will keep you ascended and moving upward. That is what will keep you safe."

"You mean that is what will keep you ascended!" Baxter yelled as he left the utility room with Candace following closely.

"I did all of this for you! How can you be so ungrateful! How dare you make me out to be self-serving!"

Baxter wheeled around so fast that she nearly crashed right into him.

He pointed into her face, a look of utter disdain filling his features. "You did this for you! You did this for this!" He spread his arms and took in the surrounding space. "And now, people need me because of what you've done, and I'm going to them."

Candace stayed where she was, unable to move. It confounded her. How could he put this on her? She was loyal. She was a superb mother to him.

"Fucking bitch," she heard him say as he went out the door.

She didn't know what that meant, but she knew it didn't sound good.

Chapter 17

WILLIAM SAT BEFORE Michael Burke knowing he had been caught dead to rights sending the map, but also knowing there was nothing Michael or the Aldergate goons could do about it.

No one else knew as much as he did about the workings of the portals, and no one was better equipped than he was to deliver a working projection portal. The Ascendancy needed the new Gates, so they needed him. He was bulletproof.

Burke opened the conversation with a formal greeting and then got to business. "William, we know that you sent a message to Laena Reisatra."

"I don't know anyone by that name."

"You sent information to the girl who escaped by getting a message to the pad she stole from the guard she killed. In a manner of speaking, you are actually an accessory to murder."

"Bullshit," William blurted.

"I do not believe it to be 'bullshit', and the Warden does not think it is 'bullshit', and the Chancellor is quite convinced that it is not 'bullshit'."

William giggled at Michael's attempt at using the vernacular.

"It is not funny!" Burke yelled at him, bringing everyone else in the room to a halt. "I need to know what you sent to her. I have known you and your family for a long time, William, which is why the Chancellor asked me to speak to you personally. He would like for this to go as smoothly as possible so that we do not have to use drastic measures."

"You can't touch me, Michael," William said knowingly. "The Chancellor needs his portals, and I am the only person who can deliver them. So what are you going to do? Take away my hotplate privileges? Hmm? The worst you could do is move me into a regular cell. You can't even torture me because it would delay my work. There's nothing you can do to hurt me, I mean, shit, you've already killed me." William could not hold back his smile, but he looked at his lap to conceal it.

Burke sat back thoughtfully and gave William a contemplative look. "Well, you've got me there, William. But apparently, you have forgotten the speech you received when you were taken into custody. You are correct, William, insofar as I will not torture you. But I most definitely will hurt you. And it will not even leave a mark on you. Not on the surface, at any rate."

A startled look of realization swept over William's face. "You had better not hurt my boy, you bastard."

"Or what, William? Will you take away my hotplate privileges?"

William hated having his own words thrown back in his face, but it forced the understanding that he had overestimated his position. "You asshole," William ground out between his teeth.

"You see, you are not actually as invulnerable as you think. You tell me what you sent to Miss Reisatra, or bad things will begin to happen to Candace and Baxter." He leaned ahead and raised his eyebrows. "But, if you are cooperative, we can make their lives enjoyable again. Did you know that they installed a buffer on your son's Ascension Points algorithm? He will have to work three times as hard to get half as far ahead in life, William. And we can torture him if it comes down to it. It won't slow your work one bit. Candace has been most helpful of late, and we have already considered removing her buffer and making things easier for her, but now your actions prevent that. Please make it easy for us to be helpful for them."

William slouched in his seat and spoke to the floor. "A map. I sent a map. That's all."

"A map of what?" Michael interrogated.

"I sent her a map of the region and showed her location on it." He looked up into Burke's smug face. "But that doesn't mean I know where she might go or what she might do."

"Okay, then. I will bring this forward, and we will continue this conversation later." He stood, and his chair raked against the floor. "Your cooperation is duly noted, but no promises about your boy. Not yet."

William turned to face his desk as Michael walked away, frustrated that the powers that be always maintained the upper hand.

WHEN BAXTER ARRIVED at the Lookout, Lila was already there. She was crying, and had been for some time if her reddened, puffy eyes were an indicator.

She ran to him when he appeared and hugged him tightly.

"It was awful," she started. "They took her, and I stayed in the dark lab all night. I was too afraid to come out, and there were policemen and Guardians, and they took the computer. And the module was still in it."

Baxter was horrified and had more information than he could process rationally. "I'm sorry, Lila. Mother held me up - it's a long story - but then I went to the Martens building and looked all over for you, but I could not find you. Are you okay?"

"Do I look okay?" Lila snapped. "You were held up by your mother? What does that even mean, Baxter? We were counting on you, and you let us down!" Baxter hung his head. "Now Raishann is with them, and everything is gone. It was all for nothing!" She sat down in her usual spot and collected herself.

Baxter sat with her, and she recounted what had happened. She apologized for insinuating that it was his fault, and Baxter admitted that he felt guilty for not being there. They consoled each other, and Baxter told her what his mother had done.

Once they talked through the personal facets of the matter, Baxter breached the subject of what to do next. "So, they have Raishann, and the computer, and the memory module."

"That is correct." Lila wiped her cheeks.

"I do not know how to deal with this, Lila," Baxter pleaded, looking for an answer where there was none.

Lila, as usual, knew what to say. "You do not have to act alone, Baxter. You may not know what to do, but perhaps you know someone who does?"

Baxter straightened as he illuminated from within. "Thanks, Lila. I have to get to Nylen." He stood and started for the door. "It's not like there's anything positive waiting for me at home, anyway."

"I NEED TO TALK TO YOU," Timoth stated flatly, standing across the open space of the house from Shawan.

His dad turned around, raising an elbow to the rear of the chair he was in to accommodate the width of his back as he turned to face his son.

"I know this isn't the greatest time for us, and we have a lot going on, and I'm about to make it worse, but I'm gonna do what's right."

"Come and sit," Shawan said, facing the table again and pulling out the chair beside him. "What's on your mind?"

Timoth crossed the room and chose another chair on the opposite side of the table. He pulled it out and sat, not looking down, but not making eye contact, either.

He had rehearsed this over and over in his head, knowing that he should share the information he had sooner rather than later, but now, none of the eloquent words he had chosen seemed sufficient.

"The Ascendancy plans to invade Sylva," he blurted.

Shawan came to attention, and his look prompted a further explanation. Timoth buckled under the weight of his deeds. Seeing his dad's unbelieving eyes, combined with the path he had explored, and the abject failure that resulted in so much misery for so many people broke him down.

"It was me, Dad," he sputtered. "I told them things, and I didn't want to be here anymore, and I put a tracer on Shadaar, and I'm sorry for everything." Shawan sat silently. "But now, they're coming for us, for everyone, and I want to fix things. I know it's gonna take a long time, and I know you won't trust me anymore, but I can't do this for them anymore, Dad. I went too far, and now I want out. But Sylva is in danger."

His dad sat unblinkingly, and had to shake his head to enable himself to respond. "So I suppose it was you who sent me off for nothing that day? When we went for the bomb?"

"Yeah, it was," Timoth admitted. Maybe he could play this up to minimize the unbelievable amount of shit he was in. "I wanted to save you."

Shawan stood, almost knocking over the chair he was on. Timoth slid his chair back. It was plain to see that his father was irate.

"I should have been there that day, Timoth!" Shawan bellowed. "A lot of good people died! Shadaar died! I honestly don't even know what to say to you right now!"

Aellana came out from the short hallway. "What is going on out here?" she demanded of her husband.

Shawan pivoted from the table and walked around the open area, rubbing his mouth with one hand. "Ask him," he said to her, gesturing at Timoth.

Aellana turned her attention to Tim. "So?" she asked, apparently puzzled.

"I gave information to the Ascendancy." His mom cringed. "I'm sorry, Mom! I just wanted to get out of here, and I thought it would be better there! But now they're coming for us, and if we don't do something, they're gonna wipe us out!"

"What?" Aellana cried out. She returned her focus to Shawan. "What are we going to do?"

"Well, I can't deal with him right now. I don't know what to do with him." He shrugged and turned away.

"No, Shawan. Not that. We'll have to deal with that later. What are we going to do to protect ourselves?"

"I don't know!" Shawan barked. "I'll tell you this, though. He's lucky he came to us with this! Anyone else might have killed him!"

"Knock it off!" Aellana bellowed. She looked her husband in the eye but pointed at Tim. "He is our son, Shawan! And it sounds like he made a mistake - a fucking huge mistake - but he came to us, and we will have to decide how to handle that!" She calmed herself, breathing deeply. "We love him, and I'm so incredibly grateful that he felt he could come to us with this." She sighed. "So, here's what we're gonna do. We will alert the Luminants to an impending attack. We'll tell them that the information came from an informant, which, in a way, it did."

His mother regarded Timoth in a way she had never done before, and were it possible to die from shame, he would have dropped out of his chair at that very moment.

She continued. "Then, we will put together a plan, just like we always have, and we will deal - with - this! And then, assuming we are still alive, we will deal with Tim."

Shawan went to her and put his arms around her. "I'm sorry," he whispered. He turned to Tim and repeated the message. "Your Mom is right. We'll talk about you later. Right now, you just need to tell us everything you know."

There was a loud bang at the door. Timoth wondered if anyone had found out what he had done already. Were they coming for him?

Shawan peeked out the window next to the entrance to their home. He immediately grabbed the handle and threw the door open.

Baxter Clarke was there, panting, with his hands resting on his knees. He stood after catching his breath and stepped into the house. "We need to talk," he said to Shawan on his way in.

"You bet we do," Shawan agreed as he closed the door.

LAENA CROUCHED DOWN in the smaller trees and brush that outlined the Ascendancy depot, watching for signs of people and their routines. She had checked the perimeter and saw only one door that connected the exterior to the inside.

She supposed that meant the Gate was in there, too. It wasn't outside; that was for sure. The possibility that it might have been easily accessible was just wishful thinking.

Okay, Laena thought, *that means I'll have to get in, then.*

She took out her pad and zoomed her map to show the depot in greater detail. She put on the data glasses from her pack and asked for a marker on the location of the Gate. A light flashed on the lenses, indicating that it was located in a room opposite the door.

She would have to get in the door, cross a hallway to the Gate room, make her way through that to reach her goal, and exit. Sounded easy enough. She tried to get the pad to show her the people and bots inside, but it told her there was no data available to respond to that query. Shit.

Laena put the glasses in the pocket of her jumpsuit and made her way to the door in one short burst. There were no cameras that she could see. She supposed the Ascendancy thought no one would come way the hell out here for whatever was inside.

The door had no visible opening mechanism. Chip implants or key cards or something must remotely activate it. Oh, well. She would have to do things the old-fashioned way. She pulled her handgun from its holster, and the weight of it settled into her hand.

Laena knocked at the door with the ion pistol ready in the other hand. When no one came, she banged loudly with the meaty part of her fist and waited, tapping her foot.

The door opened inward slightly, and a man peered out of the opening. "Holy shit," she said. "Took you long enough."

Laena kicked the door as it began to close, and hit the guard, knocking him over. She kicked it again as it bounced back, realizing that if she had to knock again, she would get a very different response.

She walked in as the sentry was recovering and going for his sidearm. She shot him in the head and kept walking across the hall.

Guards came around the corners at either end of the hallway, and she thought that was just as well because she was running straight ahead, anyway. She sprinted into the Gate room. There was no gunfire behind her; neither of those teams would risk hitting the other. Perfect.

Laena was shocked that this had been so easy.

Shit! Why did she always do this to herself? She examined the room thoroughly, thinking she may have missed it, but there was no Gate.

She wheeled to face the open doorway and fired several shots through it to hold off the guards who must surely be right outside.

Then she heard some talking, but could not make out what was being said, and she put a couple more ion bolts through the entrance.

Laena surveyed her surroundings and saw another door in the room. She went for it, putting some random shots over her shoulder as she ran.

As she passed through the next area toward an exit on its opposite side, gunfire erupted from behind her, scorching the walls to her left and right.

She ducked as she exited and quickly turned to the right. There it was!

Laena moved through the hallway with the Gate in it into another room to take cover. The guard and O-bot in the hallway between her and her objective would not make this easy.

More guards gathered across the hall in the room she had just left. She fired at them from where she was, hitting one guard, and causing the other three to scatter out of the line of her fire. She looked around the corner of the door, back into the hallway, and a guard there seized her and caught her gun hand.

They struggled, locked in a savage dance, and when he left a gap between them, she head-butted him in the nose, causing him to let go. He moved his hands to his face, and she grabbed two handfuls of his uniform and started rushing him down the hall toward her exit.

The Guardian stood its ground, and she thought she would try to force her way past it. She ran the guard straight into the bot. It shifted its weight to the side, deflecting the intended blow, and caught her around the arms from behind as she went by.

She looked ahead from its grasp and saw that her goal was only a couple meters away. Damn! She was so close!

The guards from the other room came into the hallway, and their leader halted them with a flat hand extended.

"We've got you!" the leader called to her. "Drop your weapon!"

She released her handgun, and it clattered to the ground. Her rifle dug into her back from the force of the Guardian's grip, and she could not reach it.

The leader looked into the eyes of the O-bot. "Get her out of here. Right now," he commanded.

The Guardian turned, assessing what it had been commanded, and opened its stance as it gripped Laena at the waistband and collar and threw her out the Gate.

RAISHANN HATED CONFINEMENT. She was, by nature and necessity, an outdoorsy girl, and even when they let her out of the tiny cell for short periods, she was still inside.

There were windows that allowed natural light to enter, and a courtyard beyond them, but seeing the outdoors was no consolation to her. She needed to be out there, feeling the fresh breeze against her skin instead of filtered air. Hell, even if it were raining out there, she'd rather be wet than trapped.

She longed for the forest, and her family, and her neighbours, and the village, and she found that she even missed Baxter.

She wondered what happened to him that caused him to miss the heist, and she hoped he was alright. Maybe he had been pinched, too, although she hadn't seen him since they moved her in.

From what Raishann knew of the lay of the land and the route they had taken out of the city, she assumed that she was in the facility closest to Enswell. They might have brought Baxter here, too, if they had caught him, but he may have been transported out before she arrived. Or, he may have ended up like his dad.

She put those thoughts out of her head, laying flat on her uncomfortable cot, and thought of all the people affected by the corrupt government of the cities.

The Ascendancy maintained control over their citizens, of course, but they also had dominion over the Sylvans. The people of the woods were forced to live nomadically, not because they had to follow a food source, or avoid flooding, or for any other natural reason.

They ran when it was no longer safe to be where they were. Many Sylvan tribes lived far enough away from cities to be left alone, but they also faced harsher conditions, especially in winter. Her tribe lived where it did to accommodate the Luminants, so they could be distant enough to be relatively safe, but close enough to cause problems for the Ascendancy and look for ways to undermine it.

Children who grew up in the more militant villages were taught from an early age how to fight, and to blend in with the Ascended if they needed to, and how to hide and set up an ambush. They were shown how to infiltrate and assassinate if the need arose.

She realized now that as much as she had always felt oppressed by the Ascendancy, it was ultimately the Ascended who had to endure the brunt of their injustice. They didn't suffer because of the way they lived; that was an illusion. What hurt them most was the fact that they didn't realize they were suffering. As she was taught to rebel, they had been trained to conform and to hide their pain with pills, entertainment, and comfort.

Raishann may be incarcerated, but at least she wasn't a zombie.

The Ascended shouldn't be seen as separate from the Sylvans. The real distinctions weren't because of the technology they had or the comforts they enjoyed. The differences that mattered existed because of the way those people were forced to live, and the ideas that were mandatory for them to believe.

Her head snapped up in revelation. She had heard it a thousand times before, but it held no real meaning for her until she came to the thought for herself. The Luminants relation to the Ascendancy was to spread the light of knowledge over everyone so that they might recognize their captivity for the first time.

She rolled onto her side and tucked a hand under her thin pillow, finding renewed strength in her epiphany.

It was ironic that having her autonomy taken away had enabled her to see things plainly.

An explosion emanated from far beyond her cell, and a sudden increase in pressure made her ears pop. It was distant but distinct, and she rubbed her ears as she turned to sit up on the edge of her narrow bed. She cocked her head to hear more clearly, and chaotic sounds became more frequent and rose in intensity.

Raishann went to the bars to see what was happening. She could not discern anything where the commotion was coming from, but she thought that would change soon. The noises were increasing in volume and getting closer. There was yelling, and the cracking of gunshots - both energy and projectile - and she backed against the far side of her cell. Raishann flipped her tiny bed onto its end and leaned it against the wall to protect the corner where she sheltered herself.

A distinct clicking noise came to her, mixed in with the cacophony of battle, and she flinched, pulling herself further into her flimsy refuge. But then, the familiarity of that sound made her peek out toward the bars to confirm her notion.

The door to her cell sat back far enough away from its casing to indicate it must have become unlocked. She tried to discern whether it had been a stray ion beam that had forced it open when she saw a man in a jumpsuit like she wore run past her cage, followed by another. Then two more went by, and she finally grasped what had happened.

All the cell doors were unlocked. She started to move, but paused to decide whether it was best to bug out or stay put. There was no protection for her where she was, and many more secure places outside the cell, so logic dictated that she go for the door.

A man appeared on the other side of the bars, wielding a rifle, and she dropped into a defensive stance. She focused on the moment, and her training kicked in. She reflexively performed combat step one - identify your target - then ran to the gate as it was being flung open from the outside.

Raishann threw her arms around the neck of her father and embraced him tightly. "I missed you so much! I wasn't sure I'd ever-"

"No time," Shawan redirected. He unstrapped an extra rifle from over his shoulder and gave it to her.

"There were other reasons for coming here, but this-" he held her shoulders as he regarded her, "was the best one. Come on. We have to move."

Chapter 18

THE LUMINANTS HAD SENT scouts to look for Ascendancy troop assemblage. When it was found that forces were gathering at the facility nearest Enswell, the rebels decided on a preemptive strike. Hit them before they were ready, and on ground they were not prepared to defend.

A general call-to-arms was sent through the village, and out to the surrounding communities, as well. The response was overwhelming.

Men, women, and youth from all over Sylva congregated in Nylen. Some of the youngest volunteers were denied their requests to fight and would remain there.

A small compliment was left behind to defend the village if necessary, but most of the efforts in Nylen centered on evacuation. Even though the houses were portable, they were to be abandoned. The Luminants instructed the people to travel light, bringing only necessities and their most cherished personal items.

The main forces organized themselves under the leadership of Shawan, reviewed the plan of engagement, and readied themselves for the attack. The Sylvans knew that this day was imminent, and they had discussed the pending event at great length, usually over beers an around a late-night campfire. But it was taken seriously enough that preparations were already in place.

The troops were taken to within a kilometer of the facility using any means of transportation they could avail themselves of, and they made the rest of the trip on foot.

The Ascendancy had a modest compliment posted outside the depot, apparently not expecting any trouble. They were quickly overtaken, and the next phase of the strategy was put into action.

The Luminants knew that entering through the small entrance to the facility would mean going through a choke point where they would be promptly subdued. For the plan to work, they would have to penetrate in larger numbers, which meant they needed a bigger door.

Explosive charges were placed along the length of one of the end walls of the facility, at intervals where the blast from one would overlap the explosion from the next.

The explosives were laid at a point farthest away from the cells where the prisoners were held. They were detonated simultaneously, creating a hole as high as two men, and open across two-thirds of the building.

There were casualties - some Ascendancy troops were eliminated in the blast - but the most significant injury to the enemy was also the most calculated one. On the inside of the demolished wall were the Gates that led from the depot to Enswell, and others that connected this place to other facilities.

The Luminants had, with their first move, prevented the Ascendancy forces from retreating or strengthening their numbers. Now the Sylvans had to overtake those who lived through the explosion.

Shawan led the first team into the breach and gunfire erupted immediately from the irregular hole in the wall. Then, after an interval, another group entered, shortly followed by the next.

Baxter went in with one of the last teams to enter, and he found himself in the middle of the pack due to his inexperience. He had initially hoped to be in the squad that Shawan led, but knowing that the experienced Sylvan's group moved in first and were handling the brunt of the fighting made him okay with the team they placed him in.

Most of the Ascendancy forces had been cleaned out by the waves of soldiers who preceded Baxter, and expended bodies jutted from places where they thought they would be safe.

There were a few Luminants among the dead, and it punctuated the gravity of what they hoped to accomplish.

Part of him feared for his life, but mostly he wished that there was more he could do to contribute to his comrades' success.

The mission objectives were threefold. They needed to overcome the Ascendancy forces and take control of the facility. They also had to free the prisoners, arm them, and absorb them into squads. The most critical mission parameter was the recovery of the computer that Raishann and Lila had attempted to procure, and the memory module attached to it.

Baxter hoped that the article was worth all this trouble, plus the lives of his father and all the others who would die this day.

They weren't just doing this to save the living; they would also vindicate the countless rebels who had tried to beat the Ascendancy and failed.

The Luminants had developed a belief in Baxter that he could only hope to live up to.

RAISHANN MOVED WITH her father's squad through the building. They took out Ascendancy soldiers they encountered along the way until they came to a choke point - a small bay door that separated the north and south halves of the facility. The Ascendancy forces arrived there first and had a defensive advantage over the Luminants. The soldiers took cover and held their position against the government troops there.

They had advanced as far as they could, and Raishann would have to wait for the action to come to her.

She squatted behind the cover they had chosen, and though she tried to stay focused on the mission, she couldn't help but think on the news her father had shared.

Baxter was coming with a squad at the rear. She was so thankful she had to constrain herself.

She knew that he must have given up a lot to do what he was doing now; more than the Sylvans had in some regards. But he was putting his life on the line right alongside the rest of them.

She pondered how he had been so naive when they met in the city, utterly unaware of who she was and what was going on right in front of him, or that his dad was squarely in the middle of it. The sacrifices Shadaar made had helped to bring them to the edge of freedom.

The Ascendancy had enjoyed its day, and now, in its evening, William's luminance was missing, but another bright star took its place to provide a light of hope.

Baxter was turning out to be more than she ever imagined he could be.

Maybe that was why she felt this way about him. She had never known someone to overcome so much to live up to their potential. It was funny, in a way, that by leaving something called "the Ascendancy" behind, he could now rise freely to meet his destiny.

He was unique, as only a person from such twisted roots could be, and she wanted him like no one else she had ever encountered.

Raishann checked the squad's rear more often than was necessary, aware that she was not just watching for the threat of enemy soldiers.

It disappointed her every time she looked and found that Baxter was not there.

HIS FATHER WOULD NOT have approved.

Timoth enlisted along with some youths who came from another community. He had ensured that the person doing the intakes was not from his village and he gave a false name when he reached the front of the line. They signed him up and then rallied him together with the other men and women. The soldiers fell into their ranks, and while an older man paced around them barking out what they expected of enlistees, Timoth was given a helmet, rifle, ammunition, and the other standard gear of a Sylvan soldier. He added a personal touch by putting black grease paint across his cheeks and forehead, smearing his features.

Timoth lined up with the group and was taken for a briefing. They would be split up and placed in squads with more experienced soldiers. He had a sinking feeling that they would pair him with someone who knew him or his father, and the jig would be up.

It was too late to back out now, anyway, and he was firm in his conviction that he would do anything to undo the damage he had caused.

After the briefing, they assigned him to a squad. No one recognized him, or if they did, they didn't care who he was. Timoth reminded himself that no one knew what he had done. That unpleasant secret was contained within his family for now.

They loaded him into a cramped transport with his helmet flopping slightly on his head and a rifle at his side, going into battle with his fellow Sylvans. As he bumped and jostled along with the others in the enclosed space, he could see other transports behind them and hear the engine of the vehicles they had pulled together on short notice to make this happen.

He realized that at this moment - possibly heading off to meet his end - he had never felt closer to his countrymen in all his life.

SHAWAN LED HIS SQUAD to the choke point at the bay doors, and the Ascendancy troops there held them back. They would not be making it past the opening anytime soon, and being stuck in their present position was not helping them to complete their mission objectives.

The computer and the memory module were likely held somewhere beyond those doors, and he would have to change his tactics to get at them.

He pulled together a smaller group from the numbers who guarded their current position. He included himself in the unit, and two others. A man named Malcys, who was a known and trusted comrade, and Kari Bishop, an Ascended woman who had been a prisoner here - incarcerated for hacking administrative computers - would go with him.

"Cover us," he said to the others and then, winking at Raishann, "Be right back."

Raishann swung the end of her rifle over the barrier and fired at the bay doors. Others joined her while a small group stayed focused on the area to the rear.

Shawan and his cohorts leapt from behind their cover and crossed the open area that separated them from the door he wanted to access.

He looked back at Raishann and saw her fighting like a tiger. Yeah, that was his girl.

Kari shot the locking mechanism on the door, and Shawan kicked it in. They went through, checking the area with their guns raised.

An officer appeared across the room, and Malcys hit him with two shots. They continued with Malcys on point and Shawan bringing up the rear to protect Kari.

The group made their way through a series of rooms, inspecting each of them for computer equipment as they went. They took out more Ascended soldiers, some that they encountered as they moved forward, and a couple who came at them from behind.

They entered an expansive storage area, and Shawan and Malcys provided cover while Kari searched the shelves that lined the walls within. A soldier stepped into the doorway, and Shawan put two bullets into him.

"I think I see it!" Kari exclaimed, indicating an article on a high shelf. "That looks like what you described right there. Gotta be it."

"Watch the door," Shawan directed Malcys. He shouldered his weapon as he approached Kari.

She pointed out a computer on a shelf above his head. He was able to reach it, but just barely, and he used his fingertips to inch it to the shelf's edge so he could get his hands on it.

He got it out a little further and grabbed it, and the hissing of ion fire filled the room.

Shawan looked, still holding the object as it teetered halfway off the shelf, and Malcys fell to the floor. Kari fired past him, but the bullets made holes in the wall beside the soldier who had entered. Then there was another set of ion hisses mixed with percussive bursts of gunfire, and Shawan watched Kari topple as a burning arose in his chest.

Against his will, he collapsed, first slamming into the shelves, and then into the concrete floor. The computer he was trying to preserve tumbled down beside him, and chunks of it flew out in all directions as it impacted the unforgiving surface.

He put his hand to where the burning was coming from, and he heard more cracks of bullets being issued and ion fire hissing.

Shawan turned his head and saw the bulk of the computer laying there through the shrinking tunnel of his vision, with pieces strewn all around it.

Huh, he thought, *the damned thing is in as bad a shape as I am.*

Darkness closed in around him, and he tried to resist it but, finally, everything went black.

REPORTS OF THE ATTACK on Enswell Depot came into the administrative offices, and each was worse than the last.

Marshall pounded a fist on the long desk where he had assembled his advisors, watching the latest details coming in on the giant screens at the end of the room.

"Send in more troops!" he ordered.

"Your Worship," a woman halfway down the table leaned ahead to say, "We are making preparations to send reinforcements to the site, but they have to travel the entire distance over land due to Gate failures. It's the only way to get there now. We are receiving radio transmissions, but we cannot ascertain how they are arriving here. We think one of the damaged Gates may be transporting energy, but not matter."

"Find out which Gate is allowing communications and focus all repair efforts on it. How are the troops travelling?" he demanded.

"We are sending reinforcements to the depot via aircar," a man on the other side of the table reported. "It's the fastest thing we have to move numbers that large."

"How many soldiers and Guardians are there now?"

"Not enough, sir. We had just started moving people there when the attack started, and the Gates stopped working."

"People? You mean troops; people and bots."

"No, sir. The Guardians were not finished being outfitted for field combat when the Gates were disabled. There are a few at the depot on standard duty, but that is all."

"Fine," Marshall stated, standing up and making his way out of the room.

"Do everything you can to get troops to the depot and work on getting that Gate operational."

Alone in the corridor and marching with a sense of purpose to his office, Marshall was nervous. He thought of what he had imposed on Doyle Morgan and knew that the President might now see him in a similar light.

He could not allow his subordinates to guess his feelings. He needed to find a place to melt down in private.

LAENA HAD BEEN EJECTED from the Gate directly into the offices of some Ascendancy city.

Administrative staff leapt up at her appearance, and one of them tried to overtake her.

"Fuck you," she yelled, lunging toward the worker who had apparently seen too many action holos.

The man dropped to the floor, putting his hands behind his head.

"Good idea," Laena addressed to the room as she retrieved her rifle and fired a shot into the frame of the Gate behind her. A soldier from the depot was partially through it when the portal was destroyed, and his dismembered arm and a portion of one leg fell to the floor.

"How about everybody else get down too!" The people in the room dropped to their knees and clasped their fingers behind their necks.

She put on her data glasses and scanned her environment. A point in her field of vision blinked, showing a location to her left, and she took the glasses off and put them back into the pocket of her jumpsuit.

"Everybody stay where you are! Try to follow me, and I'll - well, don't follow me!" She jammed the man who had attempted heroism on top of the head with the butt of her rifle. He fell forward, unconscious, and she turned her attention back to the gasping crowd. "Yeah, that!" she said, backing toward the doorway that led to her next jump.

She ran into a crowd of curious observers who had been working in the next room. They stood gawking at her, and she wished she had been able to disguise herself as other Sylvans did when they infiltrated cities. Not that running through towns with a big gun wouldn't draw attention, anyway. Oh, well.

"Everybody down!" she commanded and fired a shot into the lights in the ceiling. Sparks rained down all around her. It was dramatic enough to elicit instant compliance from everyone in the room. They jumped behind desks and counters, doing anything they could to get out of her way.

I like this, she thought as she picked up her pace.

She left the room, repeated the process once more, and then made the jump out of the building.

At least she got away from the Ascendancy officers. If this had been any indicator, dealing with regular people was going to be way less trouble.

THE LUMINANTS WERE pinned down. The soldiers on the other side of the bay doors were standing their ground, and Ascendancy troops had come up from behind as well. Raishann's squad was effectively boxed in.

The rebels exchanged shots to the front and back and tried to stay out of the line of fire as much as possible.

Where were the other units? Surely they hadn't all been taken out.

In the distance she could still hear, beyond the fight she was engaged in, gunfire intermingled with the whining of ion rifles. No, her squad wasn't alone.

She rose above her cover and fired toward the bay door, then came back down. Maybe they should try to get out the way Dad left.

She listened again, noticing that the distant gunfire had stopped, and wondered if she shouldn't suggest moving from their position.

Then the barrage erupted again, closer this time, and peeking over the barrier she saw that the soldiers to their rear were now engaged with forces even farther away. She fired a volley of shots at the distracted officers, and one of them fell over. She squatted back down. This may work out yet.

Raishann's squad had enough numbers to keep themselves defended front and rear, but they moved a couple more soldiers to face the back. If they could eliminate the more vulnerable target, at least they would have the choice of going in that direction.

The firefight continued, and the number of Ascendancy soldiers at the rear position dwindled.

Raishann raised herself to fire again, and she could see that the surviving soldiers there were slowly rising with their empty hands held high. She lowered herself, still wary of gunfire from the bay door.

When she rose again to look behind her, she saw a squad of Luminants taking the remaining Ascendancy men as prisoners. Sylvans had subdued the combatants and were putting restraints on them. She crouched back down. "All clear to the rear!" she shouted.

The squad leader ordered them to move, and two rebels raised themselves to fire on the bay doors while the rest of them ran to join the comrades behind them.

Raishann moved at a pace equal to her teammates until she saw Baxter kneeling and putting restraints on one of the taken soldiers.

She bolted, and shouldered her rifle as she ran. He turned in her direction, and his eyes widened. When he was finished what he was doing, he stood and moved toward her.

She was still moving fast when she grabbed him, knocking the air from his lungs. He embraced her, and while his mouth was beside her ear, he whispered, "I'm sorry."

She pulled back to face him with her arms still around his shoulders. She looked into his eyes and felt her soul pour out to him.

"So?" she asked. She knew it wasn't really the time for it, but she had lost all awareness of where she was and could restrain herself no longer. Her adoration far outweighed her sensibilities.

"So?" Baxter repeated, not sure what she was driving at.

"So, are you ever gonna kiss me, or what?"

Chapter 19

TIMOTH'S SQUAD WAS sent to do cleanup, moving into the building after the main forces had swept through. They were to eliminate Ascendancy soldiers that were left behind and acting on their own, or sneaking up on Luminant squads from behind.

Timoth had not fired a shot as his team moved from area to area. There were shouts of 'Clear!' as they entered a room, or, if there were an Ascendancy soldier or two, they were taken care of by the men at the front while Tim covered the rear.

They moved into an open storage space, and Timoth noticed that even though no one had called it as being clear, no shots were fired either. They walked deeper into the large room, and then the call came - "Wounded! We have wounded in here!"

A soldier with a medical symbol on his uniform rushed past Tim and went to the fallen Sylvan.

Tim scanned the area behind the squad for Ascendancy officers but snapped to attention when the medic spoke. "Shawan," the field doctor said. "Hang in there. We're gonna take care of you."

Timoth lowered his weapon and pushed his way between his squadmates. "Let me through!"

There were two bodies on the floor near his father: a dead man and a wounded and unconscious young woman. Shawan was semi-conscious and laying between two rows of shelves with some broken computer equipment strewn around him. There was a huge burn mark on his shirt, and the smell of scorched flesh entered Tim's nostrils.

Timoth knelt beside his dad, and when he moved to touch him, the medic blocked his attempt. Tim looked at the corpsman and saw the seriousness in his expression and complied with his gestural prompt.

"Dad," he said. Shawan opened his eyes feebly and rolled his head toward the sound. "Dad, they'll help you. You're gonna be alright."

The other men gathered around and became distracted by what was going on. The squad leader looked at Timoth. "You can stay here with the doc. The rest of you, let's move!"

The men dispersed, and Timoth returned his attention to his father as the medic examined the girl who had also been shot.

"Tim," his dad said weakly, "Tim, it's okay. I'm sorry."

"No, dad, it's me who's sorry. I'm the one who did wrong." Tears trickled down his face and neck, and he tried to look reassuring as he regarded his dad through the distorted lenses of his watery eyes. "Dad, I'm so sorry."

"You're a good boy, Tim," his father said. Shawan smiled weakly, and his head turned to one side, and then his eyes stared into nothing.

"Dad?" Tim beckoned. "Dad!"

Timoth looked at the medic as he checked for a pulse on Shawan's neck. The practitioner peered back into his red face and shook his head.

Tim held back as much as he was able, but the tears kept rolling as he repeated "I'm sorry" several more times.

The medic stood and shouldered his rifle, then lifted the wounded girl fireman-carry style before he went through the door the squad had used to exit.

Timoth hung his head and closed his father's eyes with one hand. "I love you," he whispered.

"Hello Tim," said a blurred shape in the entrance. Tim fumbled for his rifle, then realized that if the owner of the voice had wanted him dead, he would have been gone already. Tim squinted through the impairing liquid in his eyes and saw a familiar face in an unfamiliar uniform.

"What are you doing here, Mr Morgan?" he asked.

"This is what I do now," Doyle clarified. "I have something for you," he said, reaching behind him. Tim tightened his grip on his rifle and observed as the man held out what appeared to be a grenade. An unseen hiss of ion discharge came from the far side of the room, and Doyle's expression dropped.

Timoth wondered what had just happened. His rifle was pointed in Mr Morgan's direction, and he checked to ensure that he had not discharged a round, even though he knew otherwise. He hadn't.

Doyle fell to his knees, and Timoth saw the source of the shot that had taken him down. A tall man was standing behind Mr Morgan, wearing Ascendancy soldier gear and grinning.

Timoth's rifle was already pointed at the murderer, so he just pulled the trigger. His gun bucked, and the soldier reeled backwards, casting a spray of blood from his head as he went.

"Timoth!" Doyle called, and Tim got down next to him. "Did you get him?"

"Yeah. I did, Mr Morgan."

"Who did this? Who shot me in the back? I need to know - I have a bet with myself."

Tim left him for a moment and came right back. "The name on his uniform says 'M Burke'."

"I fucking knew it," Doyle sputtered. Then a smile spread across his face, and he regarded Timoth. "You got him for me, though, didn't you? I guess this will be my last chance to stick it to that bastard," he said through red teeth and some blood that spilt from between his lips. "He was an asshole, and I'm glad he's dead." He chuckled, and little splashes of blood came out with the sounds. "Take this," Doyle said, holding out the object in his hand. "It's important."

Timoth took what he had thought was a grenade but now could see was a small electronic device.

"It's the memory module from the computer that was here, Tim," Doyle said, through his bleeding grin. "I heard it might be valuable."

BY THE TIME CANDACE noticed the change in direction, she was already fed up.

She had followed the path out of Enswell that she found traced onto a hand-drawn map hanging in the hidden room. Now, she was on foreign terrain, and the anger that overcame her fear was all that kept her moving.

The tracker she had put on Baxter indicated that he had been stationary as she approached, but now he was racing toward the east.

She was forced to veer from the trail to intercept the signal that blipped on her pad. He was getting closer, and she was glad she did not have to go as far as she formerly assumed. She cut through the forest to save time, leaving the path she had followed this far in favour of the direct approach.

Candace had never been outside before. She had seen pictures of nature, and she thought it would be charming and serene, but it was not long before she hated it.

Everything was poking and scraping her, and she felt as though the forest was hindering her on purpose, just to be rude.

She clawed her way through the woodlands and brush, cursing each problematic stride until she arrived at another path that appeared to align with the direction she needed to go.

The delicate woman brushed off her clothing and pulled a broken piece of a branch out of her hair before checking her pad for the tracker signal once again.

She looked up from the device, confirming that she was indeed headed in the correct direction.

Though she had exited the forest and the trees were no longer scratching her, she continued to curse with every step she took.

DOYLE MORGAN KNEW THAT he was dying.

He felt like he was ready to go, having played a role in turning the tide on the people who had taken his life and given nothing back. At least he would have retribution.

He reached out to the young man who knelt next to him and told him to listen carefully. He had to get everything out in the short time he had remaining.

"Module will work in a Guardian," he sputtered. "But can't shoot it with ion beam - ruin circuits." He coughed and saw the red spittle that issued forth. He had to force himself to ignore it and carry on. "Power. Pack. Disable power pack."

Timoth started to ask a question, but Doyle held up a hand and shook his head. Tim would have to figure out how to do that himself.

"Take my comm badge," he said, looking down at the nameplate on his shirt. Damn, there was a lot of blood there. "Take it."

The youth unpinned the badge and examined it.

Doyle tried to point, but he was getting weaker and had trouble lifting his arm. "Press. Button. 'Bot will come to you. Homing beacon. If need their help."

Timoth put the badge into a jacket pocket and stood. He reached around and put the module into his pack, and then looked at Doyle, wondering what he should do next.

"Go," Doyle said weakly. The young man hesitated. "Go!" he barked with what little force he had left in him.

Timoth headed toward an exit on the far side of the room but stopped to kneel beside the body of a soldier. He said something Doyle could not hear and then continued out the door.

Doyle strained to look at the corpse of the Sylvan fighter, but his strength left him, and he joined the fallen rebel in death.

LAENA MADE HER LAST jump, exiting a Gate near the edge of Enswell.

She followed a sub-map that showed an exit from the city through a maintenance shaft and found herself in the forest.

She hurried, anticipating her arrival in Nylen and knowing that she would be home soon. The smells of the forest and the familiarity of her surroundings invigorated her as she left Enswell far behind.

A shape came out of the forest to her left, and onto the trail ahead of her. It was a woman, and Laena moved to the edge of the path and hid behind some brush.

The woman fidgeted with her clothes and hair and appeared to be checking a device as if verifying something. Then she marched off, tromping up the trail and not appearing to be happy about it.

Laena raised her ion rifle and came out into the trail again, moving stealthily until she was within twenty meters of the woman.

"Hey," she yelled at the lady's back. The marching ceased, and the woman froze in place.

"I'm with the Ascendancy," she said, rotating to face Laena.

"Well, I'm not!" Laena shouted. "Put your hands in the air where I can see them and keep turning around. Slow!"

The dishevelled woman raised her empty hands and appeared more insulted than threatened. Either way, she wasn't impressed.

Laena could see that she wasn't a soldier. She looked more like an Ascended business type, but she was so far out of context that Laena couldn't imagine what the old gal was doing outside the city walls.

"Who are you?" Laena demanded.

"I am Candace Clarke. From Enswell."

"What are you doing out here, Candace Clarke from Enswell?"

"I am searching for my son. He is out there somewhere, in the battle at the depot." Candace jerked her head behind her.

Laena wondered if she hadn't somehow stumbled into a bad drama. A weird woman in the middle of the forest blathering about a battle? What was going on here? But, she decided that the unlikely traveller could be trouble if left to her own devices, and maybe she had some answers.

"Well, you're coming with me, Candace," Laena said, moving forward. "You may be of use."

"No!" the muddled woman yelled. "I have to find Baxter!"

Candace lowered her hands and appeared almost crazed. Laena issued a warning, but when the lady kept moving, Laena fired two shots, the first of which hit the woman in the left thigh and as she twisted with the impact the second caught her right forearm.

The woman fell to her knees and reached for her newly scorched upper leg, but quickly withdrew her hand after touching the wound. She screamed in agony and sat down before rolling back to lay flat.

"Shit," Laena said under her breath. She walked over to the wounded woman. There was a bag next to her writhing frame, and she took it and searched its contents. There was no water or food or weapon in it, and Laena thought this person must be nuts to be out here without supplies. She threw the bag back to the ground. "Well, you're no good to me anymore. I told you not to move!"

Laena backed away from the fallen woman, toward her destination. "Sorry, but I gotta go."

She turned and picked up her pace again, heading deeper into the forest. "Crazy bitch," she muttered.

Laena wondered what the woman had meant about a battle at a depot. She checked her map as she jogged, and saw an Ascendancy outpost not too far from where she was.

Perhaps it would be best to put off her arrival in Nylen to make one last detour.

She left the wounded Ascended woman behind and made her way toward the alleged conflict.

If her friends and neighbours were in a fight, they would need Laena there more than they did at home.

BAXTER STAYED WITH the combined squad alongside Raishann. His heart was so full he thought he might burst.

He had to put it aside for now, to keep his focus on what he was doing. At the same time, her presence gave him a renewed sense of purpose.

Timoth came around the next corner, and Raishann held out an arm to the squadron who raised their weapons in his direction. The soldiers lowered their guns, and she went to him and opened her arms to receive him. Timoth hugged her, then pushed back, creating some space between them.

"What's wrong?" Raishann asked, taking in Timoth's sober features. She raised her voice. "Tim, what's wrong?"

"Dad's dead," Timoth said flatly. Raishann froze for a moment before opening her mouth to ask if he was sure, but the welling in Tim's eyes and serious look on his face answered her. She embraced him, and there were no sounds from them as large tears rolled and soaked each other's uniforms.

Baxter stood back, feeling his own sense of loss. He wanted to say or do something, but he was unsure what his level of participation should be.

Tim backed away from her, and they both wiped their eyes. Then Timoth addressed the squad. "Are any of you carrying ion weapons?" A member of the unit said he was, and Timoth told that man not to engage any O-bots. Raishann asked why, and Tim said that they needed one intact and he didn't think there were very many left. He took out the memory module and showed it, stating that a Guardian's onboard computer could run whatever was on it.

"Fine," the squad leader said. He addressed his soldiers, yelling, "No one is to engage a Guardian with an ion weapon. Clear?" The rebels grunted their acknowledgement, and the Commander turned back to Tim. "You have a mission to fulfill, and we have ours. Good luck."

The ranking soldier rallied the garrison and Raishann reached out to Timoth. They looked into each other's eyes and nodded. There would be time for grieving once this was over. For now, they had to remain focused on what they were doing. They could not allow their father's death to be in vain.

Timoth went past the squad as they continued their sweep.

Raishann soldiered on quietly, eyes streaked with vessels and lids puffy with tears. Baxter stayed close to her but said nothing.

He knew what it was to lose a father and he would share her burden later, once this was finished.

LAENA ARRIVED AT THE facility to find smoke billowing from a massive hole in the side of it and signs and sounds of battle emanating from within. She approached with her rifle ready and crossed over the rubble that separated the outside of the building from its inside. There was very little wall left there.

She ambled in, taking in every detail before her. There were dead soldiers, both Sylvan and Ascended, but there seemed to be a lot more Ascended casualties. There were a couple of unmoving bots laying among the dead, and she stepped over one as she continued her entrance.

What the hell was going on here? She considered for a moment that she might leave and finish her journey home.

The shape of a young man entered her view, obscured by the dust and smoke that hung in the air, and she raised her ion rifle, aiming it just as he pointed his at her. "What's going on here?" she asked in a sharp voice as she strained to see him better.

"Who are you?" the boy overlapped her.

"I asked you first," Laena stated as though it mattered.

"Are you Sylvan or Ascended?" came the reply. She thought it would be evident from her skin tone and features, but she was wearing a prison uniform and he probably couldn't see her clearly, either.

"What?" Laena asked.

"You have an Ascendancy weapon. If you're with them I'm not lowering this."

"Oh fuck," she said, dropping her gun to her side. "I am not 'with them'. My name is Laena Reisatra, and I'm just trying to get home to my village."

The young man relaxed and lowered his rifle. "Laena? It's Timoth Forander. They took you in the raid. How did you-" He started toward her.

An energy blast ripped the dirty air between them, and they both headed for the same source of cover. They got down behind it, and Laena peeked out. "Fucking bot," she said as she readied her weapon.

"No!" Timoth yelled, grabbing her gun. She looked back at him tersely.

"Are you nuts?" she asked.

"Not with an ion rifle. We need it."

"What? What for?"

"I actually brought it here on purpose with this." He showed her Doyle's blood-spattered comm badge. "That thing can run a memory module that's supposed to save us." He looked serious.

"Okay, fine. Sounds important enough," she said as she lowered the gun. "So, what do we do? Let it shoot us?"

"We have to disable the power supply. We can get at it through its back."

"Fine," Laena said. She moved to the edge of their cover, away from the bot. "Cover me," she ordered, already moving out.

Timoth brought his weapon to bear on the Guardian, firing a volley of bullets that would put it on the defensive without destroying it.

Laena ran as fast as she could to the edge of the corridor and passed through an open door. She checked the room as she entered, then headed for an exit on the other side.

As she went from room to room, she oriented herself so she would make her way back to the corridor, but on the opposite side of the O-bot from where she had left Tim.

After going through two more rooms, she peeked out a door and saw her goal. The Guardian was only doing a half-assed job of covering itself, taking confidence from its protective armour. It fired on Timoth occasionally, and Timoth returned in kind.

If she could just shoot the damned thing, this could be over in two seconds, but she altered her tactics to align with the new mission parameters.

Backing into the room again, she slung her gun across her back and pulled her knife from its sheath, ripped a sleeve off of her shirt, and wrapped it around the handle in anticipation of a potential electrical shitstorm.

Laena exited through the door and closed the gap silently, side-stepping toward her target with her knife-wielding hand forward. When she came upon the metal soldier, she slowed and took careful aim at a space between its armoured back panels and thrust the knife in.

The machine writhed, trying to reach her, and Laena jumped and put her legs around its waist and reached around with one hand to hang on. It fired wildly as it tried to remove her, and Laena kept pushing and twisting the knife into the tight gap between its backplates.

The metal woman twisted, trying to reach over its shoulder, and Laena could see Timoth charging toward the O-bot at full speed.

The machine turned to face its new adversary and leaned ahead slightly to engage. Laena felt the tip of the knife slide into its purchase, and she pulled down, putting all of her weight on the handle, levering a space between the plates.

Timoth hit the bot with full force, and the three of them went down in a heap. Laena felt a dull pain from her leg, where it was pinned between the Guardian and the floor. She grimaced but continued to ply the knife.

The O-bot backhanded Timoth in the face and his body slid across the floor before coming to a stop.

The robot tried to roll onto its back, but Laena stuck her strong leg out to remove any leverage it might have. It turned the other way, and the knife handle became all that Laena had to hang on to. The robot tried to rise, and the combination of her weight and the bot's movement popped the plate off its back.

Laena fell with a rude thump, and the knife flew back, clanging as it skittered across the floor. The breath blew from her body, and she gasped for air but none came.

The bot hovered over her, and its eyes gleamed without mercy as it stepped forward, confident in its victory.

It reached down, taking a handful of her shirt in its steel fist, and lifted her from the floor. Her breath came back, and Laena went for the rifle over her shoulder, forgoing the value of the mission in exchange for the preservation of her life.

The bot stopped, frozen in place with Laena partially lifted from the floor. Then its eyes became dim, and it fell forward.

Laena placed her good foot between the Guardian's breasts and ushered it past her as it slumped to the ground.

Looking up, she saw Timoth, holding the knife while blood streamed down his face and his chest heaved with full breaths.

Laena caught her breath. "Kid, you look absolutely badass right now."

He laughed, and she smiled at him.

"Now," she said dryly, "there was something about a memory module?"

Timoth said that they needed to find another O-bot that had been taken out with an ion weapon. He explained that it would have its internal circuitry fried, but its power supply would still be functional.

They would install the memory module in the unit they had taken down, then apply a fresh power cell to the system.

Laena suggested that they get on with it, and they left the disabled Guardian to find another with tell-tale ion scorching indicating its cause of death.

Chapter 20

THOUGH HE HAD RETURNED to his work in the lab, things were much more difficult for William. He was removed from his quarters and placed in general population with the other prisoners, except during work hours.

He had been limited in what he could do and watched more closely, but his rebellious spirit would not stop looking for ways to assist the Luminants. William was tracking Laena's progress by monitoring her datapad whenever it was connected to a network. When the Gates at the Enswell facility disappeared, he tapped into the audio and video on the device to find out what was happening.

He could see nothing - the pad must be in Laena's pack, but the sounds he heard did not please him. There were sounds of gunfire and people shouting. Every once in a while he heard a loud impact, and he thought Laena must be banging the pad against something.

He tapped into the pad's text to speech capabilities and sent a message: Laena? Are you there?

He waited for a response, and he could hear a female voice talking with a boy. He sent the message again.

"What the hell is that?" he heard through his earpiece. He sent it again. Then were shuffling and banging noises, and then the video feed lightened.

The pad came out of its bag, and he had his first good look at the woman he had helped. He opened his video feed so she could see him, as well.

"Who is this?" the woman on his screen asked.

William typed at his keyboard and sent the message to be spoken out loud by her pad. "I am the man who sent you the maps. My name is William Clarke."

"Holy shit!" came the male voice.

The video shifted abruptly, and then a familiar face appeared. "Shadaar!" the face exclaimed. "You're alive!"

"Hello, Timoth. Yes, I am very much alive. What is going on there?" the pad said on his behalf.

"The Ascendancy was going to attack Sylva, but we got to them first. We're in the facility just outside of Enswell."

William tapped out another message. "Is there anything you need?"

"Well, no. I guess not. Wait, can you control any of the facility infrastructure from there?"

"I can try," the pad said to them.

"See if you can close the main internal bay door, then activate the fire system on the north side of it. Think you can do that?"

"I will try. Watch for it." the pad replied.

"Bye for now," Timoth said.

The video shifted again, and Laena came back into view. "Thank you," she said, and the screen went blank.

William searched for ways to get his terminal to connect with the depot's control systems. After doing some creative programming, he accessed the building's computer and put the requests he had received into effect.

There was a tap on his shoulder, and he turned to face the guard standing behind him. William smiled weakly, and the guard furrowed his brow at him.

"You seem like a smart guy, but you simply refuse to learn," the large man said as he drew his weapon and motioned for William to get up.

William poked at a couple more controls before the guard hauled him out of his chair. He said nothing as he walked at gunpoint toward the familiar Gate in the lab.

"Man, you have brought a whole world of suffering upon yourself, do you realize that?"

William knew the potential consequences he would incur because of his actions, but he was more concerned that the Ascendancy meet its end.

"They're going to kill you, you know."

William breathed a sigh of relief. He had been enough trouble that the Warden would apply the consequences directly to him, and not Baxter.

Good.

BAXTER'S SQUAD WAS mired at the bay doors.

The exchanges of gunfire were growing tedious. Neither side was losing or gaining anything. Raishann fired over their cover and then came down slowly.

"Something weird is going on," she reported to the rest of them.

The bay doors were closing, and there was a lot of loud and confused chatter coming from the other side.

A small cadre of Guardians came out of the slowly closing doors and positioned themselves to the left and right.

The rebel squad fired on them, but only one went down after taking a precisely placed bullet in a vulnerable area. The rest of their rounds deflected off the metal bodies as the Guardians made their way out.

"They're moving to flank us!" the squad leader called out.

"What's happening?" Baxter asked Raishann.

"Now that the doors are closing, they aren't protecting those men anymore, so they're going on the offensive."

"Prepare to fall back!" came the voice of their leader. Shots rang from their position as they awaited the order to retreat.

A klaxon sounded on the other side of the doors as they sealed and a loud hissing sound began that did not stop. They could hear coughing from beyond the sealed doors which dwindled to nothing.

The Guardians fired on the Luminants' position, and a couple of them dropped to all fours. Through small gaps in their hiding place, Baxter could see the bots sneaking around them on both sides.

"Fall back!" came the order from the squad leader. He put out cover fire, and Baxter and Raishann moved with the others, staying as low as they could.

Then the Guardians all stood up straight - whether they were behind cover or not - and dropped their weapons. They lowered their hands to their sides, and their eyes faded to black.

"Hold up!" the squad leader called. The retreating Luminants stopped but stayed down, wondering what had changed. There was no more gunfire, and though the hissing behind the bay door could still be heard, there were no more sounds of people.

The Luminants at the front cautiously stood with their weapons raised, not trusting what their eyes were seeing. "The bots aren't moving! They're deactivated or something," one of them said.

Everyone stood now, looking at the mannequins who, just moments earlier, had threatened their lives.

"What happened?" Baxter asked, directing the question to anyone who may have an answer.

"I happened," came a bright female voice from behind them.

Baxter pivoted, bringing up his gun, then allowing it to fall again as he saw the answer to his question.

A Guardian was walking toward him, which would have alarmed him except that it was flanked by Timoth and a Sylvan woman striding casually beside it.

"What is going on?" Baxter called to them.

"I think that, other than cleaning this mess up, the battle is over," the Sylvan woman said. "This," she indicated their android companion, "is your memory module in action. It's an artificial intelligence who shut down all the O-bots."

Raishann recognized Laena beneath the dirt and strange garments and dropped her gun as she ran to meet her friend. They embraced one another tightly, adding to Baxter's confusion.

Raish broke the hug and regarded her brother. "What about the doors, Tim? What happened to those soldiers?" she queried.

"That," Timoth said, "Was Shadaar. He closed the doors and gassed those guys with the fire suppressors."

Baxter could not believe what he heard. "Shadaar? My father? Alive?"

"Yes, yes, and yes," Timoth said. "We were talking to him on a pad, but it got smashed when we were looking for an O-bot body for - well, for her." He gestured toward the Guardian at his side.

Raishann went to Baxter and put a hand on his shoulder. He looked at her and smiled through watering eyes and squeezed her tightly, laughing and crying at the same time. "I'm sorry about your father," he consoled.

"Me, too. But I'm glad about yours."

The squad leader called out for the soldiers to assemble and prepare to move out to take prisoners, and there were cheers from the Luminants and claps on shoulders as they reorganized themselves.

Baxter whispered to Raishann, "It's over," and she said nothing for a moment before replying that she thought this was only the beginning. Baxter agreed that it was an apt description of where they had arrived.

He pondered his journey and the irony of it all. He had come from being Ascended, oppressed and mostly unhappy, to being a criminal in the eyes of the Ascendancy, and more content than he had ever been. He was at peace with himself and what he stood for.

He studied Raishann, who was sharing the burden of her loss with her most cherished friend, and breathed easily, confident for the first time that everything would be alright.

TIMOTH SAT AT THE KITCHEN table in the Forander home. His mother and sister sat near him, and the air was thick with seriousness.

"What are we going to do with you?" his mom asked him.

"I don't know. Whatever you figure is right, I suppose."

"Yes, but what is right? You acted directly against the Sylvan people, but then were instrumental in the mission's success at the outpost."

"A real conundrum," Raishann said.

Timoth said nothing, prepared for whatever his family resolved to be the best course of action.

"We have decided not to tell anyone else about what happened. We'll keep this to ourselves," his mom delivered.

Timoth repressed a smile. It could have been a whole lot worse.

"But," she whispered as she leaned in closer, "we will be watching you."

Timoth sobered, realizing that he was nowhere near off the hook for what he had done. It would take a lot of convincing to prove that he regretted his actions.

"We need you to know that if you ever do anything to undermine the Luminants, or do anything hurtful to any Sylvan - man, woman, or child - we will turn you in and take whatever heat comes our way for protecting you. Is that understood?"

Timoth stood and projected his most sincere voice. "Yes, Mom."

Aellana extended a hand to the door, and Timoth was acutely aware of the eyes that watched him as he nervously left the house.

He had a lot of work to do. He exited into the bright daylight, and Raishann followed him outside.

Timoth turned to her. He wanted to say something but couldn't think of anything appropriate, and she put an arm around him.

"It'll be okay, Tim," she said, turning to walk up the street. "Come with me. There's someplace I want to show you."

BAXTER WATCHED INCREDULOUSLY.

There, seated before him and the others who had gathered to witness the spectacle, was the O-bot who had helped to save them all. A compartment on its chest was open, and the exposed mechanisms twitched, and indicator lights blinked as it moved.

Baxter was brought in to examine the android because, of all the people around, he would be the most familiar with the machine and its inner workings.

Everyone watched as Baxter closed up the compartment, tightening the fasteners that held it shut. "Everything seems to be working normally, except for its AI. The O-bots have a simple operating system that allows them to act on their own, or follow straightforward directives, but this is unlike anything

I have ever encountered. The AI is reconfiguring parts of the body. That's not even supposed to be possible. My friend Lila would love to study this thing."

The android looked at Baxter, and he could see its eyes adjusting to the new focal distance. "Am I a thing?" the bot queried.

"You are an artificial intelligence housed in the frame of a Guardian."

It glanced down and examined itself. "I have the outward appearance a woman," it said.

"Well, the O-bots were made to appear female to be less intimidating to the public," Baxter clarified. "But, yes, I suppose that if you see yourself as female, that is fine. What are you called?"

The bot returned its gaze to him. "I am designated as the Overwatch Geologic System Artificial Intelligence," it said.

"That doesn't work for us. It would be easier if we had something we could call you."

It regarded Baxter, calculating. "I am a female?" it asked.

"Yes, okay, if that is how you self-identify."

"And I am the first of my kind?"

"As far as I know. I have seen lots of robots and different AI, but I've never encountered anything like you."

The bot looked away for a moment. "I have searched my databases for appropriate designations." It waited, and Baxter thought it wanted choose wisely before committing. "My name will be Eve," it finally said.

"Hello, Eve," Baxter said, smiling. "It's nice to meet you."

Epilogue

MARSHALL SAT, FLANKED by a pair of Guardians, and facing a holographic projection. The holo image showed three people, two of whom he did not recognize, standing over him on either side of the President.

"Mr Marshall," the President began. Marshall was acutely aware that President Windsor had not called him Chancellor. He supposed he had lost that title already. "You have failed to uphold the expectations and high standards set forth by the Ascendancy."

Marshall said nothing but became determined to ascend once again from whatever ashes his descent would reduce him to.

"We have already deliberated and decided on justice that best suits your demonstrated lack of commitment to your superiors."

Lack of commitment? Marshall thought. No one had done more than he had to fulfill his mandates. It wasn't his fault that things happened as they did.

This was Doyle Morgan's fault! He should have eliminated him much sooner. Even in death, Morgan was still causing problems for him.

"Your sentence is as follows, and to be carried out immediately."

Marshall braced himself.

"You will be stripped of all implants and upgrades. And then you will be brought to the 13th city."

What? Maybe this would not be as bad as he thought it might be.

"There, you will act in the capacity of a domestic servant, carrying out the will of whoever you are assigned to."

Oh, no. No! A slave! He was being made a slave!

Marshall jumped from his chair, but cold metal hands on each shoulder pushed him back down and held him in place. His face reddened, and his vision blurred as his eyes welled. The Ascended predilection for using people rather than androids as servants had once given him a sense power and dominance. But now he wished he had never heard of the 13th city. A part of the former Chancellor wanted assurance that he would be treated better than those who had been under his subjugation, although he knew that would never happen.

"For as long as you have known of its existence, you have desired admission to the 13th. So, welcome."

Marshall writhed in his chair as the holos blinked out. There had to be a way out of this. The Guardians took him by either arm and led him to a Gate.

"Wait!" he called out to the holographic representation of the President, even though it was gone. There must be someone he could appeal to or something that could be done.

"Unhand me!" he commanded the androids. The bot on his right accessed the control panel, and the portal momentarily flashed, and when it came back on, Marshall saw a different destination than the one that had been there before.

"Where are you taking me?" He screamed at the bots, buckling his knees so they had to carry his full weight.

The Guardian on his left answered in its soft voice. "Home."

SURVIVORS OF THE BATTLE of Enswell Depot had been all been triaged and treated, and those who required additional care were convalescing wherever room could be found, with only the most severely injured staying in the ward. Proximity to the hospital was based on people's potential need for further medical attention.

The funeral services for Shawan and the others who died during the raid had come and gone, and the Forander family was reestablishing itself in their patriarch's absence. An Ascended woman, Kari, had been there when Shawan died, and she spoke eloquently about Shawan from the wheelchair she occupied while recovering from her injuries. It was very touching, and the speech provided the Foranders with a sense of closure.

Timoth had changed - he was quieter even than before - but Raishann thought he would be okay after some time. He carried a lot of guilt, and she did not speak to him about it directly but tried to be as supportive as she could. She had to remind him sometimes not to be angry with people who called him a hero for what he had accomplished at the depot. He had to remember that they did not know about the reestablishment of trust he was working to build.

Aellana was mourning but continued her daily routines without changing anything, except to resolve to be more active within the Luminants once again. She didn't feel guilty about her absence during her husband's death - she knew that events happened as they were meant to, and believed there must have been a reason for it - but she felt she owed it to him to continue what he had died for. When Mrs Reisatra asked her about it, she said that yes, she would have stayed with Shawan forever, but forever had come and gone, as it sometimes does, and now she had to move on without him. As the weeks went by, she even started to smile occasionally.

Raishann quickly developed a fascination with Eve and insisted to her mother that the android come to stay with them at the house. Eve was a welcomed distraction and began forging a role for herself within the family.

Baxter stayed in the village, too, and Raishann was glad to have him nearby. The pair had become as inseparable as fate could have possibly made them. He was right for her, and he was also helpful to Aellana around the house and supportive of Timoth.

Baxter came over frequently for meals and was at ease with his new love and her family, but tonight he was polite but less talkative than usual.

Raishann asked him what was going on and he said that he was thinking about his dad. He said he was sorry that Shawan was gone, and knew how that loss felt. His father had died too, and Baxter had gone through the services and the grieving process. Now, he was overjoyed to hear that Father was alive, but the knowledge of his circumstances left a burning sensation in Baxter's chest.

Baxter had asked the Luminants about the possibility of a rescue mission, but they told him there was nothing they could do.

He had been disappointed when he asked Laena about the location of Aldergate, and she did not know precisely where it was. Having come home through a series of Gates, some of which had been destroyed, left her impression of the prison's whereabouts in a perimeter of several hundred kilometers, but she couldn't even be entirely sure of that. All Laena knew for sure was that it was a long, long distance to the southwest. There was no way they could search that much ground.

Then Eve moved from where she was and came to stand beside the table. "I know where Aldergate is," she said.

"What?" yelped Baxter, nearly choking on his food. "You haven't said anything about this before now?"

"This is the first time anyone has mentioned it to me. I would be happy to show you where your father is."

They left the meal on the table as everyone got up, scrambling to find as many maps as they could.

WILLIAM SAT BACK, SATISFIED with his contribution to the attack on the depot. He wondered what it was going to cost him.

The Warden went through a tirade of procedural whatever's, and William didn't hear a word of it. It was not until they called his name twice and the guard next to him struck him that he paid any attention.

"William Clarke," the Warden directed at him. "Do you have anything to say in your defence?"

"You know you work for an evil institution, right?"

The Warden turned to the record keeper. "Strike that last statement from the official recordings." The record keeper touched some controls at her station, then confirmed that she had carried out the order.

"Very well," the Warden continued. "Being that you have nothing to state in defence of yourself, I will keep this brief. Your wife has proven to be a valued citizen of the Ascendancy, and she will continue to rise as she strives to make the 12 cities better. She is one of us, and she shall prosper." The pompous man paused, knowing the question that must be plaguing William. "Your son? It seems he has cast his lot, as well. He has left Enswell and has not been seen since the Sylvan raid against our troops."

William's mouth curled up at its corners, and the Warden stamped out his relief quickly. "If Baxter Clarke is seen either inside an Ascendancy city or is observed anywhere outside of one, he is to be put to death immediately. Shot on sight." The stern man was entertained by William squirming against his restraints and somewhat surprised that no snide comment came from the prisoner. That was more like it.

"As for you, the burdens you have placed on the Administration have finally outweighed your potential for further contribution. You will be executed." William calmed and seemed to be okay with his fate. The Warden would change that, as well. "But your sentence will not be carried out here. It will take place in Midtown Square in the city of Enswell one week from today. We wish to ensure that we have adequate time to advertise the spectacle and ensure a good turnout. The citizens of the Ascendancy will get to see a dangerous terrorist removed from society, and your death will serve as a reminder to the people of what happens to traitors."

The Warden scanned the room and saw nothing but agreement in the surrounding faces.

"Sentence is passed and scheduled for seven days from today." William was picked up from his chair and escorted from the chamber.

"Have a pleasant week, traitor," the Warden added with a grin.

AS SHE STROLLED ALONG the gently curving streets of Enswell, Lila had no way of knowing what had become of the memory module, or what had happened to Raishann. It bothered her, and she really could have used some resolution to ease her mind over the issue.

So many questions remained unanswered. The only thing she knew for sure was that Baxter was gone. But she did not know if he had left the city, been arrested or otherwise detained, or even if he was alive or dead.

A part of her carried guilt over having been involved in a failed operation because she assumed that her ineptitude had been a significant contributor to that failure. Raishann took the fall and kept her involvement in the illicit affair hidden, and Lila hadn't even been able to thank her for that. Getting caught doing those types of things must be a known risk to the Luminants, but they followed through anyway, hopeful that the gains of success would outweigh the consequences of failure. Raishann had surely known what she was getting herself into when she gave herself up to save someone she barely knew. It was admirable.

Lila had always hoped that she would have the grace and courage to rise to the occasion when it counted, and Raishann had exemplified those traits. She wondered what it would take to get from her current state to where she wanted to be.

Heading toward her home, Lila found that she looked upon the surrounding people differently as they moved past the shiny surfaces in the diffuse light of the city. She saw herself as being disconnected from them even as she existed among them and it felt strange to occupy a place so precariously balanced between those opposed points.

She automatically veered off toward the main doors when she arrived in front of her building, despite its looking like every other in her vicinage. The door opened when she walked up to it, and as she crossed the lobby, she was startled from her thoughts by an unfamiliar voice calling from behind her.

"Lila Riley?" a young man asked. Lila turned and assessed him quickly as he approached. He was not a policeman, but beyond that, she had no idea who he might be.

"Yes," she offered hesitantly.

The well-dressed man scanned the area and invited Lila to follow him back outside. The thoughts of danger she had just processed were fresh in her mind, but there were a lot of people around, and she saw no potential harm coming from being on the busy sidewalk any more than there was a threat right where she was. She started for the door, and the man cut in front of her and led her back to the street.

Once they were outside, Lila stopped, forcing the man to turn and confront her. She did not want to stray too far from the familiar surroundings and people of her building. "Can we walk together?" he coaxed, jerking his head in the direction he proposed to go.

"Not until I know who you are."

"Right now all you need to know," he stated as he faced her squarely, "is that Raishann sent me to find you."

Lila stood, stunned and processing what he had just said. If Raishann Forander had sent him, he must be a Luminant, which meant that her unspoken questions could be answered. Accompanying him was now worth the risk.

The man turned part way around again before he started down the sidewalk and Lila followed him, abundantly interested in where this might take her.

"WHAT HAPPENED? WHERE am I?"

"Hold still, Mrs Clarke."

"Who are you? Why can't I see?"

"Candace, I need you to stop moving. I am Dr Samuels, and this is Chief Technician Westerman. You have undergone a series of surgeries over the past several weeks."

Chief Westerman said hello, but Candace ignored her. "I don't understand. Surgeries for what?"

"For starters, ion fire severely damaged your leg and arm. They found you unconscious from blood loss outside Enswell after you sent a distress signal from a pad."

"Where is Baxter? Where is my boy?" She squinted, and despite opening her eyes as wide as she could, she saw only darkness.

"One thing at a time. You were brought in by Ascendancy forces whose transports ceased functioning just outside the city. Chief Westerman, can you please give her the details of her augmentations?"

"Yes, Dr Samuels. Mrs Clarke, we rebuilt your damaged leg and gave you several other upgrades. We augmented your legs, right arm, spine and eyes. You also received a prototype processor for learning new skills. You can't see because there are bandages covering your eyes. That was the most recent surgery."

"Why? I don't remember injuring all of that."

"No, your injuries were not that extensive, but we felt that the implants and upgrades we gave to you would be useful in your new capacity."

"My what?"

"Well, actually Candace," said the voice of Dr Samuels, "That brings me back to your other question. Your son has left the city."

"No. Baxter?"

"I'm afraid so. But your loyalty is undeniable, and we gave you these upgrades so that you can lead a task force charged with protecting the Ascendancy. In that capacity, you are authorized to rescue your son. Once he is retrieved, he will be reconditioned and brought back to Enswell. You will get your son back, and we will eliminate the Sylvan infiltration into the cites. The processing implant we furnished you with has allowed us to teach you all the military, combat, and other related skills you will need. It will also allow you instant access to your virtual assistant, Kyla - who has also been upgraded - any time you are connected to a network. All of that happened while you were unconscious. We are proud of what we have accomplished, and we think the results will delight you. Congratulations, Commander Clarke."

There was still a chance to have everything she wanted. She could save Baxter, and she now had the power and authority to eliminate the people who had done this to him.

The bandages around her cheeks tightened as Candace smiled wide.

Don't miss out!

Visit the website below and you can sign up to receive emails whenever

Daniel McMillan publishes a new book. There's no charge and no

obligation.

https://books2read.com/r/B-A-UTOE-FBHY

Connecting independent readers to independent writers.

Vector11 Studio

Thank you for reading this Vector11 Studio Book! If you enjoyed it
and want to see more great releases from us, the single most helpful
thing you can do is to *please post a review!* Find your preferred
vendor online, search for this book title, and put your review on their
page. Good reviews can be just a short paragraph, and are hugely
beneficial to get our books into the hands of new readers, which in
turn helps us to get more content out to you! Also, we appreciate and
listen to our readers and always take feedback and reviews into
consideration.

Thank you!

About the Author

Daniel McMillan is a Science Fiction and Fantasy author who is currently living in Brandon, Manitoba with his lovely wife, Tahera.

Read more at https://vector11books.webs.com.

Made in the USA
Columbia, SC
30 April 2019